GRAVE OFFENCE

A BERNIE FAZAKERLEY MYSTERY

JUDY FORD

Bernie Fazakerley Publications

GRAVE OFFENCE

Published by Bernie Fazakerley Publications

Copyright © 2017 Judy Ford

All rights reserved.

ISBN-10: 1-911083-30-9
ISBN-13: 978-1-911083-30-6

DEDICATION

Dedicated to the Disabled Police Association

Promoting ability in the United Kingdom Police Service

CONTENTS

ACKNOWLEDGEMENTS

I would like to thank the authors of a wide range of internet resources, which have been invaluable for researching the background to this book. These include (among others):

- Spinal Injuries Association
  (http://www.spinal.co.uk/page/living-with-sci)
- Wikipedia (https://en.wikipedia.org/)
- Google Maps (https://www.google.co.uk/maps)
- The University of Oxford (http://www.ox.ac.uk/)
- Police Oracle (https://www.policeoracle.com)
- The Disabled Police Association
  (http://www.disabledpolice.info/)

Some details of police methods and the roles of Crime Scene Investigators are based on information from *Crime Scene Management (2nd Edition)*, edited by Raul Sutton, Keith Trueman and Christopher Moran, ©2017 Wiley & Sons, Ltd. However, any mistakes in this matter are my own.

Members of the *UKMethodists* Facebook group provided valuable insight into alternative options for the minister and funeral director when faced with a strange corpse in 'their' grave.

I would like to thank Gillian Gilbert for reading the manuscript, giving helpful comments and pointing out typographical errors.

GLOSSARY OF UK POLICE RANKS

Uniformed police

Chief Constable (CC) – Has overall charge of a regional police force, such as Thames Valley Police, which covers Oxford and a large surrounding area.

Deputy Chief Constable (DCC) – The senior discipline authority for each force. 2nd in command to the CC.

Assistant Chief Constable (ACC) – 4 in the Thames Valley Police Service, each responsible for a policy area.

Chief Superintendent ('Chief Super') – Head of a policing area or department.

Police Superintendent – Responsible for a local area within a police force.

Chief Inspector (CI) – Responsible for overseeing a team in a local area.

Police Inspector – Senior operational officer overseeing officers on duty 24/7.

Police Sergeant – Supervises a team of officers.

Police Constable (PC) – 'Bobby on the beat'. Likely to be the first to arrive in response to an emergency call.

Crime Investigation Unit (CID) – Plain clothes officers

Detective Superintendent (DS) – Responsible for crime investigation in a local area.

Detective Chief Inspector (DCI) – Responsible for overseeing a crime investigation team in a local area. May be the Senior Investigating Officer heading up a criminal investigation.

Detective Inspector (DI) – Oversees crime investigation 24/7. May be the Senior Investigating Officer heading up a criminal investigation.

Detective Sergeant (DS) – Supervises a team of CID officers.

Detective Constable (DC) – One of a team of officers investigating crimes.

These descriptions are based on information from the following sources:

[1] Mental Health Cop blog, by Inspector Michael Brown, Mental Health co-ordinator, College of Policing. https://mentalhealthcop.wordpress.com/, accessed 31st March 2017.

[2] Thames Valley Police website, https://www.thamesvalley.police.uk , accessed 31st March 2017.

GLOSSARY OF OXFORD UNIVERSITY JARGON

This glossary is by no means exhaustive. A fuller list of Oxford terminology may be found on the University website here: https://www.ox.ac.uk

BA – Bachelor of Arts, the degree that is awarded to students completing an undergraduate degree programme. (Even those taking science degrees receive a BA).

Battels – The charges made to members of a college for accommodation, meals etc.

Blue – Sporting award for those who have competed in the annual varsity match for some sports. In less prestigious sports, competitors are awarded a "half blue".

Bod – "The bod" is a nickname for the Bodleian Library.

Bodleian Library – The Bodleian Library is the main university library.

Bursar – The member of staff responsible for the finances of a college.

Buttery – A college shop where members can purchase provisions.

Chancellor – The ceremonial head of the university

Collection – College examination usually set at the beginning of term to test students on work covered the previous term.

Coming up – Arriving at Oxford at the beginning of term

Commoner – A student who does not have a scholarship or an exhibition

CU – Christian Union. Most colleges have one.

Dean – Except at Christchurch, where the Principal is known as the Dean, the Dean of a college is a senior fellow responsible for student discipline.

Don – A member of the academic staff.

DPhil – Doctor of Philosophy, the postgraduate research degree that is known as a PhD at almost all other universities.

Eights – Intercollegiate rowing races.

Eights week – The week in Trinity Term when intercollegiate rowing races take place.

Exhibition – A type of minor scholarship.

Exhibitioner – A student who has been awarded an exhibition. At some colleges, exhibitioners wear scholar's gowns, while at others they wear commoner's gowns.

Fellow – A member of staff holding a Fellowship at one of the colleges. Fellowships may be Tutorial (i.e. teaching) or Research.

Finals – Also known as "Schools". Both terms are abbreviations of "Final Honours School". These are the examinations taken by undergraduate students at the end of their final year of study.

First – Abbreviation for "First class degree". This is the highest class of undergraduate degree.

Fresher – First year student

Gaudy – A college event for old members. Most colleges hold one each year during the summer vacation.

Going down – Leaving Oxford at the end of term

Gown – Members of the university are entitled to wear gowns that indicate their level of scholarship. The term may also be used to refer to the university community as a whole, as in "Town and Gown" which expresses the, sometimes uneasy, relationship between the residents of Oxford and the members of the university,

Greats – The commonly-used term for *Literae Humaniores*, which is an undergraduate degree programme comprising classical languages (Latin and Greek), philosophy and ancient history.

Hall – the dining hall of a college. This term may also be used to denote the evening meal ('dinner') served there. 'Formal Hall' means that staff and students are required to dress formally in gowns when attending.

High Table – The table in a college dining hall, often on a dais, at which the Head of House and Fellows dine.

Hilary Term – The second term of the university year,

which starts in January.

ISIS – The part of the River Thames that runs through Oxford.

JCR – Junior Common Room. This may either refer to a room for undergraduate students belonging to a college to meet or to the undergraduate student body of a college collectively.

Long Vac – Long Vacation. The period in the summer between the end of *Trinity Term* and the start of *Michaelmas Term* each year.

Long Vacation – The period in the summer between the end of *Trinity Term* and the start of *Michaelmas Term* each year.

MA – Master of Arts. A "courtesy" degree awarded to graduates of the university when they have completed twenty-one terms from Matriculation.

Master – The principal of a college. Each Oxford college is headed by a senior Fellow. Each college uses its own terminology for this. These include: Master, Principal, President, Rector, Dean, Warden, Provost.

Matriculation – The ceremony at which students are formally made members of the university.

MCR – Middle Common Room. This may either refer to a room for postgraduate students belonging to a college to meet or to the postgraduate student body of a college collectively.

Michaelmas Term – The first term of the university year, which starts in October.

Mods – Abbreviation for "Honour moderations". This is an examination taken, usually at the end of the first year of undergraduate study, which must be passed in order for a student to progress.

Norrington Table – A league table of colleges published annually, showing comparative performance of students in *Finals*.

OICCU – Oxford Intercollegiate Christian Union.

OUP – Oxford University Press

Penal Collection – College examination set if college tutors are concerned about a student's progress. Failure may result in the student being *sent down*.

Pigeon Post – Nickname for the University Messenger Service, the internal mail system.

Prelims – An alternative examination to *Moderations*, taken by students in certain subjects during their first year. Unlike Moderations, Prelims are not classified.

President – The principal of a college. Each Oxford college is headed by a senior Fellow. Each college uses its own terminology for this. These include: Master, Principal, President, Rector, Dean, Warden, Provost.

Principal – The principal of a college. Each Oxford college is headed by a senior Fellow. Each college uses its own terminology for this. These include: Master, Principal, President, Rector, Dean, Warden, Provost.

Provost – The principal of a college. Each Oxford college is headed by a senior Fellow. Each college uses its own terminology for this. These include: Master, Principal, President, Rector, Dean, Warden, Provost.

Rector – The principal of a college. Each Oxford college is headed by a senior Fellow. Each college uses its own terminology for this. These include: Master, Principal, President, Rector, Dean, Warden, Provost.

Research Fellow – A member of staff holding a Research Fellowship at one of the colleges

Rustication – Suspension from the university, usually as a result of a disciplinary offence.

Scholar – A student who has been awarded a scholarship. Scholars wear a different design of gown from commoners.

Schools – Also known as "Finals". Both terms are abbreviations of "Final Honours School". These are the examinations taken by undergraduate students at the end of their final year of study.

Scout – A college servant responsible for cleaning. Each scout is usually assigned to a specific part of the college. A student may refer to "my scout" meaning the scout responsible for cleaning his or her room.

SCR – Senior Common Room. This may either refer to a room for the academic staff (Fellows) belonging to a college to meet or to the academic staff of a college collectively.

Second – Abbreviation for "Second class degree". Until the nineteen-eighties, Oxford University, unusually in the UK, did not divide the second class. Now, students are awarded degrees designated "first", "upper second", "lower second" or "third" class. These are abbreviated as 1, 2:1, 2:2 and 3, respectively.

Sending down – A student who is sent down is expelled from his college, and hence from the university. This may be for misconduct or for failure to progress, for example failing *Mods* or a *penal collection*.

Senior Member – Anyone who has achieved an Oxford MA automatically becomes a Senior Member of the University. The Senior Members of a college are its fellows.

Staircase – The older Oxford colleges are designed on a 'staircase' system, in which a group of rooms is accessed by a staircase that opens on to one of the quadrangles around which the college is built. Typically, rooms are identified by a combination of the name of the quad, the number of the staircase and the room number within the staircase group.

Subfusc – Formal attire worn by students and academics on formal occasions, including matriculation, examinations and graduation.

Teddy Hall – Nickname for St Edmund Hall, one of the colleges of the university.

Terms – All undergraduates are required to "keep terms" which means that they have to reside in Oxford for a minimum number of nights each year during their degree course.

The Union – The University debating society, which also

has a building housing a library, bar and various other facilities for its members.

Third – Abbreviation for "Third class degree". This is the lowest class of undergraduate degree normally awarded. There are, however, three lower classes for students who fail to reach the required standard: Pass, Honours Pass and Unclassified Honours

Trinity Term – The third term of the university year, which starts in April.

Tutor – A member of staff (or a postgraduate student) who gives tutorials to undergraduate students.

Tutorial – A session in which one or two (or occasionally more) students are taught by a Tutorial Fellow or some other person appointed by their college. Typically, this involves students preparing work in advance and talking about it during the tutorial.

Tutorial Fellow – A member of staff holding a Tutorial Fellowship at one of the colleges

UCAS – Universities and Colleges Admissions Service, a central clearing house for applications to UK Higher Education institutions.

Univ – Short for University College, one of the colleges of the university.

Varsity Match – Sporting fixture between Oxford and Cambridge universities.

Vice-Chancellor/VC – The senior academic officer of the university.

Viva – Abbreviation of "viva voce", meaning an oral exam.

Warden – The principal of a college. Each Oxford college is headed by a senior Fellow. Each college uses its own terminology for this. These include: Master, Principal, President, Rector, Dean, Warden, Provost.

MAP OF BINSEY AND PORT MEADOW

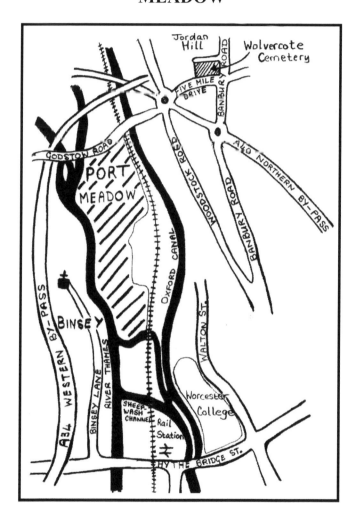

PART I: ACTUAL BODILY HARM

07.40 THURSDAY 29TH OCTOBER

'It's good of you to give me a lift, sir,' Andy said, opening the door of Peter's car, which had pulled up outside his home in Headington Quarry. 'But there was no need. I could have managed on the bus while my car's in dock.'

'Just get in and make yourself comfortable.' Peter looked up from scrutinising his mobile phone and smiled towards the young detective constable. 'I need to give a friend of mine a ring. He's left me two missed calls in the time it's taken me to drive here, so he must be keen to speak to me. It won't take long.'

He punched in the numbers and waited for the ringing tone. It had hardly started when it was replaced by the voice of Dr Martin Riess, Geology Fellow at Lichfield College and one of Peter's few close friends.

'Peter! Thank God!' Martin sounded anxious and distressed – fearful, almost. There was a pause, as if he did not know what to say next. Then, after a gasp for breath, he went on. 'We're at A and E. Can you come over?'

Peter's heart started beating faster as he tried to imagine what might have happened. He opened his mouth

3

to ask, but Martin continued, speaking quickly, stumbling over the words, his voice rising as if in panic.

'It's Lucy. Don't worry. She's not badly hurt. We brought her here just to be on the safe side. I think she probably needs a couple of stitches – but, like I said, it's nothing much really. But I think you ought to be here. Can you come?'

'Of course. I'll be right over.' Peter's training as a police officer enabled him to speak calmly, although his heart and mind were both racing. What could have happened to his young stepdaughter to require hospital treatment and to send the usually placid Riess into such a tailspin? He was about to end the call when another voice sounded in his ear.

'Don't listen to him. It's nothing much really – just a little cut on my cheek, that's all. And you mustn't blame Martin. It was all my fault.'

'Lucy!' At least she was conscious and able to speak, even if her voice did sound rather strained, as if she were finding it hard to keep back tears. 'I'll be right over. It'll only take a couple of minutes – we're not far away.'

'I'm sorry,' Martin's voice came on again, 'they're calling us in now. We'll have to go. You will come, won't you?'

'Yes, of course. I'll be over in a couple of minutes,' Peter repeated.

'Thanks. And Peter – I'm so sorry!'

Peter slipped the phone back in his pocket and turned to Andy.

'Change of plan,' he said briskly. 'As you may have gathered, my stepdaughter, Lucy, has had some sort of accident. She's in A and E. I need to get over there right away. Do you mind coming for the ride? I'm hoping it won't take long. It sounds as if it's probably just Martin getting himself worked up about nothing,' he added, more to reassure himself than for Andy's benefit.

'No problem,' Andy shrugged. 'I'm fine with that. I can

always get the bus from the hospital if it looks like taking a while.'

It was just a little over a mile to the John Radcliffe hospital, but the rush-hour traffic was starting to build and Peter had a frustrating stop-start journey. The promised *couple of minutes* stretched to five and then to ten. As he queued to turn on to London Road, he tried to close his mind to the pictures that kept forming in his head of pretty, golden-haired Lucy with her face covered in blood. How could it have happened? Would it leave a permanent scar? What would Lucy's mother say when she found out? Should he telephone her at once or wait until she got back from Manchester?

Glancing to the left as he eased the car out into the line of traffic heading towards the centre of Oxford, he realised that Andy was watching him intently. Presumably, his anxiety was evident on his face. He tried unsuccessfully to relax and to concentrate on identifying the correct road on the right to bring them to the hospital.

'Shall I ring in to let them know we'll be late?' Andy asked.

'Yes, you do that. Thanks.' Peter murmured absently, his mind still occupied with the puzzle of how things could have gone so disastrously wrong that morning.

Only two hours earlier, he had been waving off Lucy, Martin and Bernie as they cycled out into the dark October morning. Bernie had rung him from the train to say that she was on her way, and she had mentioned parting from Lucy and Martin at Hythe Bridge Street and seeing them making their way down the path to where his boat was moored. An early morning trip in Martin's narrowboat should have been a safe enough treat for a nine-year-old. She had been so looking forward to the idea of having breakfast aboard and watching the sun come up over Port Meadow. How could anyone have imagined that she would get hurt?

And Martin was a dependable sort of chap – he

wouldn't have allowed her to do anything silly. Admittedly, he didn't have much experience with children, being a single man still living quietly at home with his mother. But he was always very cautious and safety-conscious. He had insisted on Lucy wearing a buoyancy aid while she was in the boat, despite her protestations that she could swim like a fish.

Lucy must have fallen, Peter supposed, and cut her face open on some sharp object – but what could that have been? He had been on that boat – there were no obvious hazards of that sort.

At last, they pulled up outside the Accident and Emergency department. Peter got out and then leaned back inside to hand the car keys to Andy.

'Park the car for me, will you? And then come and find me.'

'Yes, sir.' Andy obediently slid himself into the driver's seat. 'See you in a bit.'

Peter was not listening. He was intent on getting inside as soon as he could and finding his stepdaughter. He waited impatiently as a casualty was wheeled out of an ambulance and in through the doors of the emergency department. Was there another entrance for those arriving on foot? No – better to wait than to wander off looking for one. He followed the trolley into the building and looked around for someone to ask about Lucy's whereabouts. At last! There was the reception desk. The woman there must surely know.

08.10 THURSDAY 29TH OCTOBER

The first thing that Peter saw, when he entered the treatment room, was a uniformed police officer. She was standing against the wall opposite, watching the proceedings. Peter got the impression that she was taking mental notes, as if she were expecting to be asked to give evidence in court about what had happened. What was she doing here? Why would the police be involved in a simple accident?

Peter studied her face for just long enough to establish that it was unfamiliar. He knew most of the officers in the Oxford area. She looked young, but her confident bearing suggested that she was not fresh out of training school. Perhaps she had recently been transferred from elsewhere.

He turned his attention to more important matters. There was a couch along another wall of the room, but it was unoccupied. Lucy was sitting on Martin's lap, on a chair in the centre of the room. A woman in a white coat – presumably the doctor – was bending over her, obscuring Peter's view. He took a step forward, hoping to get into a position where he could see the extent of his

7

stepdaughter's injuries.

The doctor straightened up and Peter caught a glimpse of a pale face framed by yellow curls with an ugly red gash on the left cheek, surrounded by an angry reddish-purple swelling. Martin's anxious eyes looked over Lucy's shoulder from another face almost as pale as hers. Peter was suddenly struck by an uncanny resemblance between the two – they had the same pale blue eyes and heart-shaped face. Martin's hair was a shade or two darker and wavy rather than curly, but ...

'Daddy!' Lucy's eyes lit up as she caught sight of Peter and broke into a smile. She put out her arms towards him, struggling to free herself from Martin's protective embrace. He released his hold on her, allowing her to slide to the floor and race over to Peter, flinging her arms around his waist. He picked her up and hugged her to him, taking great care not to touch her injured cheek, relieved beyond measure that she was safe, if not completely sound.

'Excuse me,' the young police officer stepped forward, looking first at Martin and then at Peter. 'Am I to understand that you are this girl's father?' she asked, rather coldly, Peter thought.

'Yes – or, to be more precise, I'm her stepfather,' Peter explained. 'But I have parental responsibility,' he added defensively, seeing the officer's look of disapproval, mingled with what he took to be scepticism that any stepparent could have a genuine interest in a child's welfare.

The officer treated him to a hard stare before turning to look at Martin.

'And you? Are you her biological father?'

'No.' Martin sounded apologetic. 'I'm just-'

'He's my friend!' Lucy broke in, sensing the disapproving tone in the woman's voice and determined to defend two of her favourite people against whatever accusations were being levelled at them.

'Martin's a friend of the family,' Peter confirmed. 'He works with Lucy's mother – at the university. Not that I can see that it's any concern of yours, constable …?'

'Ferrar,' she filled in the gap where he had left his sentence hanging. 'Police Constable Louise Ferrar. And your name is?'

'Peter Johns. As I said, I'm Lucy's stepfather; and this is Dr Martin Riess, who is a friend of ours. Now, can someone tell me what happened and why the police are involved?'

'According to your *friend*,' Constable Ferrar said, in a tone that endowed the word with deeply sinister connotations, 'some complete stranger hit the child with this, and then ran off.' She turned and picked up, from the floor behind her, a length of wood, such as might once have formed part of a fence. Peter inspected it, noting that there was a nail protruding near one end. He thought that it might have blood on it, but could not be sure without looking more closely.

'We *said* that, because it's true!' Lucy burst out indignantly. 'Stop behaving as if we're telling lies. And you shouldn't be holding that without gloves on – it's evidence!'

Lucy had formed an alliance with another family friend, forensic pathologist Mike Carson, and he had told her all about correct procedure for conducting a criminal investigation.

'Please,' the doctor intervened. 'Can we leave all this for later? Just now, the main thing is for me to get the child's face stitched up. I've given her a local anaesthetic,' she added, turning to Peter. 'So now I just need to wash out the wound and put in a couple of stitches to make sure it heals up cleanly and doesn't leave a nasty scar. It's just a flesh wound. I've checked the bone underneath and there's no sign of any fracture. It'll probably swell up and look dreadful for a few days, but there's nothing serious to worry about.'

Peter nodded gratefully. PC Ferrar stepped back and resumed her position against the wall, continuing to watch Peter and Martin with a critical eye.

'Now, Lucy,' the doctor went on. 'I need you lying down to do the next bit. So if your stepdad will just put you down here,' she pointed towards the couch, 'I'll get the things I need and soon it'll all be over and you can go home. Is that OK?'

Lucy nodded vigorously. Peter carried her over to the couch and laid her down carefully.

'Now Lucy,' the doctor resumed, returning with a small tray of instruments, which she laid down on a trolley next to the couch. 'I need you to be quite, quite still while I do this. So I'm going to ask your dad to hold your head for me. Is that OK?'

'Yes,' Lucy nodded again.

'Close your eyes,' the doctor instructed. 'We're all ready to start now.'

'Why?' Lucy wanted to know. 'I want to watch.'

'That's really not a good idea,' the doctor argued gently.

'I'm not frightened,' Lucy insisted. 'And I'm going to be a pathologist when I grow up, so I'd like to see how you do it.'

'But the saline that I'm going to use to clean out your cut will sting if it gets in your eyes,' the doctor replied, refusing to be deflected, despite being intrigued as to what could have prompted this unusual career choice. 'And I want to be able to concentrate on stitching up your cheek, without worrying that I could accidentally get the needle in your eye. That's why I'm going to ask your dad to put his hand over your eyes while he holds your head still. I'm sorry – but believe me, you wouldn't get a very good view anyway. I'm going to be working just below your left eye.'

'OK,' Lucy said regretfully. Then, more hopefully, she asked, 'could Martin video it on his phone? Then he could show me afterwards.'

'I suppose that would be alright,' the doctor said. She

was finding it hard to argue with this persistent child, who so clearly knew her own mind and expected to get her own way. 'Just so long as he doesn't get in my way.'

'Good,' Lucy lay back on the couch and closed her eyes. 'I'm ready.'

Peter positioned one hand over Lucy's eyes and forehead, holding her head down firmly. With his other hand, he steadied her chin, leaving the damaged cheek clear for the doctor to work. Martin fumbled reluctantly for his phone in his jacket pocket and stepped forward so that he could focus the camera on Lucy's face. He would have very much preferred not to have been compelled to watch the procedure – never mind filming it – but he did not dare to flout Lucy's wishes.

Both men watched anxiously as the doctor gently pulled back the lips of the wound and peered into it. Then she poured warm saline into it, holding a pad at the side of Lucy's head to absorb the run-off. She peered down again and then reached for a small pair of tweezers. Peter winced as he watched her probing inside the wound with them. Then, with a swift movement of her hand, she brought them out again and held them aloft.

'Look what we've got here!'

Peter looked closer and saw a tiny sliver of something in the tweezers. The doctor put it down in a kidney dish and bent down to inspect it.

'What is it?' Lucy asked eagerly. 'Can I see?'

'You can have a look after I've finished,' the doctor promised. 'Not that there's much to see. I think it's a tiny splinter of wood. The main thing is – I've got it out now. Lie still again now and I'll just give it one final wash to make sure we won't be sewing up anything inside. And then I'll stitch you up.'

Peter and Martin held their breath as they watched the doctor expertly closing the lips of the wound and stitching them together. Constable Ferrar scrutinised their faces with a sceptical expression, as if she did not believe that their concern for Lucy's welfare was genuine.

In a matter of minutes, it was all over and the doctor stepped back and started taking off her surgical gloves.

'OK, Lucy,' she said. 'You can open your eyes now. I'm done.'

Peter released his hold and Lucy opened her eyes and sat up. She looked towards Martin eagerly.

'Did you get it all?' she demanded.

'I think so.'

'Can I see?'

'Perhaps that could wait until later,' the doctor intervened. 'I just want to tell you and your dad about the stitches. They're dissolvable, so they'll disappear after a couple of days. If there are any bits left after it's all healed up, you can make an appointment to see your GP to have them removed – or you can just leave them until they dissolve completely by themselves.'

She handed a typewritten sheet of paper to Peter. 'Here's some information about looking after the wound. It's all simple enough. The main thing is to keep it clean and check it regularly for signs of infection. Don't worry,' she added, seeing his anxious expression. 'Kids heal really quickly. In a few days she'll probably have forgotten she's got it.'

Peter nodded gratefully, pocketing the paper and turning back to Lucy, who was now sitting up on the edge of the couch about to jump down.

'You be careful now,' the doctor said, bending down to speak to Lucy. 'Keep your face as clean as possible, but don't rub the wound with your face flannel – just dab it very gently with cotton wool, if you absolutely have to. The best thing is if you can stop it getting dirty in the first place – do you understand?'

Lucy nodded.

'Can I see that splinter you found now?' she asked.

The doctor held out the kidney dish and Lucy gazed down with interest. At first, she could not see the splinter, which was surrounded by pieces of blood-stained gauze.

'It's very small,' she observed, when she at last identified the tiny object, 'but I expect forensics could match it up with the stick that hit me. 'You'd better keep it safe. It's evidence that Martin and I are telling the truth.' She gave constable Ferrar another hard look.

'When it starts healing up,' the doctor went on, ignoring this remark, 'you may find that it starts to itch. However bad it gets, don't scratch it, because you could pull the stitches out before they're ready.'

'OK,' Lucy nodded again.

'Right then,' the doctor straightened up and turned to address Peter.

'You can take her home now. The anaesthetic will wear off in a couple of hours. She should be fine, but if she complains of pain, you can give her paracetamol – just the usual dose. Keep an eye on her and if you're worried about anything see your GP.'

'Thanks. Come along, Lucy – time we were off! The doctor's got other people to see to.'

08.45 THURSDAY 29TH OCTOBER

Peter caught Andy's eye in the waiting area and headed across the room towards him, holding Lucy's hand tightly in his. Before he had gone more than a few paces, constable Ferrar stepped in front of him, barring his way.

'Before you go, I need you to answer some questions.'

'Can't it wait? I want to get Lucy home.'

'Non-accidental injury of a child is a serious matter,' Ferrar's voice was calm, but it had a hint of menace in it. 'It's important that I have all the relevant facts.'

'Very well,' Peter answered, seeing that the young policewoman was not going to give way, and deciding that to argue would only cause delay. 'Do you mind if we sit down?'

Peter settled down on the nearest vacant seat and lifted Lucy on to his lap. Martin took the seat next to him. Constable Ferrar hesitated for a moment, as if uncertain whether to sit or to remain standing; then she perched herself on the edge of the seat opposite them and took out her notebook.

'First, can I have your name and address?' she said to

14

Peter. 'I have this as the little girl's address – do you live there too?'

She held out the notebook and Peter saw Lucy's name and address written in a clear, rather immature, script.

'Yes. That's right.'

'And your name?'

'Peter Johns.'

'So, although you say you have parental responsibility, the child hasn't taken your name? I've got her down as Lucy Paige.'

'No. She wanted to keep her father's name,'

'I see. And where is he now? Does he live locally?'

'No,' Lucy answered, before Peter could think of the best way of explaining. 'Don't be silly. My dad's dead – or Peter wouldn't have married my mam.'

Ferrar hesitated for a moment and then resumed her questioning of Peter.

'And the child's mother? I assume she lives with you too?'

'Yes.'

'Of course she does!' Lucy broke in. She felt that the young officer was unfairly criticising her family, although she could not work out what it was that they were supposed to have done wrong, and was determined to stick up for her mother and stepfather.

'And where is she now?'

'On her way to Manchester for a seminar,' Peter answered. 'She'll be back this evening.'

'And she left her child in your care? Does she know that you let her go off alone on the river with this man?' Ferrar asked aggressively, gesturing towards Martin, who was hunched up in his chair, gazing despondently at his feet.

'Excuse me, constable,' Andy Lepage, who had come up silently while they were talking, held up his warrant card in front of Ferrar's face. 'I think you ought to know that the gentleman you're speaking to is Detective Inspector

Johns.'

'I don't care if he's the Chief Constable,' Ferrar retorted, turning to face Andy with eyes blazing. 'When it comes to child protection, rank doesn't come into it. A young girl has been assaulted, and I need to know how it happened.'

She had recently attended a course on dealing with domestic violence and was well aware that abuse occurred in all classes of people and all walks of life.

'We *told* you what happened,' Lucy protested. 'But you won't believe us. Why won't you? I don't tell lies.'

'No, of course you don't, Lucy,' Ferrar said soothingly, 'but sometimes people's memories get a bit muddled up – especially when something painful or frightening has happened. And sometimes it can feel wrong to tell the truth in case it gets someone else into trouble.'

She turned back to face Peter.

'Now, Mr Johns – sir – please will you answer my question? Was Lucy's mother aware that she would be going off with Dr Riess in his boat this morning?'

'Yes. It was her suggestion. Lucy's off on half term this week and she'd been hankering after watching the sun rise over Port Meadow, ever since Martin told her about it months ago. Bernie said that, since we'd all be up early for the train, this would be a golden opportunity.'

'Bernie? Who's he?' Ferrar asked sharply, wondering how many more adult male friends this little girl might have in her life and imagining that she could be about to uncover a paedophile ring.

'My mam, stupid!' Lucy said rudely. She had lost all patience with Ferrar's questioning and no longer cared how much offence she might cause.

'Dr Bernadette Fazakerley,' Peter explained. 'Shall I write it down for you? People often get the spelling wrong. She kept her maiden name when she married Lucy's dad and again when we got married. As I said, she and Martin are colleagues. They both hold tutorial fellowships at colleges in the university. Martin often takes Lucy out in his boat. We never had any concerns about that. We know we can trust him to take care of her.'

'He didn't do a very good job of that today,' Ferrar observed, still reluctant to let go of her idea that, at very least, some negligence had been committed by the two men who had been charged with Lucy's care.

'It wasn't Martin's fault!' Lucy shouted, slipping off Peter's lap and stepping forward to look Ferrar in the eye. 'He tried to stop me. It was all *my* fault she hit me. I should have done what he told me.'

'Is that what he told you to say?' Ferrar asked quietly, putting both hands on Lucy's shoulders and looking into her face. She had learned that abusers could be very manipulative and often succeeded in convincing their victims that they were to blame. 'Did he tell you that you deserved to be hurt because you wouldn't do what he wanted?'

Lucy pulled herself away angrily and stood glaring at Ferrar, feeling puzzled and frightened. She did not understand this line of questioning but sensed that the policewoman was attempting to allot blame to one of her favourite people.

'It's alright Lucy,' Ferrar said softly, wishing that she could speak to the child alone, away from the watchful eyes of the two men who seemed to have such a hold over her. 'You're safe now. Nobody is going to hurt you. And you mustn't think that it's your fault that you got hurt earlier. That's very important for you to remember – none of this is your fault.'

'But Martin told me to wait in the boat,' Lucy argued dogmatically. 'If I'd done what he said, she wouldn't have hit me.'

Peter got up and put his hand on Lucy's shoulder. She looked up at him and put her arm around his waist, resting her head against his body.

'This has gone on long enough,' Peter told Ferrar.

'You've got our names and addresses. If you need Lucy and Martin to give statements, you'd better arrange interviews for them at a better time. DC Lepage and I have work to go to and it's time Lucy went home.'

'If you're going to be at work and your wife is in Manchester, who will be looking after Lucy?' Ferrar asked sharply.

'Her grandparents,' Peter replied shortly. 'Come along, Lucy, we're going now. Good morning Constable Ferrar.'

'Very well,' Ferrar answered, bowing to the inevitable. 'I'll be preparing a report for Social Services. You can expect them to be in touch within the next few days.' She put away her notebook and bent down to speak to Lucy, slipping a small card into her hand as she did so. 'Bye, bye Lucy. I hope your face is better soon. Here's a number you can ring if you want to talk to someone about it ... or about anything else that's bothering you.'

Lucy looked down, read the words on the card, considered the option of tearing it into pieces and scattering them on the floor in a dramatic gesture, and then changed her mind and thrust it back towards Ferrar.

'No thank you,' she said politely. 'I already have the Childline number on my phone. And I've got *plenty* of people I can talk to. You'd better keep this in case you meet someone who needs it.'

Peter took Lucy's hand and they walked to the door, followed by Martin and Andy. Andy paused as he passed Ferrar and spoke to her in a low voice.

'Believe me; you're making a big mistake picking a fight with DI Johns. Ask anyone. He's one of the most popular men in the force, and completely devoted to his stepdaughter. There's no way he'd put her at risk.'

'You drive, Andy,' Peter said briskly as they crossed the car park. 'I'll go in the back with Lucy. We'll drop Martin off so he can rescue his boat from wherever it is, and then we'll take Lucy to the friends who are going to be looking after her today. I'd better give them a ring to let them know she'll be coming a bit earlier than planned.'

Peter held open the door while Lucy climbed into the car and settled herself in the back. Martin came up behind Peter and spoke to him in a low voice, so that Lucy would not hear.

'I'm so sorry. I shouldn't have let this happen.'

'Don't,' Peter said, opening the front passenger door and ushering Martin into the car. Then he bent to speak in his ear. 'I know you would never do anything to hurt her, whatever Constable Ferrar may think.'

09.00 THURSDAY 29TH OCTOBER

'Sylvia? It's Peter here. There's been a bit of a change of plan. Are you OK to have Lucy over now, instead of later?'

'Of course. Whenever you like. But I thought you'd be at work by now.'

'So did I, but something's cropped up. Lucy's hurt herself – nothing major, but Martin took her to A and E and she's had a couple of stitches – so we thought it was best if she came straight to you. Are you sure it's OK?'

'Yes. We're not doing anything – and you told us Martin would be bringing her over mid-morning, so it's not much different is it?'

Peter looked at his watch. Nearly nine o'clock. Sylvia was right, by the time they had dropped Martin off and driven to her house, it would not be so very much earlier than planned.

'No, I suppose not. Anyway, I thought I'd just let you know. See you in a bit.'

They deposited Martin on Godstow Road, close to the

narrow stone bridge that spanned the Thames. Lucy watched him through the window of the car as he carefully closed the gate behind him and descended to the towpath.

'Where to now?' Andy asked.

'Get us to Cowley Road and then I'll direct you,' Peter answered. He sat back and pondered on how best to find out from Lucy what had actually happened in the boat that morning. He did not want her to feel that she was being subjected to yet another interrogation, but he needed to know – both for his own peace of mind and because he would have to give an account to Lucy's mother

'Why did you tell that policewoman that Stan and Sylvia were my grandparents?' Lucy asked, while Peter was still trying to formulate his opening gambit.

'Because it would have been too complicated to explain who they really are,' he told her.

'And grandparents sound like nice safe people?' Lucy asked with surprising perspicacity.

'Yes,' Peter agreed with a smile, 'that as well. And it wasn't really a lie, because Stan and Sylvia are the nearest you've got to grandparents and I'm sure they think of themselves as honorary Gran and Granddad. Now, I know you've been over it all with Constable Ferrar, but do you mind telling me what really happened to give you that gash on your face? I'm going to have to ring your mam to warn her what to expect and she won't be impressed if all I can say is that you were hit by a strange woman, will she?'

'There were these two men,' Lucy began. Peter opened his mouth to ask a question and then shut it again and allowed her to continue. 'They were running after a woman – across the fields, just before we got to Godstow Lock. One of them caught up with her and I saw him holding up something above her head. It looked like a knife. Then she got away again, and ran down towards the river and hid in some bushes. I shouted to Martin to go over and help her. I think the men must have seen us then, because they turned and went back into the trees at the other side of the field. Martin said it was none of our business, but I thought we ought to see if she was OK. So he took the boat over to that side and found somewhere that we could stop.'

'Go on,' Peter said gently, noticing that Lucy had stopped speaking and was gazing out of the window as if deep in thought. 'What happened next?'

'Martin told me to stay in the boat while he tied her up,' Lucy answered in a whisper. 'But I didn't take any notice of him. I got out and went over to the bushes to look for the woman. I ... I think she must have thought I was one of the men coming to get her. She hit me with that piece of wood you saw and then she ran off. And then Martin came and found me, and he called the police and an ambulance and ...,' she trailed off. Peter reached out and put his arm round her shoulder.

'I'm sorry, Daddy.'

'Don't be silly. There's nothing for you to be sorry about.'

'But if I'd done what Martin said she wouldn't have hit me, and that horrid policewoman wouldn't have been angry with you and wouldn't be reporting you to Social Services!'

'Don't you worry about that,' Andy called over his shoulder. 'Your daddy is a much more important policeman than Constable Ferrar. Nobody's going to take any notice of anything she says against him.'

'More to the point,' Peter added, 'Social Services are far too busy to spend time worrying about a little accident like this. As soon as they hear what really happened it'll be the end of the matter – just you wait and see. Now, Andy and I are already late for work, so I'd better just drop you off and then go. You'll have to explain everything to Stan and Sylvia – is that alright?'

09.15 THURSDAY 29TH OCTOBER

Sylvia was watching out for them and she came out to greet them when the car pulled up outside the small terraced house in East Oxford. She and her husband, Stan, were spritely seventy-year-olds; Geordies, who had moved down to Oxford when they retired in order to be closer to their friend, Bernie, and to be able to help with caring for her daughter, Lucy. They were the preferred babysitters whenever both Bernie and Peter were at work.

She held the car door open while Lucy climbed out, and looked closely at the angry looking swelling on the little girl's face. However, sensing that Lucy did not want a fuss, she said nothing. Then she looked across the car at Peter, who had got out of the other side.

'I'll leave Lucy to explain what happened,' he said. 'I'm not that clear on it myself yet. The main thing is: it's nothing serious. Now, I must dash – we should have been in a briefing with Superintendent Brown half an hour ago.'

He reached for the front passenger door and got in beside Andy. Lucy waved as she watched them drive away.

'Well, Lucy,' Sylvia said briskly, as soon as the car

disappeared round the corner. 'We'd better be going inside – can't stop out here all day.'

'Hello, Lucy. Been in the wars I see,' Stan greeted her, looking up from his newspaper and smiling as she entered the small front room. 'What was it? An argument with a boat hook? Should have known something would happen – these Oxford dons!' He shook his head in mock despair. A welder by trade, and proud of his working-class credentials, it amused him to make fun of Bernie and her academic colleagues. 'Heads in the clouds! Don't know what day of the week it is half the time!'

'It wasn't Martin's fault!' Lucy said indignantly. 'Why is everyone blaming him?'

'Hold hard there!' Stan said anxiously, seeing tears welling up in Lucy's eyes. 'I was only joking. Of course I'm not blaming Martin. Come and sit down. I didn't mean to upset you.'

'I thought I might make some gingerbread men this morning,' Sylvia said from behind Lucy. 'Would you like to help me?'

Lucy wiped her eyes on her sleeve. Then she turned and nodded at Sylvia, who ushered her out of the door, giving her husband a look that told him that he would not be welcome in the kitchen until she had found out from Lucy what the problem was. He turned back to his newspaper, wondering to himself what could have provoked her unexpected reaction to his little witticism. She was not usually so sensitive about his mild mockery of the educated classes.

For about half an hour the conversation was exclusively about weighing and mixing ingredients, rolling out dough and cutting out shapes from it. It was only as they put the last tray of gingerbread figures into the oven that Sylvia ventured to broach the subject of Lucy's injury.

'Did the doctor say how long the stitches would have

to stay in?' she asked casually, trying to speak as if this were a matter of very little importance. 'I remember when I was a bit younger than you, falling over on some glass and having to have stitches in my knee. I had to go back to the hospital a week or two later for them to take them out. And then they gave them to me to keep – the other kids at school were very impressed to see them!'

'These are dissolvable stitches,' Lucy told her. 'They don't have to be taken out.'

'That's good. I remember it wasn't very nice having them out. That sounds like a much better idea. Right! Now, while the gingerbread men are cooking, will you help me to clear everything away and wash up?'

Lucy nodded.

'Can I wash and you dry?'

'Yes, of course.' Sylvia fetched a low wooden stool and placed it in front of the sink so that Lucy could reach to wash the baking utensils. 'What was it that you cut yourself on?' she asked cautiously, watching Lucy carefully for signs that she would prefer not to talk about the incident.

'It was a nail – in the end of a piece of wood.'

'You mean part of the boat?'

'No. I wasn't on the boat. I got out. Martin told me not to, but I still did. If I'd done what he told me it wouldn't have happened.'

'What wouldn't have happened?' Sylvia asked, deciding that her oblique approach was getting nowhere and that she would have to be more direct in her questioning. 'Do you think you could tell me all about it from the beginning?'

'Yes. Peter said I had to tell you, but I thought you didn't seem interested.'

'I'm *very* interested,' Sylvia assured her. 'I just didn't want to make you talk about it if you didn't want to.'

'We-e-ell,' Lucy said slowly. 'We'd watched the sun coming up over Port Meadow, and we'd had breakfast sitting up on the deck – that's what Martin calls the roof of the boat – and Martin had got down to drive the boat a bit further. I was looking round and I saw some people running out of the trees and across the field. It was a woman and two men. The men were chasing the woman.'

'Really?' Sylvia said encouragingly.

'Yes. One of the men caught up with the woman. It was still a bit dark, so I couldn't see what they were doing properly, but he held something up in the air. It looked a bit like a knife, but it could just have been a stick. I thought he was going to hit her with it, but she got away again and ran off. I shouted to Martin to look, and he did and he saw them too.'

'And what happened then?'

'I think the men must have heard me shouting. They stood there together for a little while and then they turned round and went back.'

'And what happened to the woman?'

'She ran and hid in some bushes near the water. I told Martin we ought to go and see if she was alright. He didn't want to, but he drove the boat over to the other side and started to tie her up. He told me to stay in the boat until he was ready – but I got out and went to find her!' Lucy's voice rose as she recounted her disobedience. 'When she heard me coming, she hit me with this long piece of wood – I think she must have found it lying around there in the bushes – and then she ran away. And Martin came and found me and took me back to the boat. He said he'd got some sticking plasters in his first aid kit, but then afterwards he said I had to go to hospital. So he rang 999 and the police came – and then an ambulance. I wish he hadn't.'

'Why? I would have thought it was a good thing to get you to hospital right away.'

'A horrible policewoman came. She told me to call her Louise. I showed her the piece of wood – I'd been ever so careful not to leave my fingerprints on it – and she just took it and looked at it, without wearing gloves or anything. I told her it was important evidence and she said she'd keep it safe – but she didn't mean it, she was just …'

'Humouring you?' Sylvia suggested, keeping a straight face with some difficulty as she imagined the officer's surprise at being lectured on correct police procedure by a nine-year-old.

'Yes. But that's not what was so horrible about her.'

'Oh?'

'She didn't believe me when I told her about the woman and the two men. She *pretended* to believe me, but I could see she didn't really. She didn't try to find them! She didn't even ask me to describe them!'

'I suppose she probably isn't a detective,' Sylvia suggested. 'Perhaps she'll get someone else to do all that.'

'No she won't, because *she* thinks it was Martin who hit me. And she thinks that Peter shouldn't have let me go out in Martin's boat. She even thinks that Mam shouldn't have gone to Manchester and let Peter look after me!'

Lucy stepped down off the stool and flung her arms around Sylvia's waist, burying her face in her apron. Sylvia hugged her close. Then she crouched down so that she could look Lucy in the eye.

'Lucy, pet,' she said gently. 'I'm sure you must be wrong about that. I expect she was just worried that your mam didn't know what had happened and wasn't able to be at the hospital with you. Most little girls aren't as brave about that sort of thing as you are.'

'No, that wasn't what she meant,' Lucy insisted tearfully. 'She called Martin *this man* and she talked about *child protection* and she said she was reporting Peter to Social Services.'

'I expect she just meant that she had to tell Social Services that you'd been hurt, that's all. You mustn't worry about it. Social Services are just nice people whose job it is to see that children are safe. Now those gingerbread men will be ready to come out of the oven and I need you to help me to put the icing on them.'

'I think they're cool enough for you to decorate now,' Sylvia told Lucy a few minutes later. 'And while you're doing that, I'll look out a box for you to take some home for your mam and Peter.'

'Can I have two boxes? I want to take some to Jonah when I go to see him this evening. Nurse Jeanette says he needs to eat more to build himself up.'

'Of course,' Sylvia agreed, looking round from rummaging in a tall cupboard on the other side of the kitchen. 'But will you be going this evening? I mean ...,' she broke off, unsure how best to explain her doubts without upsetting Lucy again.

DCI[1] Jonah Porter was a great friend of Lucy and her mother. He had worked with Lucy's father and, since his untimely death, had taken on the role of a favourite uncle to the little girl. He was currently in hospital, making a painfully slow recovery from a bullet wound in his neck, which he had received some four months previously. Lucy took great pride in being allowed to play a part in his rehabilitation by visiting every evening to give him his dinner, now that the damage to his spinal cord prevented him from feeding himself. Sylvia was not sure that it would be helpful to Jonah to see Lucy's cut and bruised cheek and red eyes, and she would have liked to suggest that it would be better to put off her next visit until the swelling had gone down and the colour faded. She was also of the opinion that, after an early start and the traumatic events of the morning, Lucy would benefit more from an early night than from a forty-mile round trip to the spinal injuries centre. However, she was reluctant to voice these concerns for fear of further upsetting the little girl.

'I mean, I thought you might not get over there today, with your mam being away,' she finished eventually.

[1] Detective Chief Inspector. See Glossary of UK Police Ranks.

'It's OK,' Lucy assured her. 'Peter's going to take me. He promised to come home early so we can.'

'I see. That's alright then.' Sylvia gave up any thought of argument. It was clear to her that, if Lucy's visit to the hospital were to be cancelled because of her injury, she would consider herself to have let down her friend. The little girl was already irrationally blaming herself for having caused the incident. The last thing she needed was this added burden of guilt. Sylvia made a mental note to telephone Peter later to warn him of his stepdaughter's determination to stick to her agreed routine, and to offer Stan's services as Lucy's chauffeur if Peter were to be delayed at work and unable to fulfil his obligations in this respect.

14.00 THURSDAY 29TH OCTOBER

'You've lost weight again,' Margaret said sternly, striding into the room and flopping down into the high-backed chair that stood next to Jonah's bed in his room on the rehabilitation ward. She set her pillar-box red crash helmet down on the floor beside her, packed her brown gauntlet gloves inside it, and gave her husband a hard look. 'And Danielle tells me you didn't eat your lunch today.'

'She always feeds me too fast,' Jonah complained. 'Anyway, I wasn't hungry.'

'You ought to have been. She also said that you only had coffee for breakfast. You need to make more effort.'

'I'm sorry,' Jonah said defensively. 'But it's hard when you don't fancy anything. You know what hospital food's like.'

'It was liver and bacon for lunch,' Margaret countered. 'You always used to like that.'

'It's different the way you make it.'

'Would you eat properly if I cooked meals and brought them in?' Margaret snatched eagerly at the thought that this might be a way of tempting her husband out of this

30

downward spiral of low energy, lack of appetite and listlessness.

'No – I don't want you going to that sort of trouble. It's bad enough for you having to trail over here every day, without turning yourself into a meals-on-wheels lady as well. I'll be alright. It's just this chest infection that's the trouble. Once I'm over that, I'll be able to –'

'That's another thing,' Margaret broke in. 'I've had reports that you aren't co-operating with the physios. You aren't going to get over this infection if you don't work on clearing your chest. No pain, no gain, as they say.'

'Well, if you only came here to nag …,' Jonah grumbled.

'I'm sorry,' Margaret apologised, sighing and trying to speak in a less hectoring tone. 'It's just that I'm worried about you – and so are the doctors. You were doing so well over the summer, and now you're back to the weight you were right back at the beginning of July – before Lucy took you in hand. I was hoping you'd be fit to come home for Christmas – at least for a visit, if not to stay – but, to be honest, it's not looking very likely at the moment.'

'I told you – it's this chest infection that's getting me down. Once that's out of the way –'

'But I keep telling you,' Margaret's voice rose as she became more frustrated with her husband's attitude. 'You won't be able to fight it if you don't eat properly. How can you expect to get over a serious lung infection when you're heading rapidly for malnutrition?'

'Now that's just ridiculous!' Jonah protested. 'Don't exaggerate. I finished up my meat and two veg like a good boy yesterday dinner-time, when Lucy was here.'

'Yes,' Margaret admitted, 'they tell me you always manage to eat everything for her. I suppose that's something.' She sat thinking for a few moments. It was supremely frustrating to watch her husband wasting away, apparently simply through an unwillingness to take sufficient food to sustain him, but she was afraid that continuing to press the point would only antagonise him and make him more stubborn in refusing to eat. Then her rising irritation got the better of her.

'But that's not enough. You need to be eating three proper meals a day, at least until you're up to a safe BMI. The doctors were telling me that if you don't start putting on weight again soon they'll have to consider intravenous feeding.' Jonah maintained a stony silence and stared out of the window. 'If you can do it when Lucy feeds you, why can't you eat properly for anyone else?'

Jonah continued to stare at the window for several minutes. Then he turned his head and looked at her.

'It's different with Lucy,' he said at last. 'It's more like a game with her. I can see how much she enjoys being able to tell a grown-up to eat his greens!'

'I'm sure *she* doesn't see it as a game,' Margaret observed drily. 'She's a very serious-minded little lass and she thinks she's helping you to get better.'

'And so she is. I always feel better after she's been.'

'But it's no good, is it? Not if you're starving yourself the rest of the time. You're not playing fair. You owe it to her to do your best to make sure you *do* get better.'

'Look, I *am* doing my best,' Jonah said testily. 'I know she'll be upset if I don't finish everything when she's there. I know she's only nine and doesn't understand. I know I've got to try to put a brave face on things for her sake. But for goodness sake! Can't you give me a break? I can't always be acting as if everything's hunky-dory and it's all going to be alright in the end. It isn't and it won't be. Is it any wonder I feel depressed sometimes?'

'No, of course not. Actually, that was something else I wanted to talk to you about. I know you don't like the idea of taking antidepressants, but– '

'Dead right, I don't,' Jonah said sharply, becoming more animated than Margaret had seen him for some time in his determination not to admit to any sort of mental illness. 'I'm not clinically depressed! I'm just understandably less than over the moon about getting a bullet in my neck and being paralysed from the chest down.'

Margaret leaned forward and hugged Jonah round the shoulders, resting her head on the top of his so that he could not see the tears gathering in her eyes. Her hair, currently died a rusty brown with creamy-coloured streaks, fell forward and brushed across his forehead. She breathed deeply, trying to compose herself. After what seemed like an age, she felt sufficiently in control of her voice to speak. She sat back and looked at her husband He was staring vacantly out of the window again.

'I'm sorry,' she said softly. 'I know it's bad for you – and I know that none of us can imagine how bad. But I do wish you'd try to see that it's bad for us too.'

'Oh, I know that alright,' Jonah interrupted. 'Don't think I don't care about the effect it's having on you all. I know how difficult it is for you to get time to come over here every day. And I know it's probably spoiling Lucy's childhood thinking she's got to look after me instead of doing all the things normal kids do at her age. I keep wondering whether I ought to tell her to stop coming, but I know she wouldn't agree to it and it would only upset her all the more to think that I didn't want her. And I know Nathan hasn't been able to concentrate on his university course because of worrying about me. And–'

'But that's not what I meant. I mean that it's tearing us all apart seeing you going downhill like this. You were so positive a couple of months ago – really determined not to let this defeat you. But these last few weeks, it's been as if you don't care anymore. And we really don't want to lose you. Can't you see that? I thought, maybe, having Reuben and Ann coming down to show you your first grandchild would help to buck you up. But, if anything, it seemed to make things worse.'

'Of course it made things worse!' Jonah growled. 'How d'you think I feel, not even being able to hold my own grandson? And I saw Reuben's face when he walked in the door. I could tell he was thinking, *what a pity the bullet wasn't a couple of inches higher so it'd have been in the brain instead of the neck and-*'

'That's ridiculous!' Margaret exclaimed. 'He never thought anything of the sort. You're just being-'

'But he did though,' Jonah insisted. 'He was thinking that a nice clean assassination would have been so much better than … this! And sometimes … well, sometimes I think maybe he's right.'

Margaret could not think of anything to say to this. She had looked forward to the visit from their older son, Reuben, and his wife. They did not see them as often as she would have liked, because they lived far away in County Durham and Reuben's job kept him busy. It had been good of them to take out four days from his two weeks of paternity leave to bring their newborn son down to Oxfordshire to see his grandparents. And she had expected it to be a treat for Jonah, and something to make him realise that life was worth living. Instead, it would appear that it had only brought home to him how much he was going to miss out by being paralysed and confined to a wheelchair.

She became aware that Jonah was speaking again and turned to listen.

'When they told me George was on the way, I thought how nice it would be to have grandchildren. I thought it would be like when the boys were young – only better, because we'd always be able to hand them back again afterwards! I thought we'd take them to the park and go for walks on the Ridgeway and play games with them in the garden and help them get up to all the mischief that we complained at Reuben and Nathan about. But now …,' he trailed off into a long sigh. 'A fine Granddad I'm going to be!'

'But you will!' Margaret insisted, forcing herself to sound cheerful, while feeling far from it. 'Just not doing the things you were imagining back then.' Back then! It sounded as if she were talking about the distant past, rather than six months ago. 'Kids don't want their grown-ups to be racing round doing things all the time. Sometimes they're glad to have someone who'll just sit and talk … or read to them! Think about all the books you and Lucy have got through together since you've been in here. And you'll still be able to go to the park – maybe even to the Ridgeway – in your wheelchair.' She paused, wondering whether to go on. Then she took a deep breath and added emphatically, 'provided you buck up your ideas and start eating and exercising again.'

Jonah said nothing. He was staring out of the window once more. Margaret racked her brains for more examples to focus Jonah's mind on the things that he could still do and stop him dwelling on all the things that were now denied him.

'What about your computer,' she said at last. 'Since you got that special mouse and keypad that the guy from the university rigged up for you, you were getting on really well with that. A few weeks ago, every time I came you were full of all the new things you'd found on the internet. And it meant you could keep in touch with people too. But it's ages since you said anything about what you've been looking at, and Reuben told me he hasn't had an email from you for weeks.'

Jonah sighed.

'I got out of the habit when I had those pressure sores, back in September,' he explained eventually, still staring into the distance. 'I was kept lying on my front or my side for nearly two weeks while they healed up. I couldn't get the screen arranged so that I could see it and work the mouse at the same time. And then, by the time I was able to sit up and take notice again, it was too much of an effort trying to re-learn how to use it.'

'You never used to be afraid of a bit of hard work,' Margaret commented, trying to speak normally, as if they were at home together discussing a particularly difficult case that he was working on or contemplating some heavy digging in the garden. 'Where's all your *get up and go* got to?'

'I'm sorry.' Jonah turned his face to look at her briefly, before returning to his contemplation of the view through the window. 'It's this awful chest of mine. It makes me feel so lethargic. Once the antibiotics get that sorted, I'll have another go.'

Margaret decided against repeating her view that it was the lethargy that was preventing Jonah from throwing off the infection and not the infection that was causing the lethargy. She watched him in silence for a few moments and then looked down at her watch. She stood up and gave him another hug around his shoulders, kissing him on the cheek.

'I'm sorry. I'm going to have to go. Give my love to Lucy when she comes. And ... and you will think about what I said, won't you?'

Jonah nodded absently. Then, with a great effort, he turned to look at her and forced a weak smile.

'I'll try. Once I've got over this chest infection, things will be better – you'll see.'

Margaret bent down to pick up her crash helmet. She stood there with it in her hands, looking at him for a few seconds before giving him a final kiss and turning to go. She hurried past the nurses' station, nodding in response to the cheery greeting from Danielle, the nurse on duty. She did not trust herself to speak and wanted to get out before anyone saw the tears that she could feel coming, now that she was starting to relax her self-control.

As soon as she was out in the corridor, she put on the helmet. It would look rather odd to be walking through a hospital like that, but at least it obscured her face from prying eyes. Her brown, calf-length culottes swished against her leather cowboy boots as she hurried on down the now-familiar route to where she had left her motorbike. In the cold air outside, her visor steamed up and she had to take the helmet off in order to see. She fumbled in the pocket of her leather jacket for a handkerchief and wiped her eyes, still striding purposefully on across the car park.

She sat astride the motorbike, slowly wiping the inside of her helmet with her handkerchief, struggling to compose herself sufficiently to make the journey back to the hospital in Reading where she worked. What was she going to say to Reuben when he rang that night? After his recent visit, he had been so concerned about his father's condition that he had demanded to be given daily updates. What about Nathan? He was such a worrier! Up until now, she had kept her anxieties to herself, making reassuring noises whenever he suggested that Dad was not making as much progress as he had been led to expect. Was it time now to start preparing him for the worst?

18.10 THURSDAY 29TH OCTOBER

'Hi there Lucy!' Staff nurse Robert Overton greeted them as they entered the ward that evening. 'We've got your patient all ready for you, but the dinners aren't here yet. That's a nasty bump you've got there,' he added, seeing the purple bruising and line of stitches on Lucy's face. 'What happened?'

'She had a bit of an argument with an old fence post with a nail sticking out of it,' Peter said hastily, trying to play down the incident. 'It looks worse than it is. They said at the hospital that once the swelling goes down you'll hardly be able to see it.'

'You go right on in,' Robert continued, realising from Peter's tone that he did not want any further discussion of Lucy's injury. 'He's waiting for you. I'll bring the dinner in when it comes.'

'Is there something I can put these in?' Lucy asked, holding up a large bunch of Michaelmas daisies, which she had picked from her garden.

'I don't think there is – not in Jonah's room. You go on in and I'll hunt out a vase for them and bring it in to you.'

'Thanks.' Lucy trotted off down the ward carrying the flowers.

'Jeanette not around?' Peter asked. He had struck up a friendship with one of the other nurses, whose family, it had turned out, came from the same small town in Jamaica where Peter's first wife had been born. Often, when it was Peter's turn to bring Lucy to visit Jonah, he would spend the time chatting with Jeanette. This suited Jonah, who still felt embarrassed at being fed like a baby in front of his colleague.

'No,' Robert told him. 'She's on nights this week.'

'Ah,' Peter nodded understanding. 'Well I'd better go and say hello to Jonah.'

He hurried after Lucy, anxious to be there when her friend was confronted with the disturbing contusion on her face.

They entered the room together. Jonah was sitting up next to the bed, in a high-backed chair, specially designed to provide good support for patients with spinal injuries. He appeared to have become smaller since Peter last saw him. He had always been a lightly built, wiry type, but now he was gaunt, rather than slim, and his clothes hung loose about him.

He looked up and smiled to see Lucy. Then his face changed as he took in the angry purple-and-red swelling on her face, and he looked towards Peter with an expression of anxious enquiry. Peter smiled back. He was about to say something reassuring about the injury being merely superficial, but Lucy spoke first.

'I brought you these,' she said, holding out the flowers. 'There are loads of them all along the border under the big pear tree. Nurse Robbie says he's going to bring us a vase for them.'

'Thank you, Miss Paige,' Jonah said solemnly, addressing Lucy in the formal way that he had used with her ever since their first encounter when she was only a few weeks old. 'Put them in the sink for now and come and tell me what you've been doing to yourself.'

'It's a long story,' Peter began, hoping to deter further questions. 'The main thing is it's not serious. It just looks awful, that's all.'

'Let's hear it then!' was Jonah's response. 'I like a good story and there's plenty of time – it's not as if I'm going anywhere, is it?'

Lucy, returning from the sink, put her arms around him and kissed him tenderly on the cheek.

'I'll tell you all about it while you're eating your dinner,' she offered. 'But *only* if you *promise* that you'll eat it all up.'

'You drive a hard bargain, Miss Paige,' Jonah grumbled. 'What if it's something I don't like?'

'We all have to do things we don't like sometimes,' Lucy said primly, repeating a favourite saying of a teacher from her time in the Infant School. 'And I've got something special for you, for when you've finished it.'

She turned to Peter and held out her hand. He obediently reached inside a canvas bag, which he had brought with them, and took out a plastic container. Lucy took it and held it in front of Jonah. She removed the lid to reveal a small pile of gingerbread men, decorated with blue icing.

'Sylvia and I made them today,' she told him. 'I've brought you four. That's one to eat now, one with your bedtime drink, one with elevenses tomorrow and one for afternoon tea.'

'They look very good,' Jonah said, trying to sound appreciative. 'But I'm not sure that I'll be able to eat as many as that. Don't you want to keep some for yourself?'

'I already have – and some for Mam and Peter. These are for you.'

'Well, thank you very much.'

Lucy put the lid back on the box and put it down on the top of the bedside locker.

'Here you are!' Robert came in carrying a large glass vase. 'Shall I put the flowers in it for you?'

'No. I'll do it.' Lucy took the vase and went over to the sink to fill it.

'The dinners are here,' Robert told Jonah. 'I'll send yours in as soon as we've sorted out whose is whose.'

'Thanks,' Jonah said without enthusiasm.

Robert left. Lucy carried the full vase carefully over to the bedside locker and set it down next to the box of gingerbread.

'Thanks, Lucy,' Jonah said, looking at the flowers and wondering whether Margaret would have remembered to tie up the tall Michaelmas daisies in his own garden. The recent spell of windy weather was sure to have ruined them, if not. 'Now, tell me how you come to look as if you've gone three rounds with Mike Tyson '

'Not until you promise,' Lucy insisted.

The door opened and one of the Healthcare Assistants entered carrying a tray of food. She set the meal down on a table-on-wheels that stood next to the bed, adjusted it to the right height for Jonah's chair and positioned it over his lap.

'There you are Nurse Lucy. All ready for you. Ring the bell when you're finished and I'll come and take away the empties.'

'Thank you, Susan. I can manage now,' Lucy said, impatient to be left alone to care for her patient.

Peter settled down in a chair in the corner of the room and took out a book. He knew that Jonah did not like being watched while he was fed – and Peter himself felt embarrassed at seeing his colleague's helplessness exposed in that way. So he positioned the chair at an angle to avoid catching Jonah's eye whenever he looked up from his reading.

Lucy lifted the lid from the dinner plate and inspected its contents. 'It looks like curry and rice,' she said. 'I know you like that, so now will you promise?'

'All right – I promise. Now can I have my story?'

Lucy nodded and smiled.

'I told you I was going out in Martin's boat this morning, didn't I? Well, he came round, just like we'd planned ...'

She recounted everything that had happened, starting with their bicycle ride down Headington Hill and through the city to Hythe Bridge Street. She told him how they had waved goodbye to Bernie before heading down the path between Castle Mill Stream and the Oxford Canal to where the *Maid of Saxony* was berthed. She described in detail everything that they had done, said and seen during their leisurely journey along the canal, through the Sheepwash Channel, into the River Thames and on past Port Meadow. All the time, she skilfully fed Jonah with small spoonfuls of food, watching carefully to see when he was ready for more and, in between mouthfuls, offering sips of water from a plastic cup with a long straw.

By the time that she reached the point in the story where the three strangers appeared in the fields next to the river, Jonah had consumed the first course and Lucy was engaged in cutting up a small treacle pudding into bite-sized pieces.

As she started to describe the drama that had unfolded on the bank, Lucy was gratified that she had at last found a grown-up who was taking serious interest in the unknown woman and her pursuers. As they reached the end of the story – and the end of the pudding – Jonah became more animated than she had seen him for some weeks.

'Do they know who the woman was?' he demanded, swallowing the last spoonful. 'Have they found her yet?'

'I don't think so,' Lucy shook her head. 'I don't think anyone's looking for her.'

'But why on earth not? She assaulted you *and* she may be in danger from the two men that you saw. There ought to be a team of officers out there – with dogs – searching the area. Peter!'

Peter looked up from his book.

'Do you know if they've found the woman who hit

Lucy yet?'

'No. You know I can't get involved. I've got a conflict of interest.'

'You must know whether they've had people out looking for her,' Jonah persisted.

'As far as I know, they haven't,' Peter said, wishing that Jonah would drop the subject.

'That horrible policewoman doesn't believe there *was* a woman on the bank,' Lucy said resentfully. 'She thinks I'm just making it up.'

'Why on earth would you do that?' Jonah asked in astonishment.

'*She* thinks that Martin hit me. *She* thinks that he told me to say there was a woman who hit me and ran off, so that he wouldn't get into trouble.'

'Did she say that? Did she actually accuse you of lying?'

'No – but she did accuse Peter of not looking after me properly,' Lucy said indignantly. 'Andy told her off about that,' she added with satisfaction.

'Andy?'

'DC Lepage,' Peter explained. 'My current bag-carrier. I was giving him a lift into work when Martin called me. Look, I'm sure it isn't really how Lucy thinks. Constable Ferrar just didn't put things very well.'

'Then why didn't she let me tell her about the man with the knife?' Lucy demanded. 'That was before you got there. I tried to tell her about those two men who were chasing the woman and she said not to let my imagination run away with me and to stick to how I got my face hurt.'

'Well, tell me about it now,' Jonah urged her. 'I'm listening. What did the men look like?'

'I didn't get a very good look at them,' Lucy admitted regretfully. 'They were a long way away and it was still a bit dark.'

'Were they tall or short?' Jonah prompted. 'Fat or thin? What sort of clothes were they wearing?'

'I don't know.' Lucy thought hard. 'They were both

about the same height, I think, and not very fat or very thin – but I wasn't noticing really. I think the first one – the one with the thing that I thought was a knife – I think he wasn't as old as the other one.'

'What makes you think that?' Jonah asked.

Before Lucy could answer, Susan the healthcare assistant returned to bring in cups of tea for them all and to see whether Jonah had finished his dinner. She smiled to see the empty plates.

'My, my, Lucy!' she said heartily. 'We could do with having you around to deal with all our difficult patients! I wish you'd tell me how you do it.'

She cleared away the dirty dishes and went out again. Jonah immediately turned back to Lucy.

'You were telling me about the men on the river bank,' he reminded her. 'What made you think that one of them was older than the other?'

'I'm not sure,' Lucy answered. 'Something about the way they ran, I think. The second one just looked old somehow.'

'Old like Stan or old like Peter?' Jonah wanted to know, realising that anyone over the age of about forty probably seemed old to Lucy.

'I don't know,' Lucy shook her head. 'Anyway,' she added, fixing him with a stern gaze. 'I'm not answering any more questions until you start drinking your tea and eating your gingerbread man.'

In between taking small bites of the biscuit, which Lucy offered up to his mouth, Jonah continued with his interrogation.

'Forget about the men for now – what about the woman? You must have got up close enough to her to see her face. What was she like?'

'She was facing away from me,' Lucy told him. 'I think that's why she hit me. I think she thought I was one of the men coming to get her.'

'OK then. What *did* you see? What about her clothes

and her hair?'

'Her hair was dark – I think – unless it was just because it was dark in the bushes. And she was wearing a dress – a long dress – all pink and glittery. I remember because it was a silly thing to be wearing for running across the fields.'

'Now that's interesting,' Jonah said thoughtfully. 'I wonder how she got there. Maybe the men were holding her somewhere near there – in a barn or something – and she escaped. Now, is there anything else you saw that could help identify who she is?'

'She had a picture on her arm,' Lucy said, suddenly seeing in her mind the pale hand, sweeping round towards her, gripping the improvised weapon. 'The one that was holding the piece of wood that she hit me with.'

'A tattoo?' Jonah asked eagerly. 'What was it like?'

'It was a plant.'

'What sort of plant? Can you draw it for me? Peter! Have you got a pen there?'

'I'm not very good at drawing,' Lucy said anxiously. 'And I don't remember it very well. It was just some wiggly stems and some leaves and some purple flowers.' She thought hard, trying to remember more details. 'It looked like a climbing plant – it had curly bits, like sweat peas do.'

'That's excellent! A climbing plant with purple flowers. Well done, Lucy,' Jonah praised her. 'Let's see if we can work out what sort it was. Take away this cup – it's alright, I've finished it,' he added, seeing Lucy's disapproving frown. 'And bring over the computer. There must be some pictures we could have a look at to get some ideas.'

Peter got up and picked up a laptop computer from a shelf at the side of the room. He brought it over and placed it on the table in front of Jonah. Lucy plugged in a specially-designed miniature keypad and mouse combination and gently placed Jonah's left hand over it. Since his injury, the only movement that he had below shoulder level was in the thumb and first two fingers of his left hand.

At first Jonah struggled to manipulate the controls. Skills that he had acquired over the summer months had been forgotten during weeks of disuse and he was now having to learn them again. Gradually it became easier, however, and it was only a matter of ten minutes or so before they were all looking at a picture of a purple-flowered clematis.

'No,' Lucy said decidedly. 'The flowers weren't like that at all.'

'How about this then?' Jonah navigated to another page.

'No. That's wisteria, isn't it? We've got one on the back of our house. It wasn't that. It was more like a wild flower.'

Jonah continued to search for more plant species for Lucy to consider. She looked at each carefully and then shook her head. They had just decided that the tattoo on the woman's arm might perhaps have been of a flower from the pea family when Peter announced that it was time for them to go.

'I promised your mam that I'd have you in bed before she got home,' he told Lucy.

Lucy kissed Jonah goodbye and got up to leave. Jonah called after them as they opened the door.

'Get on to Missing Persons, Peter,' he said. 'And see if they've got a woman on file with a tattoo on her forearm. If my theory's right and those men had kidnapped her, she may have been reported missing.'

'You know I'm not allowed to interfere in this,' Peter sighed, turning back. 'And if she was being held against her will, isn't it more likely that she's been trafficked from abroad?'

'Probably, but you never know. Go on – you needn't tell them why you want to know. Just a quick search of their database, that's all.'

'OK,' Peter conceded reluctantly. He would much have preferred to try to forget about the whole incident – and to encourage Lucy to do so too – but he did not want to refuse Jonah's request point blank. The idea of identifying the mysterious woman seemed to have raised his spirits so much (compared with the low mood that he had exhibited when they arrived that evening) that Peter felt obliged to go along with the plan. 'I'll see what I can do. Now, we really must go.'

20.05 THURSDAY 29TH OCTOBER

They found Martin waiting on the doorstep when they returned. He was holding Lucy's bike, which she had left chained up by the boat moorings that morning and subsequently forgotten about. Peter invited him in, telling Lucy to make them all a drink while he put the bike away. When he got back, he found Martin sitting at the kitchen table watching Lucy as she stirred a pan of cocoa.

'When will Bernie be back?' he asked Peter anxiously. 'Does she know yet?'

'I sent her an email once I knew she'd be on the train back,' Peter told him. 'I thought that would be easier than trying to explain over the phone, and better than waiting until she got home. That way she's got the whole story in front of her and she can't interrupt before I've explained properly.'

'How's she taking it?'

'She didn't say much – just thanks for letting her know.' Seeing that Martin was continuing to watch him anxiously, Peter added, 'She'll be here soon. Her latest update said that the train was just coming into Banbury, so she'll be here in about three quarters of an hour – which means that you'd better hurry up and drink that cocoa and get off to bed or I'll be in trouble,' he added to Lucy.

They sat round the table making rather stilted conversation while they drank the cocoa and ate one of Lucy's gingerbread men each. Martin's eyes kept being drawn to the ugly swelling on Lucy's face, and he kept looking away again quickly hoping that she had not noticed him staring at it.

Peter wanted to reassure Martin that he was not to blame, but he also wanted to avoid speaking about the incident in front of Lucy for fear of reawakening her anxiety on the subject. He talked with a rather false cheerfulness about Lucy's plans for the remainder of her half-term holiday and made polite enquiries about Martin's work and his mother's health. Getting very little encouragement from either of his companions, eventually he relapsed into silence.

'Martin?' All of a sudden, Lucy put down her mug and fixed him with her eye. 'Will you show me the video you took of the doctor sewing up my face?'

'Are you sure you really want to see it?' Martin asked dubiously. 'It wasn't very nice to watch.'

'Yes, of course!' Lucy insisted. 'Come on – let me see. Please!'

Martin reached inside his jacket pocket and got out his smartphone. He selected the video app and set it running. Then he put the phone down on the table in front of Lucy. She snatched it up in her hand and held it in front of her face, gazing down at it intently. Peter, who was sitting beside her, leaned towards her so that he could see the screen over her shoulder.

'The picture isn't very clear,' Lucy complained. 'And you keep letting the doctor's head get in the way.'

'I'm sorry,' Martin apologised. 'I didn't want to put her off. It wasn't very easy to get a clear view.'

Lucy watched intently, taking in every movement of the

doctor's hands as she expertly stitched up the wound. She smiled with satisfaction that Martin had left the camera running afterwards and had managed to take a close-up of the splinter of wood lying in the kidney dish. Then her expression changed to a frown as she saw the doctor's hands picking up the dish and then a jumble of images as she crossed in front of the lens. The picture jerked and swayed as Martin struggled to stop the recording, but Lucy could see the doctor tipping out the contents of the kidney dish into a yellow bin.

'What she doing?' Lucy demanded. 'What's she done with the splinter?'

'I suppose it will have been thrown away with the swabs that she used to clean the cut,' Martin suggested.

'But it's evidence!' Lucy protested. 'Isn't it, Daddy? It must have come off that piece of wood. It shows we were telling the truth!'

'Well, yes,' Peter admitted, 'but it isn't really that important.'

'Mike says, you've got to preserve every little bit of evidence just in case it turns out to be important later,' Lucy objected.

'But Mike's a pathologist,' Peter argued. 'His patients are all dead – so they can't tell him what happened. We know you were hit with that piece of wood because you and Martin told us.'

'But that horrid policewoman thinks we're lying.'

'No. I'm sure she doesn't really.'

'And Martin didn't see what happened. He was in the boat.'

'Well, if that was what hit you, there'll be your blood on the end of it,' Peter pointed out, trying to close down the subject. 'Now, hurry up and drink that cocoa. It's past your bedtime and I don't want to catch it from your mam.'

Lucy finished her drink in silence. Then she put down her mug and slipped off her chair. She went and stood in front of Martin, looking up at his face.

'Good night. Thank you for taking me out in your boat and showing me the sunrise,' she said politely.

'That's alright. I just wish you hadn't ended up in hospital.'

'That wasn't your fault,' Lucy said earnestly, her face falling as she went over in her mind, yet again, the conversation with Louise Ferrar. 'I'm sorry I got you into trouble. I didn't mean to.'

She flung her arms around Martin's chest and hugged him as hard as she could. 'Good night,' she said again, kissing him on the cheek.

'Come along Lucy,' Peter said, taking hold of her by the shoulder. 'Stop procrastinating. It's time you were in bed.'

Martin gently unwound Lucy's arms from around his waist and got to his feet.

'I'd better be off. Good night Lucy. I hope your face is better soon.'

'You don't have to go,' Peter told him. 'You're welcome to wait until Bernie gets home, if you'd like to …'

'No. I'd better go. She'll be busy. She'll want to see that Lucy's OK. She won't want me around,' Martin said, mentally adding, *because she'll want to be able to say what she thinks of me without having to be polite about it.*

'Well, alright – if you're sure. Thanks for bringing the bike back.'

20.30 THURSDAY 29TH OCTOBER

'Here you are, young Jonah!' Nurse Jeanette Slater came into Jonah's room carrying a plastic cup, with a long straw protruding from a hole in its lid, and a plate on which there lay another of Lucy's gingerbread men. 'I've brought your bedtime malted milk and I've got special orders from Nurse Lucy to see that you eat this.'

'Uh-huh,' Jonah murmured absently, without looking up from his computer screen.

Jeanette came over to the bed and started making adjustments to get Jonah into a better position for drinking. In doing so, she moved his hand off the computer control panel. He grunted annoyance and looked at her sullenly.

'Can't you wait a bit? I'm busy.'

'Are you now? What is it you're so interested in all of a sudden?' Jeanette looked at the picture on the screen. 'Tattoo studios!' she exclaimed in surprise. 'Don't tell me *you're* planning to get one done.'

'No,' Jonah explained. 'I'm just researching designs. Lucy was telling me about one she'd seen and I was

52

wondering if it was a standard motif or something bespoke. Now, will you please put my hand back on the mouse so I can carry on?'

'Not so fast, young man! First, drink this all up. Then, if you eat Lucy's gingerbread man too, I'll let you have half an hour playing on your computer before lights out.'

'I wish you wouldn't keep treating me like a child,' Jonah grumbled irritably. 'I'm not at prep school.' He knew that his complaint was entirely unreasonable. He knew, if he bothered to think, that Jeanette would never have dreamed of addressing him in this teasing way had it not been part of the friendly relationship that they had built up over the months that he had spent on her ward. Normally – or what had been normal until recent events had blighted his sense of humour – he would have happily responded in similar vein; but right now he was in no mood for joking.

'I do beg your pardon, Inspector Porter.' Jeanette sounded serious, but her eyes were shining with amusement. 'In that case, I'll just remind you that it's important for your kidney function to take in plenty of fluids and that the doctors are still concerned about your recent weight loss. And I know that, as a responsible adult, you won't want to cause your young friend distress by refusing to eat the biscuits that she baked for you.'

'Oh alright!' Jonah said ungraciously. 'I suppose we'd better get on with it. I can see I'll get no peace unless I do.'

He had no intention of disappointing Lucy, but at the same time, he resented the power that she exercised over him – and especially the fact that Jeanette was aware of it and was prepared to use it to force him into co-operation. Jeanette sat down on a chair next to the bed and started feeding him gingerbread, encouraging him to take small bites in between sips from the cup.

'Why do women have tattoos?' He asked her a few minutes later.

'Now that's something I've never thought about. I

don't think there would be much point *me* having one.' Jeanette looked down at her own dark brown arms and hands. 'Why do you ask?'

'Just wondering. It's this woman who lashed out at Lucy – you've presumably heard about what happened?'

'Not about that. Robbie told me she had a big bruise on her face when she came in this afternoon, but he didn't know how it had happened. He seemed to think it was some sort of accident.'

'Well, it wasn't. She disturbed some woman who was hiding in the bushes along the river, and the woman hit her. The only thing Lucy can remember about her is that she had a tattoo on her arm. I was wandering if it might help us to identify her. You haven't answered my question. You must know lots of young nurses. Don't they ever have tattoos?'

'We try to discourage them. Lots of patients – especially the older ones – don't like them.' She thought for a few moments. 'Danielle has one – on her shoulder. She said she had it done for a bet when she was at uni.'

'I suppose at least she had the sense to have it somewhere that she can keep hidden if she wants to. I hope nobody would be stupid enough to get themselves tattooed somewhere prominent like their forearm just for a bet.'

'I read an article about people using tattoos to disguise birthmarks,' Jeanette remembered. 'It was in one of the medical journals, because there had been some cases of melanoma not being detected because the tattoo covered up changes in the skin pigment.'

'And presumably some women get them done just because they like them,' Jonah muttered. 'I can't imagine why. I mean – however much you like a picture, you'd want to be able to change it if you got bored with it, wouldn't you?'

'I think it's mainly a fashion thing – and peer pressure. And I have seen some very attractive designs. Now you've reminded me about it, there was a young woman on the ward a couple of years back who had tattoos all over her. She was like a walking picture gallery!'

'What sort of pictures?'

'Flowers mainly – and birds of paradise with long, curling feathers. Lots of blues and greens and reds.'

Jeanette fed Jonah with the last piece of biscuit and got up to go, carefully positioning his hand on the computer keypad before she left, carrying the empty cup.

'You can have twenty minutes,' she told him. 'Then I'll be back to settle you down for the night.'

21.00 THURSDAY 29TH OCTOBER

The solar powered light over the side gate came on as Bernie brought her bicycle to a halt in front of it. She fumbled in her pocket for the key. Soon she was pushing her bike down the side of the house to the large brick-built outbuilding, which had once been the wash house and now contained an array of gardening equipment, bicycles for all the family and an assortment of old toys belonging to Lucy.

Peter was waiting for her in the kitchen when she came in at the back door.

'How is she?' Bernie asked at once.

'Fine. It looks awful, but the doctor was convinced it wouldn't leave much of a scar. Poor Martin's terribly cut-up about it. I think he's more bothered about it than she is.'

'Well, I won't go up now.' Bernie looked at her watch. 'Time enough in the morning for me to inspect the damage.' She crossed the room, making for the door to the hall. 'Make us a brew, will you, while I hang my coat up?'

'Mam?' Bernie finished taking off her fluorescent

cycling jacket and hung it on its peg in the hall, before looking up to see her daughter, standing in her pyjamas at the top of the long flight of stairs. 'Mam! Will you come and tuck me in?'

'Alright. I'll be up in a moment. Go back to bed.' She went back to the kitchen and put her head round the door. 'Her ladyship wants me,' she told Peter. 'I'm going upstairs – and I may be some time!'

She found Lucy sitting up in bed with her legs bent up under the duvet and her arms around them. She watched her mother with anxious eyes as she crossed the room. In the dim light from the bedside lamp, her face looked swollen and misshapen, but Bernie could not see the line of stitches or the bluish colouration of the bruising

'I thought you wanted me to tuck you in,' she said, trying to speak normally and not to look at the wound. 'I can't do that with you sitting up like that, can I?'

Lucy obediently lowered her legs and slid down into a lying position. Bernie pulled up the bedclothes around her and leant forward to kiss her on the cheek.

'Mam?'

'Yes?'

'Will Social Services have me taken into care?'

'No, of course not! Whatever made you think of that?' Bernie sat down cross-legged on the floor beside the bed and looked Lucy in the eyes, trying to puzzle out what could be going on in her head.

'There was this awful policewoman – didn't Peter tell you about her?'

'No love. I've only just got in. He hasn't had time to tell me anything. I only know what he put in his email.'

'She thinks Martin hit me. And she thinks Peter shouldn't have let me go out with him. And she thinks you shouldn't have left me at home with Peter when you went to Manchester. And she said she was going to tell Social Services. And-'

'Hang on! What makes you think all this? Who was this

policewoman? What did she actually say?'

Lucy took a deep breath as she tried to decide where to start. Then she let it out in a sigh, still thinking. Bernie waited patiently.

'She came when Martin called 999,' Lucy said at last. 'I thought she'd want to know about the men with the knife and the woman who was running away from them, but she wouldn't listen.'

'Sorry, love – you've lost me. What men?'

'I saw these two men on the bank, chasing this woman. And I *think* one of them had a knife. They ran away when they saw us looking at them. We went to see if the woman needed us to help her. At least, I did. Martin was still tying up the boat.'

'And she hit you?' Bernie asked. 'Peter said it was some stranger on the riverbank.'

'Yes. She was hiding from the men – in the bushes. She must have been scared that I was them coming to get her. I told that policewoman that she ought to find her – and the men – but she wouldn't listen. She just kept saying all these silly things about me being a brave girl and the ambulance being there soon.'

'I expect she was just wanting to make sure you were safe before trying to find the men and the woman,' Bernie suggested. 'If she was on her own, she couldn't look after you and go chasing after three people going in different directions, could she?'

'She could have radioed for help,' Lucy argued, unwilling to be convinced. 'And she could have listened to me properly and not kept telling me not to be afraid of saying what really happened. I *know* she thinks it was Martin that hit me. And then, when Peter got there and she found out that Martin wasn't my dad, she said that you shouldn't have left me alone with Peter and he shouldn't have let Martin take me out. And she said she was going to tell Social Services. They won't take me into Care, will they? I want to stay here with you and Peter.'

'No, of course not,' Bernie assured her. 'Social Services don't have nearly enough places to take every little girl who has an accident and ends up at A and E. All she was saying was that she'll have to file a report.'

'Isn't that a bit silly – if she doesn't think they ought to take me away?'

'Lucy, love, it's more complicated than that. They don't just rush in and take children away from their families the first time something happens – but they do make a note of incidents that might mean that there's something wrong. Anyone can have an accident, but if the same kid keeps turning up at A and E week after week, it suggests there's something wrong. So it's important that someone makes a note of it, so that they'll spot if that's happening. If Peter and I really *were* battering you, we'd probably take you to different hospitals each time to stop anyone realising. I expect that report to Social Services is just to make sure that there's someone, who would notice if it happened again.'

'Are you sure?'

'Positive. Taking a child into Care is a last resort – honestly! The absolute worst that could possibly happen to you is that you'll be added to the local authority risk register for a bit – until they're satisfied that we're looking after you properly.'

'And Martin?' Lucy persisted. 'He won't be in trouble? I'm sure she thinks *he* hit me.'

'Even if she does – and I think you may be wrong about that – he can't be prosecuted without any evidence. *You* say it was someone else and the only other evidence is the lump of wood-'

'Which *I* carried to the boat and gave to the policewoman,' Lucy said, cheering up a little at the recollection of the pains that she had taken to preserve this important piece of evidence. 'And I didn't let Martin touch it, so it won't have his fingerprints on it.'

'There you are then!' Bernie said triumphantly, feeling

relieved that her daughter appeared, at last, to be coming round to the idea that the adults in her life were not all doomed to spend the rest of their lives in jail, condemned for crimes that they did not commit. 'Whatever PC Childprotection *thinks*, there's no evidence that any of us did anything wrong – or that you are in any danger of abuse – so just try to stop worrying about it. Now settle down and go to sleep. Everything will seem better in the morning – it always does.'

She leaned forward and gave her daughter another kiss on the cheek. Then she got to her feet and turned to go.

'Mam?' Lucy called after her. 'If Social Service *do* take me away, do you think they'd let me stay with Karen?'

Karen Witcombe was a neighbour of theirs. She had been a short-term foster carer since before Bernie had first come to live in the house in Headington, on her marriage to Lucy's father. Over the years, dozens of children had spent time living with her and her husband, Roy, during family crises or while Social Services were arranging more permanent homes for them. Occasionally she would invite Lucy to play with members of her ever-changing family.

'I wouldn't mind quite so much then,' Lucy continued, 'because I'd only be over the road and I could come and see you and Peter.'

'I told you,' Bernie said, with a warning tone in her voice that made it clear to Lucy that no more discussion was allowed, 'they aren't going to. So I'm not going to talk about what would happen if they did. Now settle down and go to sleep.'

12.00 FRIDAY 30ᵀᴴ OCTOBER

Dr Martin Riess, meanwhile, was doing more than his fair share of worrying on his own account. He sat in his room in Lichfield College staring morosely at the computer screen in front of him. The program that he had been attempting to de-bug all morning was still not functioning correctly. Indeed, it was arguably in a considerably worse state than when he began. He had started the day with an apparently working simulation of rock deformation under pressure, which had been producing results that did not agree with his expectations based on experimental data. Now he had a program that crashed out after a few minutes of run-time with the mysterious error message, "stack overflow". It must be looping, he decided. But where? He didn't remember changing anything that could have caused that to happen.

He sat back in his chair and put his hands on his head, ruffling up the flaxen hair. He closed his eyes, trying to concentrate on the problem in front of him. It was no good! All morning he had only had half a mind on his work, while the other half had been occupied with thinking about the events of the day before. He could not get out of his head the persistent images of Lucy, which kept appearing: Lucy smiling a welcome as she opened the front door to him; Lucy slipping her hand into his, as they stood at the stern of the *Maid of Saxony* watching the sky growing lighter beyond the dark line of trees at the eastern edge of Port Meadow; Lucy shouting out that they *must* help the woman on the bank; Lucy's face, with blood streaming from her cheek, looking up at him with incredulity that anyone could have deliberately hurt her; and – worst of all – Lucy's troubled face and trembling arms as she embraced him and kissed him goodnight.

It was no good. He could not concentrate. He had to do something about this, or he would end up wasting the afternoon as well as the morning. He reached across to the telephone on his desk and dialled.

'Hi Martin!' came Bernie's unmistakeable Liverpudlian accent a few moments later. 'Is it something quick, or shall I ring you back? I've got a couple of students with me at the moment.'

'I was hoping we could meet. Are you free later today?'

'I've got tutorials until four. I could come over then, if you like; or I could bring my sandwiches to your room and we can talk over lunch. That'd be in about … twenty minutes – just as soon as I've got rid of these two.'

'Yes please. Lunch would be great. Thanks. See you later.'

Martin hastened to get ready for Bernie's arrival. First, he made a quick trip across the quad to the Buttery[2] to purchase sandwiches for his lunch and a packet of biscuits to offer her with coffee afterwards. Back in his room, he re-filled the coffee machine and switched it on. Then he hunted for clean mugs. He had a set of six, each with a different view of the college printed on it, a gift from the Master to each Fellow on the occasion of the 500th

---

[2] A college shop where members can purchase provisions.

anniversary of the founding of Lichfield College a few years previously. They were all dirty – evidence of his distraction that morning. Had he really consumed six mugs of coffee since breakfast?

He took the mugs to the small kitchen on the floor below and washed them. Returning to his room, he arranged them neatly on the shelf next to the coffee machine. Then he hastily gathered up some papers that were lying strewn about on the two easy chairs and deposited them on an already overflowing desk in the corner of the room. Then he hesitated and selected one from the top of the pile and put it down on a small table next to the easy chairs, to remind him to read it after lunch. He was still standing in the middle of the worn carpet, gazing around for any further preparations that were needed, when there was a knock at the door and Bernie walked in.

'How's Lucy?' Martin asked at once.

'Absolutely fine,' Bernie assured him. 'Really,' she added, seeing his sceptical expression. 'She says it hardly hurts at all and she's absolutely adamant that it's not going to stop her going to football practice this afternoon. Honestly – she really isn't bothered about it.'

'But it's her face. What if it leaves a scar?'

'What if it does?' Bernie shrugged. 'She knows she'll get short shrift from me if she starts whinging about her looks being spoilt. Come on, Martin! This isn't the eighteenth century, where a woman's future happiness depends on her being pretty enough to bag a wealthy husband. Lucy's far too sensible to care about a little mark on her cheek. And, in any case, Peter told me that the doctor said it would probably heal up without leaving a noticeable scar. Oh! Just stop worrying, can't you?' She sighed. 'I never knew anyone so determined to make problems where none exist. What's that quotation? *If you see ten troubles coming down the road, you can be sure that nine will run into the ditch before they reach you.* Just forget about it. I told you – Lucy's fine.'

'Good, good. Well ... sit down! The coffee's ready.' Martin busied himself with pouring a mugful for each of them, while Bernie settled into one of the easy chairs and unwrapped her sandwiches.

'So! What was it you wanted to see me about?' Bernie asked, once he was seated on the chair opposite her.

'It's ... well ... I don't think I ought to take Lucy out on her own anymore.'

'Why on earth not?'

'I just don't think it's a good idea,' Martin hedged, reluctant to explain his real concerns.

'Because of what happened? That's ridiculous! It was just a fluke accident. It wasn't anything to do with you.'

'No – it's not that. It's ...,' Martin struggled to put his feelings into words. 'I'm afraid ... I don't know ... Isn't it a bit odd? You know ... a middle-aged bachelor and a little girl going out together - alone.'

'I don't see that it's odd at all. And I won't have you claiming to be middle-aged, seeing as you're eight and a half years younger than me,' Bernie said, trying to make a joke of Martin's fears. 'What's brought all this on?' she added, seeing from his face that he was serious and not intending to back down. 'Is it that idiotic policewoman? Lucy said she wouldn't believe it wasn't you who hit her.'

'No – it's not that! Or, at least ... no ... no, it's ...,' Martin took a deep breath and tried to explain. 'It was afterwards. I came round yesterday evening to bring Lucy's bike back and check that she was alright. When Peter told her it was time for bed, she came over and put her arms round me and I felt ...,' he was conscious of his heart racing in his chest and his cheeks flushing hot. 'Well, it felt good. And that can't be natural, can it? Me getting a kick out of having a little girl hug and kiss me? And it made me think ... maybe there's something wrong with me, to make me feel that way.'

For a moment or two, Bernie was lost for words. Martin's statement was so unexpected. Was he seriously suggesting that he might be a paedophile?

'That's preposterous!' she said vehemently, as soon as she had collected her thoughts sufficiently to speak at all. 'There's nothing unnatural about feeling good when a kid hugs you. I'm sure you didn't feel any different about getting a kiss from Lucy from how I feel when she does it to me.'

'But that's different – you're her Mum.'

'Peter then – or Stan and Sylvia. Everyone loves Lucy. You know that.' Martin looked sceptical, so Bernie continued, 'Look, Martin – think about it. The survival of the human race depends on adults looking after kids. If we didn't get a kick out of it then we wouldn't bother to do it and the whole species would die out, wouldn't it? So we're all programmed to enjoy it when a child shows appreciation. It's the most natural thing in the world. I won't have you suggesting that you're some sort of pervert. It's utter nonsense.'

'I hope you're right,' Martin sighed. 'But I still think it would be better if I stopped taking Lucy out in the boat.'

'She'll be tremendously disappointed if you do. And she'll think that you're angry with her.'

'Why would she think that?' Martin asked, puzzled.

'She'll think you're cross because she got out of the boat when you told her not to.'

'Can't you tell her it's not that – that I don't blame her at all?'

'I've already told her, but that isn't stopping her blaming herself. Come on, Martin! For Lucy's sake, don't let this stupid incident change everything between you.'

'I'm sorry.' Martin sat with his elbows resting on his knees and his hands clasped together in front of him, staring downwards. 'I just can't get the idea out of my head, now that I've thought of it. I just keep thinking, maybe that's the way these things start. I don't suppose child abusers start out planning to hurt kids. Don't you think it could start with hugs and cuddles and then … well

... develop into ... I don't know ... a craving for something more?'

Bernie leaned forward and took both of Martin's hands between her own.

'Oh Martin!' she said, looking up into his eyes. 'I'm so sorry you feel like this. I'm sure you're wrong. I really can't believe you're a paedophile. I'm sure if you were you wouldn't be telling me this now – you'd be wanting to keep your feelings secret and looking for more opportunities to get Lucy on her own.'

'Only if I didn't want to fight it – if I was happy with the idea of giving in to my urges and ending up hurting her. I'm trying to do the responsible thing and just keep away.'

'I just can't believe in you hurting anyone,' Bernie sighed. 'OK. If you don't want to take Lucy out any more, you must at least keep coming to see us. She'll be devastated if you just disappear out of her life without a word. Come to tea on Saturday. Bring your mother if it makes you feel safer.'

'OK.' Martin sat back, drawing his hands out of Bernie's grasp and attempting a weak smile. 'We'll be there. The usual time?'

'Yes – or Lucy's team has got a match in the afternoon; you could come and watch that and then come home with us afterwards. She'd like that.'

'I'll see what Mutti says about that.' Martin and his mother had fled East Germany when he was a child and he still addressed her by this term of endearment. 'She may not fancy standing around in the cold watching girls kicking a ball. But we'll definitely come to tea.'

'After all,' Bernie added, trying to lighten the atmosphere, 'if you never darken our door again, how are you ever going to win your bet with Peter?'

It was a standing joke in the family that Peter had challenged Martin to seduce Bernie[3] and that his continued association with them was directed towards that end.

'I dunno,' Martin tried to speak casually in an attempt to follow Bernie's lead. 'They say absence makes the heart grow fonder. Perhaps if I kept away for a while, you'd come chasing after me!'

'In your dreams! Now, tell me about those interesting-looking equations that you've got there.'

Martin saw that she was looking at the research paper that he had left out ready for getting back to work that afternoon.

'It's a model of rock deformation,' he explained 'I've written a simulation program based on them, but it wasn't getting the right answers and now I think I've broken it altogether.'

'Can I have a look at it? I do know a thing or two about numerical solution of differential equations, you know,' Bernie added, seeing Martin's sceptical expression. 'In fact, I would go so far as to suggest that I probably know more about it than you do – with you being a mere geologist and me being a mathematician and all.'

For the next ten minutes, the conversation was all about mathematical equations and computer algorithms. Then Bernie looked at her watch and jumped to her feet, hastily pulling on her cycling jacket.

'Sorry! Got to go – my afternoon tutorials start in ten minutes. But I think we could work together on this. You really do need a mathematician to get you on the right track with solving these equations. I think we ought to apply for a discipline-hopping award – you know, one of those joint research council grants to encourage academics to share different areas of expertise. I'll look into it and we can talk about it on Saturday.' She opened the door, still talking as she went. Martin came with her down the stairs to where she had left her bicycle. 'Meanwhile, you might as

---

[3] You can read about it in *Murder of a Martian* ISBN 978-1-911083-10-8

well try to fix that program, so that it doesn't crash any more – probably going back to the version you started with will be the easiest thing to do – but I'm not the least surprised it's getting the wrong answers. You're using an inherently unstable method. I'll explain later. Now, I must go.'

She gave him a quick hug and a peck on the cheek before mounting her bike and sailing off back to her own college. Martin stood looking after her, trying to work out how he really felt. If Peter's first wife had not died, so that Bernie had not married him, would he eventually have plucked up the courage to ask her to be his wife? If he had, then he would have been Lucy's stepfather. Would he still have been worried at finding himself feeling affection towards her then? Was Bernie right and he was mistaking a natural feeling of pleasure at the little girl's tenderness towards him for something more sinister? Or was he right to be concerned and to want to nip such feelings in the bud?

12.30 FRIDAY 30TH OCTOBER

'Did you have a good time at Karen's?' Sylvia asked Lucy, when she returned for lunch. Sylvia and Stan had come round to look after Lucy, while Bernie was busy with her tutorials.

'Yes. It was very interesting.' Lucy sat down at the kitchen table and waited for Sylvia to dish up.

'Were you playing with that little girl from Summertown – Kimberley, wasn't it?'

'No. She's gone back home now. Her mum's got a court order to stop her dad from coming round, so it's safe for her now.'

'Hi there Lucy! You're back, I see.' Stan came in from the garden, where he had been tending his racing pigeons. There was no room for them in the yard of their small house in Cowley, so Bernie had allowed him to erect a loft at the bottom of her extensive garden. 'How are things at Karen's? Any new arrivals?'

'She's got two little boys who are staying while their mum's in hospital,' Lucy told him. 'And that's all at the moment. I was just telling Sylvia that Kimberley has gone

69

back to her mum, and Beth and Neil have gone to live with some people in Hungerford. So, she *would* have room for me, if Social Services do decide I'm not safe staying here,' she added, grinning round at them both.

'Now, Lucy, let's not have any more of that nonsense,' Sylvia began. She was busy turning sausages in a pan on the cooker and had her back to the little girl, so she could not see the grin. 'There's no question of ...,' she stopped, as she turned round and saw Lucy's face. 'Alright. Let's just have our lunch now, shall we?'

'Karen says that you'd all have to do much worse things than this to me, before I'll get taken away,' Lucy went on cheerfully. 'So it looks as if you're stuck with me for a bit longer after all.'

'And there was I planning what to do with all the free time I was going to have with you off our hands!' Stan joked.

'Well, I'm glad she's managed to put your mind at rest,' Sylvia said firmly, hoping to steer the conversation on to a less emotive subject.

'I'm still not sure about that Constable Ferrar, though,' Lucy went on, ignoring Sylvia's discouraging tone. 'I wouldn't be surprised if she tries to charge Martin with assault. I'm sure she thinks *he* hit me.'

'But you say different, don't you pet?' Stan reasoned. 'And there aren't any other witnesses, so she'd never make it stick.'

'Just eat up your lunch and stop worrying about it,' Sylvia advised with a small sigh, glancing across at her husband with an expression of exasperation. 'Never trouble Trouble till Trouble troubles you. I'm sure Martin can look after himself without you worrying about him.'

'Karen said I shouldn't blame constable Ferrar, because she was only doing her job,' Lucy prattled on as she and Stan washed their hands together at the sink. 'She says that she probably didn't think I was a liar, just that I was frightened of telling her what really happened, in case I got

Martin into trouble. She said that when grown-ups hurt children, they often tell them to keep it secret.'

'You wouldn't ever do that, though, would you?' Sylvia said, trying to keep any hint of anxiety out of her voice and to speak as if this were a topic of only minor interest. 'You'd tell us if anyone did anything to you that you didn't like, wouldn't you?'

'Yes, of course,' Lucy said dismissively, keen to continue her story. She dried her hands on the towel that hung on the back of the larder door and then sat down at the large wooden table in the centre of the kitchen. 'Karen told me about a boy who came to stay with her once whose dad used to lose his temper sometimes and hit his mum. His mum and dad both told him not to say anything to anyone about it. Then one day, his dad hit his mum so hard that she fell down and stopped breathing. And the little boy got so frightened that he rang 999 and an ambulance came, but his mum died and his dad got put in prison. Karen said that the boy thought it was all his fault, because he called the ambulance and the ambulance men called the police. She said *that* was the sort of thing Constable Ferrar was thinking about when she kept trying to get me to say that it was Martin who hit me.'

'I'm not sure Karen should have been telling you all that,' Sylvia said, when Lucy paused for breath. 'You don't want to be worrying about that sort of thing at your age.'

'Karen said it was OK so long as she didn't tell me any names,' Lucy told her earnestly. 'She said that would be a *breach of confidentiality*, but just telling me what happened is fine. I think the boy was very silly,' she went on. 'I don't see why he didn't want his dad sent to prison for killing his mum. I think he ought to have called the police before – to get them to stop his dad hitting her – instead of waiting until she was really badly hurt.'

'But didn't you say that his mum, as well as his dad, told him not to?' Stan asked.

'Yes – I didn't understand that either. I think the boy

and his mum were both very silly.'

'I think they probably both loved the boy's dad,' Stan began.

'But he hit his mum!' Lucy protested. 'How could they?'

'The thing is, Lucy,' Stan said seriously. 'People are more complicated than that. There aren't good people and bad people – everyone's a bit of a mixture of the two. I expect he was a good dad in lots of ways. And I expect that every time he hurt his wife he was sorry afterwards and said that it wouldn't happen again – and the boy and his mum wanted to believe it, so they did. That's not to say it wouldn't have been better if one of them had told the police about it sooner, but not necessarily the first time it happened – and probably not the second. There was always a chance they could have worked it out for themselves, without getting anyone else involved. I've known men who used to get drunk every payday and beat their wives about, but they always made up afterwards. I'm not saying it was right, but it happens and the wives don't always want their men punished for it.'

'And you're right, Lucy,' Sylvia added, keen to make it clear to Lucy that she should never go along with concealment of any sort of abuse, 'the boy ought to have told someone about what was going on. Perhaps his dad needed help. He may have been ill, or had a drink problem. Like Stan said, drink often is at the bottom of that sort of thing.'

Lucy sat in silence, eating her sausages and digesting this information. It all seemed very strange to her. She could not imagine any of her family deliberately hurting one another. So what could it be like to have one parent attacking another? Could you really continue to love them both?

15.45 FRIDAY 30TH OCTOBER

Amy Clinton drove slowly along the road, peering out at the house numbers, trying to identify her destination. Ten, twelve, fourteen, it must be the next house, somewhere behind this tall copper beech hedge. But where was the entrance? Ah yes! Here it was! It was further along than she had expected because this house had a much wider frontage than the others in the road. She pulled up and got out of the car.

She stood for a few minutes gazing down the long drive, which curved around a large lawned area to an imposing L-shaped house. Then she looked down at her diary, where she had written the address, and double-checked that she had come to the right place. It was not at all the type of property that she had been expecting. However, the number painted on the stone gatepost was correct. Beneath the number was a name, *Llanwrda*, carved into the stone. The house was older, as well as grander, than the others in the road, and presumably the number was a more recent addition, when its splendid isolation was eroded by the gradual encroachment of new houses as the suburb of Headington had grown during the first half of the twentieth century.

Amy reminded herself that domestic abuse was no respecter of class or income bracket and that it was just as likely that a child might have been beaten or neglected in a house such as this as in one of the council flats on the Blackbird Leys estate. This was the address that the girl had given to the police and that her stepfather had confirmed; so this must be where they lived. She put her diary back in her briefcase and walked briskly up the drive.

The green-painted door was answered by a woman who looked to be in her sixties or early seventies. She had dark brown eyes beneath black brows, but her hair was white. She looked at Amy with an enquiring expression on her face. Amy held up her identity badge.

'I'm Amy Clinton,' she said apologetically. 'I'm from Social Services. Is there a little girl called Lucy Paige living here?'

The woman studied the badge carefully and then scrutinised Amy's face, checking that she was who she said she was. Then she nodded slowly, looking thoughtful.

'Yes. But I'm afraid she's out at football practice at the moment.'

'I see. And you are …?'

'Sylvia Corbridge. My husband and I are looking after Lucy today, while her mother's at work. We're …,' Sylvia hesitated, wondering how to describe her relationship to Lucy. Then she remembered Lucy telling her that Peter had described them to the officious policewoman the previous day as her grandparents. 'We're sort of honorary grandparents.'

'I see,' Amy said again, although in reality she was feeling somewhat confused. 'When are you expecting her back?'

'She won't be long now,' Sylvia told her, glancing down at her watch. 'Ten minutes I should think – twenty at the outside.'

'Can I come in and wait?'

'If you like.' Sylvia stepped back to allow Amy to enter and then closed the door firmly behind her. 'Come through to the kitchen.'

As she followed Sylvia through the hall and into the kitchen, Amy looked round her, taking in as many details as she could, trying to assess what sort of family it might be who lived here. The walls of the hall were painted primrose yellow over textured wallpaper. There was an old-fashioned dark wood hall-stand with a mirror and hooks for hats.

She noticed a group of slightly yellowing black-and-white photographs hanging on the wall. There was a portrait of a man in his fifties in a dark suit and tie. Beside it was a rather stern-looking woman of similar age with a string of pearls around her neck. Beneath them, there was a full-length picture of a young man in police uniform, gazing at the camera with wide, pale eyes and looking rather self-conscious. As she passed the stairs, she noticed a group of three porcelain ducks attached to the wall so that they appeared to be flying up towards the first floor.

On entering the kitchen, Amy became aware of a pleasant smell of baking and saw a batch of scones cooling on a wire rack on the working surface next to the large cooker. The room was dominated by a huge wooden table in the centre, surrounded by wooden chairs. At one end of the table lay a chopping board with a parsnip and three carrots lying on it. The house looked clean and tidy. This was very different from the chaotic scenes that so often confronted her on her home visits.

'Sit down,' Sylvia invited her. 'If you don't mind, I'd like to carry on. I want to get this stew in the oven before Lucy gets back.'

'Yes, of course – go ahead. Don't let me interrupt you.' Amy pulled out a chair and sat down. 'Perhaps you wouldn't mind answering a few questions while you work?'

'Fair enough,' Sylvia answered, picking up a vegetable

knife from the table and cutting into the parsnip. 'What is it you want to know?'

'Just a bit more background to the little girl, Lucy. You presumably know about the incident down by the river yesterday?'

'Yes. I assumed that was why you're here.' Sylvia looked for a moment as if she were about to say more, but then she closed her mouth and looked down, apparently concentrating on slicing up the parsnip.

'Whenever we get a report of a child sustaining a non-accidental injury, we have to follow it up,' Amy explained. 'Just as a matter of routine. We can't risk missing any signs. So-o-o,' she said slowly, taking out a pocket folder from her briefcase and sifting through a sheaf of papers. 'Let's start with the basics. She lives here with her mother and stepfather, is that right?'

'That's right,' Sylvia confirmed.

'And that's all? No other kids? You and your husband don't live in?'

'No. It's just Bernie, Peter and Lucy.'

'Bernie?'

'Lucy's mum. Her name's Bernadette but everyone calls her Bernie.'

'I see. And what about Lucy's dad? Does she see anything of him at all?'

For a few seconds there was complete silence. Sylvia paused from chopping the carrots and stood motionless at the far end of the table, the knife in her hand. She seemed to be thinking. Amy opened her mouth to prompt her with a supplementary question, but Sylvia recovered and got in first.

'He died before Lucy was born.'

'Oh! I'm sorry.' Amy did not know what to say.

'Yes. It was very sad,' Sylvia agreed, resuming her chopping. 'He was a lovely man. But then, so is Peter. And when we retired, we moved down to help. So Lucy's well looked after.'

'And what exactly *is* your relationship to the family?'

'Bernie – Lucy's mum – was engaged to our son. That was years and years ago, when they were both students at the university. After he died, she became like a daughter to us. We didn't have any other kids, you see and her mum was already dead and her dad not long after. That's why I said we were like Lucy's grandparents.'

'OK. I think I get the picture. You must know the family as well as anyone. How long has Lucy's mum been with her stepdad?'

'They've been married three and a half years now.'

'How did Lucy feel about having her stepdad move in?'

'She was over the moon. She always loved Peter He's always been like a father to her even before he married Bernie. He's *very* fond of Lucy. I sometimes think he's closer to her than to his own kids.'

'So he has children from a previous marriage? Where are they now? Living with their mother?'

'No. They're both grown up and moved away. Hannah's up in Leeds and Eddie's married and living in Jamaica.'

'And their mother – his first wife?'

'She died in 2003. She and Peter were Lucy's godparents, and Angie had always been best friends with Bernie. It was only natural that, after a decent interval, Peter would move in here.'

'So this house belongs to Lucy's mother?'

'Well, strictly it was her father's – Lucy's father, I mean – which he inherited from his father. His grandfather – Lucy's great grandfather – built it, way back at the turn of the century – the twentieth century that is – for his family, and Bernie's husband was the only one who survived. So it became his and then Bernie's.'

'I see.' Amy scribbled a few notes in a small spiral-bound book. Then she looked up at Sylvia, who had finished chopping the vegetables and was tipping them into a large enamel stew-pot that was simmering on one of the gas rings. 'Now tell me about this friend who took Lucy out yesterday. I've got his name down as Martin Rice. Do you know him at all?'

'It's pronounced *Reece*,' Sylvia told her. 'R-I-E-S-S. It's a German name. He and his mother escaped from the DDR before the Berlin Wall came down. His dad was killed trying to follow them. He's a tutorial fellow at one of the colleges – like Bernie.'

'Would you say you know him well?'

'I suppose so – well enough to know that there's nothing wrong with Bernie allowing him to take Lucy out in his boat.'

'That was a regular occurrence?'

'Yes. They probably went most weekends in the summer. Not so much at this time of year and not so much since …'

'Yes? Since what, exactly?'

'Since a friend of ours was injured. You may have seen it on the news. DCI Jonah Porter? He was shot in the neck and paralysed.'

'Yes. I think I do remember something about a policeman being shot a few months back.'

'That's right. He was an old friend of Lucy's dad – her real dad I mean, not Peter, although he knew Peter too – and he used to give her presents on her birthday. Anyway, since he's been in hospital, she likes to go and see him regularly, so that cuts down on her free time.'

'I see.' Amy made some more notes. 'Getting back to Martin Riess, was yesterday the first time anything untoward has happened while Lucy was out with him?'

'Yes.' Sylvia replied shortly, putting the lid on the stew-pot and lifting it off the hob and into the oven.

'So, you would say–,' Amy began. Then she stopped short as the backdoor opened and a small girl with a mop of curly yellow hair burst in carrying a bright red cycling helmet in one hand and a pair of extremely muddy football boots in the other. Beneath a fluorescent yellow cycling jacket, she had on red shorts – also very muddy – and thick red socks. Her left cheek was obscured by a grubby gauze dressing, which was starting to peel off.

She stopped dead and stared at Amy, looking in turns puzzled, angry and then scared as she took in the dark blue business suit and the notebook that lay on the table in front of her. Amy got to her feet, intending to go over to the girl and introduce herself, but before she could say anything, they were joined by a man of a similar age to Sylvia, who came in behind Lucy. Seeing Amy standing there, he put his hand protectively on Lucy's shoulder and looked across at Sylvia enquiringly.

'This is Amy Clinton,' Sylvia told them. 'She's from Social Services.'

'Stan Corbridge,' the man said, stepping forward and holding out his hand.

'I'm very pleased to meet you,' Amy replied, shaking the hand briefly, before turning to look down at the girl, who was now staring up at her with a defiant look. 'And you must be Lucy!'

Lucy continued to stare back without speaking. Amy crouched down so that her face was level with Lucy's and smiled in a friendly way.

'That's a nasty bump you've got there, isn't it? Would you like to tell me about how you got it?'

'No.'

Amy hesitated, trying to decide on her next move. The child's antagonism towards her was unmistakable. Was this because she was fearful of being punished if she said the wrong thing to someone in authority – or indeed to anyone outside the family circle? Or was she simply a shy girl who did not find it easy to talk to strangers? She was clearly not going to open up in front of her minders. The only way to get to the truth was to get her away from them for a while. Amy stood up and looked round at Stan and Sylvia.

'I'd like to have a word with Lucy on her own now, if you don't mind. Is there somewhere we can go where we'll be private?'

'There's the living room,' Sylvia began, but Lucy interrupted, speaking in a very clear decisive voice, as if giving instruction to a class at school.

'That doesn't sound like a very good idea to me. Aren't you afraid that I might make false accusations about you afterwards? My mam says there are rules that you always have to have at least two adults present to protect children from abuse and so there would be a witness in case of malicious allegations. That's why they always have to have two people taking Junior Church, even when there are hardly any children.'

'I don't think we need to worry about that,' Amy said with a nervous little laugh, very much taken aback. 'I'm sure you aren't going to make up any nasty stories about me, are you?'

'I might,' Lucy insisted. 'If you try to take me into Care, I might say that you threatened me to make me say things that weren't true. Or I might tell people that you hit me and made this bruise,' she added, pulling up the sleeve of her jacket and exhibiting a swelling on her right forearm.

'Except that we've all seen it now,' Stan pointed out, trying to calm the situation. 'And I know how you got it too.'

'And how was that?' Amy asked, trying to sound interested but not accusing.

'I hit it on the goalpost when Melanie Trotter brought me down with a foul tackle. I took the penalty and scored,' Lucy added in a satisfied tone.

'It sounds as if you're very good at football,' Amy ventured, in an attempt at conciliation. 'Perhaps you'd like to tell me about it?'

'No thank you.'

Amy gave up and addressed the adults again.

'I really do need to speak to the child on her own,' she

reiterated. 'So that I can confirm that there's nothing wrong.'

'I tell you what, Lucy,' Sylvia suggested. 'Why don't you take Amy into the living room and we'll leave both the doors open so that we'll hear if you shout for help, but we won't be able to eavesdrop on your conversation? How's that?'

'Alright,' Lucy said, sounding reluctant but resigned. She put down her helmet and boots on the table and stripped off her jacket, hanging it on the back of one of the chairs. 'It's this way.'

16.30 FRIDAY 30TH OCTOBER

Amy followed Lucy out into the hall, past the foot of the stairs and into a large, bright room, with a window facing on to the front garden and glass doors overlooking the back. She looked round, taking in a piano standing against the wall opposite the door, a large fireplace with an embroidered screen across it and an ornate mantelpiece above, a huge Welsh dresser housing an array of calendar plates, and a rather dowdy three-piece suite. She walked over to the sofa and sat down, placing her briefcase on the floor beside her. Lucy hesitated for a moment and then took a seat herself – perching on the edge of the easy chair furthest from where Amy was sitting.

'You mustn't be frightened of me,' Amy said, smiling at Lucy in what she intended to be a friendly manner. 'I'm here to help you.'

'No you're not,' Lucy replied truculently. 'You're here because that stupid PC Ferrar told you a load of lies.'

'Well, perhaps you'd like to tell me what really happened,' Amy suggested.

'Will you promise to believe me?' Lucy asked

suspiciously.

'Yes, of course.'

There was a long silence.

'Tell me about that bump on your cheek,' Amy said at last. 'How did it happen?'

Lucy recounted her story of the strange woman on the riverbank and the men who were pursuing her. Amy jotted down notes, thinking as she did so that Lucy was remarkably articulate for a nine-year-old and used an unusually mature vocabulary for her age.

'So you see, it wasn't Martin's fault at all that I got hurt,' Lucy finished, looking Amy in the eye for the first time. 'And it wasn't Peter's fault – or my mam's – for letting me go out with him. And it's all just so unfair that you're all blaming them!'

'I'm not blaming anyone,' Amy assured her. 'I'm just here to make sure that you're safe and that this sort of thing isn't going to happen again.'

'Well, now you've seen, will you go back and tell PC Ferrar to start looking for those men with the knife? Those are the people the police ought to be after. And Jonah agrees with me about that – and he's a DCI, so he knows loads more about police work than she does. Only he's in hospital, so he can't investigate it at the moment.'

'Jonah? He's the policeman who was shot, is that right? Your gran was telling me that you go to visit him in hospital sometimes.'

Lucy nodded.

'I like Jonah a lot.'

'And you like this Martin too, don't you?'

'Yes. He's one of my best friends.'

'But he's your mum's friend really, isn't he? What about you? Do you have many friends of your own?'

'Of course! I've been telling you about them. There's Martin and Jonah and Peter – only he's my stepdad now, so he's more family, I suppose – and Stan and Sylvia, and Mike Carson. He's a forensic pathologist. He showed me how to do a post-mortem. Not on a person,' she added hastily, seeing the surprised look on Amy's face. 'It was a squirrel. It was dead interesting looking at all the internal organs and taking its temperature to estimate time of death. And then there's Karen. You might know her, because she's a foster carer. She lives just over the road. And –'

'What about friends of your own age?' Amy cut in gently. 'Girls in your class at school maybe?'

Lucy thought for a few moments.

'Well, there are the other girls in my football team,' she said eventually. 'And there's Junior Church, but most of them are younger than me.'

'What about at school?' Amy pressed her. 'Do you get on OK with the other kids there?'

'I'm not being bullied, if that's what you mean,' Lucy said defensively.

'No, I was just wondering if you had any special friends.'

'There's a girl in the top class who isn't bad,' Lucy conceded, 'but most of the ones in my class are rather silly. The boys are a bit better. At least I can talk about football with them.'

There was a tapping sound on the open door, followed by a woman's voice, speaking in a broad Liverpool accent.

'Can I join you? Sylvia told me you were in conference, but I hope you don't mind me butting in.'

Amy turned to see a woman of short to medium height with very short mousey-brown hair, greying slightly at the temples, and grey-blue eyes behind metal-framed glasses. She was wearing black trousers and a purple-and-black roll-neck sweater.

'I'm Lucy's mother,' she explained, holding out her hand towards Amy.

'And I'm Amy Clinton, from Social Services.' Amy got up and shook Bernie's hand.

'So Sylvia told me. I hope Lucy hasn't been too harsh

with you. She doesn't have a very high opinion of Social Workers just at present.'

'No, no,' Amy assured her, unsure what to make of this woman who was quite different from the mental picture that she had formed of what Lucy's mother would be like. The police report had led her to expect a young mother, very much under the thumb of a controlling husband. This woman did not look as if she had ever permitted herself to be controlled by anyone. 'We've been having a very interesting discussion. I think you can go back to your gran now,' she added to Lucy, 'I just want a few words with your mum now. OK?'

Lucy got up to go. Then she hesitated for a moment before going over to Amy and holding out her hand. 'Goodbye Ms Clinton. It's been nice meeting you.'

'Goodbye Lucy,' Amy responded, after a brief pause while she recovered from her surprise at this formality from a child so young. 'It's been nice meeting you too.'

Lucy left the room and Bernie gestured to Amy to indicate that they should both sit down.

'I'd offer to make you a brew,' she said, 'but I don't want to prolong this more than necessary. We need to have tea promptly because I'm taking Lucy out this evening.'

'Going anywhere nice?' Amy asked, hoping to build up a rapport.

'To the hospital to visit a friend of ours. He was injured a few months back and the rehab is taking a long time.'

'That would be the policeman who was shot?' Amy asked. 'Lucy told me about him. She also told me about a pathologist who helped her cut up a dead squirrel and someone who takes in foster kids. But she didn't have much to say about any friends of her own age. Doesn't it worry you that she spends so much of her time with adults and doesn't mix with other children?'

'She does when they've got a common interest – her football team, for instance,' Bernie countered. 'But most of the time she finds other children a bit … well, childish. She's always had a lot of adults around her, so it isn't that surprising that she finds it easier to relate to them. And, let's be honest, mostly they're a lot nicer than kids are – especially if you're a blue-eyed, golden-haired little girl whom everyone's a bit sorry for because she hasn't got a dad.'

'Still,' Amy persisted. 'Don't you think she's missing out on her childhood?'

'Not really. It's her choice. We've never done anything to discourage her from playing with other kids. But Lucy's very utilitarian. She can't see what they have to offer her. Martin's got his boat and he's teaching her German. Mike tells her about his work. Martin's mum is teaching her the piano. Jonah has lots of stories about his detective work. Sylvia does baking with her and Stan lets her help with his racing pigeons. With all that going on, how can you expect any of the children she comes across to be able to compete?'

'I see. Now, I'm afraid I have to ask,' Amy began, selecting her words carefully, aware that what she said next was liable to cause offence. 'How well do you know this Martin – the man she was out with yesterday?'

'I've worked with him for just on ten years, but I only got to know him really well in the last two or three. Before that, I knew his mother, but we drifted apart for a while. She used to be a great friend of my late husband – Lucy's father. I would say that I know them both extremely well and they are both totally trustworthy.'

'So you believe Lucy's story that it was a stranger who hit her?'

'I would believe that whatever I thought of Martin,' Bernie said coldly. 'Lucy doesn't tell lies.'

'No, I'm sure she doesn't' Amy said hastily. 'But, sometimes children find it difficult to distinguish between reality and make-believe – especially if someone they're close to tells them that something is true.'

'Like believing in Father Christmas, do you mean?'

'Yes, I suppose that would be an example. But I was thinking more, if she was afraid of getting this Martin into trouble and he asked her to tell a story that he'd made up, she might do what he said, and start believing it herself.'

'I'm afraid Lucy doesn't have that sort of vivid imagination. If she says she saw two men chasing a woman on the bank of the Thames, then that's what she saw. Look – I know Lucy. If Martin ever did anything that she wasn't completely happy with then she'd tell me about it. She says that he was tying the boat up when a woman hit her with a lump of wood with a nail in the end of it, so that's what happened. End of story.'

'Yes,' Amy conceded, closing her notebook and putting it back in her briefcase. 'I'm inclined to agree with you. But you do see why I had to come to check? After the police report suggested that …'

'Yes. I do see,' Bernie sighed. 'I just wish Constable Ferrar could see how much damage she's done with her silly prejudices. Lucy has been worried sick that someone's going to snatch her away from home and put her into Care – or else that poor Martin might be sent to jail for something he didn't do. And that's all on top of her indignation at being called a liar. Now, are we done? And can I tell Lucy that you'll be taking her off the Local Authority Risk Register?'

'Please. She was never on any register. This is just an informal visit to follow up on a police report which, as it turns out, was just an over-zealous officer letting her imagination run away with her.'

'Thanks. I'm glad you've come round to seeing it that way. Would you mind telling Lucy that? I'm sure she'll be easier to convince if she hears it from the horse's mouth.'

While Amy had a short conversation with Lucy, Bernie stood by the front window looking out at the drive, waiting for Peter's car to appear. She hoped that he would not be late, so that they could all have tea together before she and Lucy set off on the twenty-mile drive to see Jonah. She pondered on everything that had happened that day. Poor Martin! At least she would now be able to set his mind at rest as far as any possible investigation into his conduct by the Police or Social Services was concerned. But would that quieten his anxieties about his own feelings towards Lucy? Then a horrible thought – an idea that had been hovering at the back of her mind ever since his confession that afternoon – surfaced and insisted that she confront it. What if his fears were not unfounded? What if he did have some sort of unnatural attraction towards Lucy? Was it irresponsible of her to urge him to continue seeing her and taking her out with him?

18.15 FRIDAY 30TH OCTOBER

'Hi Lucy! You're doing a grand job there,' Margaret said cheerfully as she entered Jonah's room and saw the little girl with a spoon in her hand carefully feeding Jonah with a thick creamy-coloured soup. 'I must be early,' she went on, turning to Bernie, who was sitting with her laptop computer on a chair in the corner of the room. 'Why don't we go and get ourselves a coffee and leave these two to finish dinner in peace?'

Bernie looked up and their eyes met. Realising that Margaret wanted to speak to her out of Lucy's – or was it out of Jonah's? – hearing, she nodded and closed the lid of the computer.

'Sounds good to me.'

They made their way down the long hospital corridors to the coffee bar. Margaret's cowboy boots made a loud tapping sound on the polished vinyl floor as she walked briskly with her hands in the pockets of tight-fitting jeans, which were topped by a cream-coloured shirt and a waistcoat and jacket in matching blue denim.

'I wanted to talk to you about Jonah,' Margaret said,

89

once they were settled in a corner of the coffee shop with their drinks in front of them. 'I'm sure you'll have noticed that he's losing weight again and he seems to have lost all his … oomph. He can't be bothered to try things anymore.' She sighed. 'I'm worried about him.'

'I know what you mean,' Bernie agreed. 'I'd noticed he seemed to be going downhill a bit these last few weeks, but isn't it understandable with these setbacks he's had recently. Don't you think he'll perk up once this chest infection is sorted?'

'I hope so.' Margaret sighed again. 'It's just so unlike him to let anything get on top of him like this. And I worry that he's using the chest infection as an excuse not to keep working at things … no, maybe that's unfair, not so much an excuse as just that he doesn't feel able to do anything until it's better and he's not facing up to the fact that it won't get better if he doesn't try. Eating, for example – he keeps telling the nurses that he's not hungry and won't accept that he needs to eat whether he *feels* hungry or not.'

'He always eats everything up when Lucy feeds him,' Bernie pointed out. 'At least that's something, isn't it?'

'Yes. And I am really grateful to you and Lucy for coming over every day the way you do. If it wouldn't be so outrageously unreasonable, I'd ask her to come three times a day to force him to eat properly. But that's out of the question and anyway Jonah would know what an impact it was having on her and her education and it might make his depression even worse.'

'I agree. He already says periodically that Lucy shouldn't feel obliged to come every day – as if he didn't know that wild horses wouldn't keep her away.'

'A bit of me wants to shout at him, "if you can eat for Lucy, why can't you do it for me or the boys or for the sake of your own health?" I sometimes feel he just won't make the effort, except when he's afraid of disappointing Lucy,' Margaret admitted. 'And then I think: what if he's putting all his energy into keeping up appearances when she's there and he hasn't got any left for any other time? So I try not to nag, but it's difficult when I can see the effect that his behaviour is having on his own health. I do wish he was able to admit that he needs help, but he's always seen depression as something that weak people use to excuse lack of backbone. He thinks he ought to be able to just pull himself together by pure will power.'

'I can sympathise with that attitude,' Bernie said. 'I'm sure I'd be the same. I know that depression is a mental illness and that mental illness is just as much out of the sufferer's control as physical illness, but I still wouldn't want to admit that *I* needed treatment.'

'I know. And, although I know that drugs can help a lot, I admit that I'd find it hard myself to ask for them to be prescribed for me,' Margaret agreed. 'So I've given up trying to get Jonah to accept that his mood is anything more than a natural reaction to his circumstances, which of course it is in lots of ways. But that leaves me wondering what I can do to help get him back on his … I was going to say, back on his feet again, but you know what I mean.'

'Maybe these students that we've got lined up to design gadgets for him will help,' Bernie suggested. 'I assume he's told you about them? Ken Thomas, my colleague from the Engineering department, has organised for two of his students to do it for their final year project. I'm bringing them over next week to introduce them to Jonah. They seem like really nice lads and very keen to help.'

'I hope so. He certainly needs something to buck him up. It's so frustrating to see him like this, especially after everything seemed to be going so well over the summer. I know I shouldn't complain, because it must be so much more frustrating for him not being able to do all the things he used to, but I really feel like shaking him sometimes and telling him to …'

'Pull himself together?' Bernie suggested with a smile.

'Yes,' Margaret laughed. 'You're right. I'm being

completely unreasonable, aren't I? But if he won't talk to the doctors about his depression, what *can* I do? Ever since September, it seems to have been just one thing after another. There was that UTI[4] and then pressure sores and now this pulmonary infection. And every time, he comes out of the crisis that bit worse. It's one step forward, two steps back all the time – and how many more steps can he take before he falls backwards off the cliff?'

They sat in silence, drinking their coffee.

'I'm worried about your Lucy,' Margaret said, after a while. 'She's invested such a lot in caring for Jonah. It's going to be awful for her if …'

'It's going to be awful for us all, if it comes to that.'

'But she's so young,' Margaret insisted. 'Will she understand? Has anyone close to her ever died before?'

'Yes,' Bernie answered simply. 'Peter's wife. She was Lucy's godmother. They were very close. Lucy was only three when it happened, but she insists that she can remember it. And she certainly does remember the effect that it had – that it still is having – on Peter.'

'How …?' Margaret asked, a little awkwardly. 'I mean what …?'

'She was knifed to death in her own kitchen.'

'A deliberate attack? Why on earth would anyone …?'

'We never found out.' Bernie shrugged. 'I just arrived one morning to find the kitchen smashed up and Angie lying there on the floor. Poor Peter had gone to work only a couple of hours before. I'm only glad I'd left Lucy strapped in her seat in the car, so she didn't see it all.'

'I never knew,' Margaret said, shaking her head.

'Why should you? Jonah had got his promotion and wasn't working with Peter any longer by then. And I only saw him once a year, when he used to come round for Lucy's birthday. It happened not long after her third, so it was old news by the time I saw him again.'

[4]Urinary Tract Infection

'And you never found out who was responsible?'

'No. It's like with Jonah. I don't suppose they'll ever find out who shot him – not after all this time.'

'No. Maybe that's another thing that's contributing to his depression,' Margaret said thoughtfully. 'At first, he had all sorts of ideas for how the investigation ought to be taken forward. I think he was half hoping to solve the case from his hospital bed! But now, he doesn't seem to be taking any interest in how it's going anymore.'

'He probably thinks they haven't any hope of solving it without him out there telling everyone how to do it,' Bernie joked, trying to lighten the gloomy atmosphere. 'Peter says that he never was one to doubt his own abilities. Well,' she added, with a grin, 'Peter didn't quite put it like that. His description was something along the lines of there being a mismatch between the size of his feet and the smallness of his footwear.'

Margaret laughed.

'I'd imagined it was more like how difficult it must be for him to find a suitably large hat to fit his outsize head! Yes, he's right. Jonah always has been supremely self-confident as far as his work was concerned. I'm sure your Peter found him quite insufferable at times. You know, I think that's one of the things that's really getting him down. Not being able to work, I mean. I think it's probably just beginning to dawn on him that he's going to be pensioned off, and it's making him think that, in that case, there's not a lot of point carrying on.'

'Didn't seeing his grandson help?' Bernie asked. 'I would have thought that was something to live for. A lot of people would be jumping at the idea of early retirement to spend time with the grandkids.'

'No,' Margaret sighed. 'I think it only made it all the more obvious to him how little he's going to be able to do for the boys and their families. It was good of Reuben and Anne to come all that way so soon after George was born. But of course they're new parents and very excited about it all, and their talk just reminded Jonah of what it was like when our two were babies – and all the things he did with them then and won't be able to do with little George. And Reuben couldn't hide his shock at how much his dad had deteriorated since last time he was down, back in July. And that made him anxious and set him off talking too much with a sort of false cheerfulness that Jonah saw right through and got annoyed about. So no, it wasn't a great success to be honest.'

'Do you think it would help if we showed him the video Peter took of him with Lucy out in the hospital garden?' Bernie suggested tentatively. 'To remind him how much he was able to do, even after he was shot, and encourage him to work on getting back to that stage – and then beyond?'

'I don't know. I suppose it's worth a try. He certainly needs something to convince him it's worth fighting, and to get him out of this downward spiral.'

'I'll ask Peter to look it out,' Bernie promised. 'And now we'd better be getting back. I know Lucy will be delighted to have more time alone with your husband, but I'm trying to maintain discipline and proper bedtimes!'

14.00-19.00 SATURDAY 31ST OCTOBER

Margaret spent Saturday afternoon with Jonah, arriving shortly after Lucy and Bernie had departed for Lucy's football match. As she usually did at the weekend, Lucy had given Jonah his lunch instead of his evening meal. He had forced himself to speak cheerfully with her and to eat all the food that she gave to him, despite feeling that he would much rather simply have stayed in bed or dozed in the chair. Now he was feeling tired after the effort of entertaining his young guest and, although he forced himself not to show it, he would have preferred not to have had any more visitors that day.

Margaret tried to think of interesting topics of conversation, but her husband replied languidly as if it were something of a trial having to concentrate on what she was saying. She racked her brains to think of something to lift his mood.

'It's a lovely day,' she said, at last. 'Why don't I ask one of the nurses to help me put you in your wheelchair and we could go outside for a bit – get some fresh air? It's a touch nippy, but we can wrap you up.'

'They're very busy,' Jonah objected. 'And I'm not sure I'm up to it yet. Not with this cough of mine.'

'We could just go for a wander down to the coffee bar, if you're afraid of the cold air getting on your chest,' Margaret suggested.

'What's the point? They bring me more drinks than I want here.'

'The point,' Margaret said, trying unsuccessfully to keep the irritation out of her voice, 'is to get you out of yourself a bit – to give you something a bit more interesting to see than these four walls.'

'I don't need taking out of myself.'

'Well you certainly need something to buck you up and get you going. I hope you're going to be a bit perkier when those two students come to talk about their project. It won't be much fun for them trying to design gadgets to help you if you can't be bothered to try any of them.'

'I'm wondering if that's such a good idea after all,' Jonah muttered. 'I can't imagine they'll be able to do much and I'll feel partly responsible if it stops them getting their degrees.'

'And so you should!' Margaret said, unable to contain her exasperation. 'I'm sure they'll be able to come up with all sorts of good ideas, but only if you enter into the spirit of things. Bernie says that her friend Ken has hand picked two of his best students. If they don't come up with something good it'll be because *you* haven't co-operated, because you're too busy feeling sorry for yourself.'

Jonah received this castigation in stony silence, staring straight ahead to avoid catching Margaret's eye. She sighed and tried again, speaking in more measured tones this time.

'Look – I know it's hard, but I keep thinking about how well you were doing only a few weeks ago. You were excited then about trying out new things. I remember when Ken finally fixed you up with a keyboard that you could type on. I seemed to be getting emails from you every five minutes. I could hardly keep up. It must be weeks now since you sent me even one.'

'This chest infection makes me tired all the time,' Jonah complained. 'And typing is so slow with only two fingers that work. I thought I'd get quicker at it, but I never do.'

'You probably would get quicker if you started putting in the effort again. The technology can only help you so far – you've got to work at it to learn to use it. Like with the chair. You made a right hash of steering it the first time you tried. But after a month or so, you were getting it around all over the place. Everything just takes time.'

'Too much time,' Jonah complained. 'It's all so frustrating. And I keep thinking, what's the point anyway?'

'The point is getting you well enough and independent enough to come home,' Margaret told him firmly.

'I don't know why you would want me home.' Jonah refused to be heartened by the prospect of leaving the hospital. 'I'd just be a millstone round your neck. Either you'd be spending all your time looking after me or you'd have to put up with paid carers invading your privacy and interfering with how you do things around the house. However you look at it, you'd all be better off without me.'

'No!' Margaret got up, came over to Jonah and put her arms around his shoulders. 'Don't you dare say that sort of thing,' she said fiercely. 'We all want you back home with us, just as soon as you can get your finger out and get yourself fit to go. And you should be pleased to have those students coming in to design customised devices to help you. Most people have to rely on off-the-shelf appliances. You can decide what's important to you and they'll invent something that fits with what you can manage.'

'That's the theory,' Jonah agreed sceptically. 'But I don't know how realistic it is. Anyway, we'll just have to wait and see,' he added, hoping to close down the subject. 'They're coming on Tuesday to talk about what sorts of things they might do. They're a Wayne Major and a Dean something-or-other. Bernie says that Dean is the organ scholar[5] at her college, but she doesn't know Wayne. Anyway, as I said, we'll just have to wait and see what they come up with.'

'No. I think you ought to start thinking *now* about what you'd like them to come up with. What are the things that most frustrate you and what would you most like to be able to do that you can't?'

'I'd have thought that was all pretty obvious,' Jonah grumbled. 'Everything frustrates me and there's pretty well nothing that I can do for myself anymore.'

'Don't be like that.'

'Why not? That's what everyone else thinks. This chap came round the other day from Human Resources, wanting to talk about Medical Retirement. He seemed to think that, seeing as I've paid in enough years to get a full pension, I ought to be *pleased* to be able to retire at fifty-one instead of going on to normal retirement age. I'll go down to half pay in another month and then ...,' he sighed. 'What's the point of me getting out of here if I'm going to be stuck at home all day? What use will I be to anyone?'

'Under the Disability Discrimination Act, they're obliged to *try* to enable you to continue working,' Margaret reminded him. 'But the way you're acting at the moment, I'm not surprised if your HR chappie thinks you ought to bow out. Where's your get-up-and-go? You used to be a *can-do* person, now you seem to be determined to think that you can't do anything. You ought to be taking hold of this opportunity with the university lads to find ways round your disabilities. Think of all the things you need to be able to do in your job and then ask them to think about how to make them possible.'

[5] Many Oxford colleges award scholarships to talented musicians on condition that they play the organ in the college chapel and, in some cases, act as choirmaster.

'I can't see how a couple of students can fix things,' Jonah said dismissively.

'Not everything, no, but I'm sure they could sort out a few problems. Why not start with the typing. There must be some way of making it quicker for you. How about something like the predictive text that you get on mobile phones? If you can get that sorted, you can lobby your HR department with emails telling them all about what a big mistake it would be if they insist on putting you out to grass.'

'I suppose there is that,' Jonah said, smiling in spite of himself. 'I could quite enjoy getting up his supercilious nose.'

'That's the spirit!' Margaret said warmly. 'You give him what for. Show him he can't keep a good man down.'

'There's someone else that I'd like to give a piece of my mind,' Jonah went on. 'Whoever it was who made the decision not to pursue the woman who gave Lucy that cut on her face. Since when has *assault occasioning actual bodily harm* been something that the police can simply ignore? It's a disgrace. And the way Lucy tells it, it sounds as if the woman may be in some sort of danger herself. I wouldn't be surprised if she were the victim of sex-trafficking.'

'There you are then,' Margaret said eagerly, pleased to see some of Jonah's usual irrepressible enthusiasm returning. 'Why not ping off a stiff email to the Chief Constable? And then get on with getting yourself back in shape so that you can get back to work and help stop the rot in the Police Service.'

A knock at the door signalled the arrival of dinner. Margaret took the tray and placed it on the table-on-wheels that stood next to Jonah's chair. Then she lifted the covers to inspect the food.

'It looks like tomato soup, shepherd's pie and then tinned pineapple to follow,' she said. 'Was that what you asked for?'

'Probably,' Jonah answered without enthusiasm. 'I

forget. It all tastes the same anyway.'

'I'm sure that's not true,' Margaret sighed. The sight of food seemed to have caused her husband's better humour to evaporate. The lopsided smile had vanished and his expression was glum and sulky. 'Let's start with the soup. It certainly smells good to me.'

'Why don't *you* eat it then?' Jonah grumbled. Then he caught his wife's eye and looked a little shamefaced. 'Sorry. I know I ought to eat, but I never seem to fancy anything these days. Go ahead. Let's give the soup a try.'

Margaret tied a large white bib around Jonah's neck to protect his shirt. Then she adjusted the table so that it was over his legs at a convenient height for her to spoon-feed him. She scooped up a spoonful of the thick red liquid and tested it for temperature on her hand to check that there was no danger of scalding Jonah's mouth.

He had eaten about half a dozen mouthfuls when Margaret tipped the spoon a little too steeply and the soup slipped into his mouth too fast and made him choke. He coughed and spluttered, going red in the face and seeming to find it hard to catch his breath. Margaret put down the spoon and watched anxiously. Just as she was about to seek help from the nursing staff, the coughing subsided and his breathing returned to normal.

'I'm sorry,' she said. 'That was my fault. Have some water to help clear your throat.'

Jonah sipped cautiously from the plastic beaker of water that she held up to his lips.

'Ready for some more soup?' Margaret enquired, dipping the spoon in the bowl again.

Jonah shook his head. 'No. I really don't feel hungry.'

'Shall we go on to the shepherd's pie then?'

'No. I said I'm not hungry.'

'Honestly Jonah!' Margaret sighed. 'It's like trying to deal with a recalcitrant two-year-old. You're just being stubborn. Try a bit – you might like it.'

'If I were a two-year-old,' Jonah retorted, 'I'd have

thrown the shepherds' pie on the floor by now and be upending that bowl of pineapple on my head!'

Margaret laughed. Their eyes met and Jonah grinned back. Margaret put down the spoon and rotated the table so that she could lean forward to give Jonah a hug and a kiss on the cheek.

'That's better,' she said. 'Can't you see? I didn't marry you for your body. It's your personality and your weird sense of humour that I chose you for. And that's why I miss you and want you back home as soon as you're ready to go. I've been talking to the OTs and they've come up with a list of modifications for the house to help with managing your care at home – and it isn't as if we can't afford it, what with my surgeon's salary and both of the boys off our hands now. Which reminds me: Bernie's bringing Nathan with them tomorrow. You *will* make an effort not to look too much like death warmed up when he comes, won't you? You know what a worrier he is.'

Their younger son, Nathan, was studying Jurisprudence at the University of Oxford. During term-time, it was more convenient for Bernie to give him a lift to the hospital in her car than for Margaret to make a lengthy detour on her way from the family home in South Oxfordshire to pick him up from his college room.

'I'll do my best,' Jonah replied, forcing another lopsided grin. 'But I can't guarantee that he won't think up some awful imaginary problems. You know what he's like. With him, it's not so much a matter of always seeing the glass half empty, it's more that he's suspicious that full or empty it must be a poisoned chalice!'

Margaret hugged him again and then sat back in her chair looking at him. He looked back and caught her eye.

'OK,' he said in the end, 'I suppose I'd better do my best to get in shape before tomorrow. Give me some of that pineapple, will you?'

11.50 SUNDAY 1ST NOVEMBER

During the drive from Oxford to the spinal injuries unit where Jonah was being treated, Bernie tried to prepare Nathan for what he was going to see. It was more than a month since he had visited his father, and Bernie was all too aware that the deterioration in Jonah's condition was likely to come as a shock. Moreover, Nathan was bound to work out that the reason that his mother had repeatedly found excuses not to bring him with her when she came was that she had been hoping to shield him from knowing that the steady progress that his father had been making over the summer had been reversed.

'Your dad's lost a bit of weight since last time you were over,' Bernie said as they turned into the hospital car park. 'It's the chest infection that's at the bottom of it. The doctors say that they've got it under control now, so I expect he'll start putting it back on soon.'

'Nurse Jeanette says he's naughty not eating his food properly,' Lucy chipped in. 'But I expect that's just because of his bad chest,' she added hurriedly, catching her

102

mother's eye in the rear view mirror and realising, from her frown, that she was not supposed to say anything about Jonah's lack of appetite.

'Lucy's right,' Bernie said. 'He's been a bit down because of his chest and that's made him tired and not feeling like eating a lot. The doctors say he'll soon be back on form once the antibiotics have done their job. That's why I thought I'd mention it before you saw him – in case you thought it was something more serious that was making him a bit low.'

'OK. Thanks,' Nathan said, feeling obliged to acknowledge what Bernie had said, while suspecting that she was concealing a darker truth from him. He had been wondering why it had been more than two weeks between his return to college for the Michaelmas Term and the first occasion when it had been convenient for Bernie to give him a lift over to the hospital to visit his father. Clearly, his mother and Bernie were trying to hide something from him.

Bernie locked the car and led them briskly into the building and through the corridors to Jonah's ward. She pressed a buzzer on the wall to announce their arrival and soon a nurse appeared to let them in. It was Danielle Rogers, a young nurse with bubbly blond curls and an equally bubbly personality. She immediately recognised them and opened the door wide to admit them.

'Come in Lucy! You know the way, don't you? The lunches will be here in a few minutes.'

When he followed Lucy into the room, Nathan's first thought was that they had come to the wrong place. Who was that old man propped up in the bed with his eyes half closed? Then Lucy ran across to the bed, put her arms around the bony shoulders and kissed the sunken cheeks. Nathan saw the man's eyes light up as his cracked lips broke into his father's familiar lopsided smile.

'Hi Dad,' he said awkwardly.

'Nathan!' the greeting sounded forced, as if his

presence were not really welcome. 'How are you doing? Are they working you hard?'

'Well – you know. A couple of essays every week. The Collections[6] went OK,' he added, trying to make conversation. 'For me that is. But Simon – the guy who was sharing my rooms last year – failed badly and his tutor is threatening to send him down if he doesn't do better when he re-sits them next week.'

'That's good,' Jonah answered absently. 'I mean you doing OK, not your friend getting sent down.'

Lucy climbed on to the bed and settled down with her head resting under Jonah's chin.

'I've brought a new book for us to read together,' she told him. 'But Mam says it'll have to wait 'til tomorrow, because you'll want to talk to Nathan while you've got the chance. So I'll leave it in your locker for another time.'

A long silence followed. Neither Nathan nor Jonah could think of anything to say to one another and both Bernie and Lucy held off to allow father and son to converse.

'Let's all sit down,' Bernie said at last, moving a chair from the side of the room, placing it next to the bed and indicating to Nathan that this was for him.

Nathan sat down and found himself face-to-face with his father. Jonah's eye sockets seemed to have grown cavernous and his skin had taken on a strange greyish hue. Nathan could hardly believe the change that had taken place during the weeks since he had seen him last.

They were still struggling to think of anything to say when the door opened and one of the healthcare assistants came in carrying Jonah's lunch. Lucy immediately slipped

---

[6] Collections are a peculiarity of the University of Oxford. They are college exams taken at the beginning of each term to test knowledge of material covered during the previous term. See Glossary of Oxford University Jargon

off the bed and went over to receive it.

'Give that to me, Susan,' she said confidently. 'I can manage it.'

'I'll just put it down on the table for you,' Susan Hammond replied, keeping hold of the tray, which Lucy had put out her hands to take from her.

Lucy looked disappointed, but stepped back to allow Susan to cross the room and put the food down on the tray-table next to Jonah's bed.

'There you are, Lucy. It's all yours. I'll come back in about half an hour to collect the empties. Any problems, just give us a shout.'

Bernie got up and turned to Nathan.

'Let's you and me go and get ourselves something to eat in the restaurant,' she suggested, knowing how much Jonah hated being watched while he was spoon-fed like a baby. 'I'm starving and we're surplus to requirements here.'

'What about Lucy?' Nathan asked. 'When does she get to eat?'

'We can bring her back some sandwiches,' Bernie told him. 'Now stop arguing and come along.'

Realising that she was deliberately trying to get him away from his father, Nathan bowed to the inevitable and followed Bernie meekly out of the room and down the long corridor to the hospital restaurant, which was busy with staff and visitors having lunch. Bernie paid for food for both of them, which they took over to a small table in a secluded corner of the room. For several minutes, they sat facing each other, eating in silence. Then Nathan looked up and caught Bernie's eye. She saw that he had an anxious frown on his face.

'He's not going to make it, is he?' he said at last.

Bernie could not think of anything to say.

'I'm right, aren't I?' Nathan went on, after a short pause, taking Bernie's silence to indicate agreement.

'No,' Bernie said firmly. 'No, you're not. Or at least, it's not inevitable. His spinal cord injury is serious, but not life-threatening. You know that – think about how well he was in the summer before this series of infections set him back. It's just going to take some time to get him back on course, that's all.'

'Are you sure he wants to get back on course?'

'Of course he does. He just finds it difficult to motivate himself sometimes, that's all.'

'I'm not so sure that *is* all,' Nathan persisted. Now that he had plucked up the courage to broach the subject, he wanted to deal with it thoroughly. 'And to be honest, I can't blame him. He hasn't got a lot to look forward to, has he?'

'Oh yes he has,' Bernie said quickly. 'He's just become a grandfather and there's your graduation and–'

'But those are all other people's achievements,' Nathan argued. 'I suppose he'll like getting pictures of the baby and seeing me dressed up in my gown, but it's not the same as …,' he sighed. 'Dad always used to be such an energetic sort of person. The things I remember us doing together are all active things: walking the Pennine Way, Youth Hostelling on our bikes, playing tennis. And then there's his garden. He'd hate to see the state it's got into now, with nobody taking care of it all over the summer while he's been in here. However much better he gets medically, he's always going to be paralysed. And what sort of life is that going to be for him? I can't help feeling that it might be better for him if he did just slip away with this chest infection he's got, instead of prolonging the agony for maybe years. And I think that's probably what he's thinking too.'

'I'm sorry Nathan, but you're wrong,' Bernie said in a very decided tone.

'How can you be so sure? He was trying to put a brave face on it just now, but I could see that he wasn't really interested in anything. And it's not surprising, is it? I'm sure I wouldn't want to carry on if I was going to be stuck in a wheelchair for the rest of my life, not even able to feed myself.'

'I still say you're wrong,' Bernie insisted. 'You may be right that, just at this moment, your dad isn't much bothered about whether he lives or dies. But that's not him, that's the depression. If we can help him to get through that, there's plenty for him to live for.'

'Such as?'

'Like I said: his grandchildren, you, your mum, all his friends …'

'But I know Dad,' Nathan persisted. 'He hates having to admit that he needs help with anything. He always has to be the best at everything. He–'

'Then it will do him good to learn to rely on other people a bit more,' Bernie cut in sharply

'What a callous thing to say!' Nathan was genuinely shocked at this statement. 'How *can* you suggest that he deserves to be shot in the back and paralysed for life?'

'I never said anything of the sort!' Bernie retorted, beginning to lose patience with the young man. 'We *all* need to learn to accept help graciously and, as you have pointed out, your dad has been one of those who needed to learn it more than most. We none of us get what we deserve in this life – thank goodness! Look – I know I didn't express myself very well. What I'm trying to say is that Jonah is quite capable of coming round to accepting his dependency. And, once he does, there will be all sorts of things that he *can* do, provided he doesn't get bogged down in regretting all the things he *can't* do any more.'

'It's all very well for you to talk,' Nathan grumbled, still unconvinced. 'You aren't the one who's paralysed.'

'No, but please believe me that I *do* know what I'm talking about. I've seen people with disabilities just as bad as your dad's – worse in fact – and I *know* that they had a good life.'

Nathan still looked dissatisfied, but did not dare to contradict this statement. Bernie watched his face and debated in her own mind whether to say any more. When she was only a small child, her mother had been diagnosed with Motor Neurone Disease. Throughout her childhood, she had seen the disease progress, restricting her mother's physical activity more and more until she had become unable to breathe unaided. She had died shortly before Bernie left school for Oxford. Bernie rarely spoke about her mother to anyone. She had not even, as yet, told Lucy about the caring responsibilities that she had shared with her father from as early as she could remember, and which had dominated her early life. It was her anxiety lest Lucy should hear about her grandmother from someone other than herself that made Bernie reluctant to tell Nathan the whole story, even though it might have convinced him that his father's condition was by no means the total disaster that it seemed to him now.

'Please believe me,' she said again. 'I know how it must look to you. And I admit that you may be right about how your dad feels right this minute – what with this chest infection and him being run down and tired and everything – but I *know* that he's got a good future if only we can help him to start thinking positively about it again.'

'I hope you're right. That's what I'd like to believe, but …'

'Where's the problem then?'

'I can't help thinking that it's … maybe … wishful thinking? Or even …,' Nathan paused, unsure whether he dared to go on.

'Yes?'

'I just wonder sometimes whether it might not be a bit, well … *selfish* of us to want to keep him alive and dependent on us – if he'd rather not be, I mean.'

'Oh Nathan!' Bernie looked across the table at him and sighed deeply. 'I *do* know what you mean, and all I can say is what I've already told you. I *know* for absolute certainty that the right thing for your dad is for us all to do our best to help him get out of this black mood and start looking forward to a bright future ahead of him. And that needs to start with you going back in there with a smile on your face and something cheerful to talk about. OK?'

PART II:
POTENTIALLY
HARMED BODY

09.30 MONDAY 2ND NOVEMBER

'Peter! I want you to take Davenport and Lepage and get over to Wolvercote Cemetery right away.'

Peter looked up from the pile of Leave Request Forms that he was studying preparatory to drawing up the December off-duty rota, and saw Superintendent Alison Brown standing over him.

'We've had reports that they've found a body in one of the graves and they need CID over there right away.'

'No problem. I'll do this later.' Peter, grateful for the excuse to set aside the thankless task of deciding who would be permitted to spend Christmas with their family and who would be condemned to turn in for work, paper-clipped the forms neatly together and put them away in a drawer. 'But did I hear you right? Aren't graves *supposed* to have bodies in them?'

'Not before the funeral takes place,' Alison said drily. 'And only the one specific body that the grave was made for. Apparently, one of the cemetery staff went out this morning to get things ready for their first funeral of the day and found that the grave they'd prepared for it on

113

Friday already had an occupant. Nobody knows who it is or why anyone would have put it there.'

When they arrived at the cemetery, on the northern outskirts of Oxford, Peter saw that the small tarmac area around the chapel was congested with vehicles and people. A police patrol car with its familiar blue and yellow stripes stood between a shiny black limousine (presumably one of the funeral cars) and the ancient soft-topped Citroën 2CV belonging to forensic pathologist Mike Carson. Standing in front of the door of the small, stone-built chapel was a hearse, with its rear door gaping open to reveal a coffin surrounded by floral tributes. Four men in dark suits and long black coats, whom Peter judged to be the pallbearers, stood in a line as if guarding the casket. A little way away, he could see another man in black, apparently deep in in conversation with a uniformed officer, whom Peter identified as Sergeant Jordan Fox. Next to them stood a short, dumpy woman in a black trouser suit and clerical collar who kept looking anxiously back and forth between the hearse, the entrance to the chapel and the driveway down which he had come. Her face looked vaguely familiar, but Peter could not recall where he had seen it before.

Seeing Peter and his assistants getting out of their car, Sergeant Fox excused himself from the man in black and hurried over to greet them. He was a tall gangling man of around thirty with rusty brown hair and deep brown eyes that looked anxiously into Peter's green ones. Peter knew him well and, despite a rocky first encounter[7], had great respect for his conscientious and caring approach to policing.

'I've taped off the area around the grave where they found the body,' he told Peter. 'Constable King is there

[7] See Chapter 5 of Two Little Dickie Birds, © 2015, ISBN 978-1-911083-13-9

with the men who found the body. Oh! And Dr Carson's there too. The big problem at the moment is the funeral. The undertaker's wanting to know what they can do with the body – *their* body I mean, not the unidentified one in the grave – and what to say to the family. The guests are all in the chapel, but they don't know whether to have the service or … Please, sir, could you come and have a word with them?' He half-turned towards the man in black and the woman in clerical costume.

'Yes, I think I'd better do that,' Peter agreed, speaking in a low voice. 'And while I'm talking to the funeral director, will you show DS Davenport and DC Lepage where the body was found? After that, come back here. I may need you to keep order when the funeral party discover that they won't be able to bury their loved-one today after all.'

Peter watched as Fox escorted Anna Davenport and Andy Lepage to the area of the cemetery where the most recent graves were. Peter noted the piles of flowers, lying on the tops of low rectangular heaps of orangey-brown earth. Then, they came to a larger pile of soil and he could see that it was cordoned off with blue-and-white tape, indicating that this was the centre of the crime scene. He saw another uniformed policeman stepping forward to speak to his colleagues.

Peter recollected himself and walked over to the man in black and his clerical companion. He held up his warrant card as he introduced himself.

'I'm DI Peter Johns,' he told them. 'I'm the officer in charge of investigating how a strange body got into the grave and who it is. I gather that you are in charge of the interment that was supposed to be taking place here?'

'Yes. That's right. I'm Raymond Ferris of *Ferris and Blythe.*' The man in black handed Peter a business card. 'And this is Reverend Barfield,' he added, gesturing towards the woman in the clerical collar.

'Mandy,' she said, holding out her hand. 'I'm here to

take the service. The family are all waiting inside. They'll be wondering what the holdup is. I do hope it won't be long before …'

'I'm sorry,' Peter said, still trying to remember where he had seen this woman before. 'I'm afraid it won't be possible to go ahead with the burial today.'

'But some of the family have travelled down from Darlington,' Mandy Barfield protested in the quiet voice of someone who does not like to make a fuss on her own account, but is quite determined to protect the interests of other people. 'We arranged to have the funeral early so that they could get home afterwards and not have to stay for another night.'

'I really am very sorry,' Peter repeated. 'I do realise how distressing it is for them, but I also have to think of the family and friends of whoever it is that is lying dead in that grave right now. At the moment, we don't know who it is or how they died or who put them there. And in order to find out those things – and to give that person, whoever it is, justice – we have to carry out a minute investigation of the grave and the ground around it, as well as allowing our experts to examine the body in situ.'

'Is there another grave that we could use?' the woman asked, turning to the funeral director.

'No.' He shook his head. 'These days interments are relatively uncommon. Most of our clients choose cremation. It would take several hours to prepare a new grave – always assuming that we can get permission from the cemetery authorities to do so.'

'In any case,' Peter intervened. 'I'm afraid that I couldn't sanction that. We need our forensics team to check over the whole cemetery for evidence of exactly what went on. I'm going to be closing the cemetery completely until that's done. What I need to discuss with both of you is the best way of getting you and your funeral party off the premises with as little distress to them and as little disruption to the police investigation as possible.'

'I suppose we could still go ahead with the service in the chapel,' Mandy suggested. 'And then, could you take the coffin back to your chapel of rest?'

'I suppose so,' Raymond Ferris agreed, reluctantly at first and then more supportively. 'Yes. I think you're right. That will be the best plan. Perhaps you could come in and explain to everyone?'

'Of course,' Peter agreed, trying not to sound as reluctant as he felt. 'Unless ...,' he turned to Mandy. 'Might it not come better from you? I mean – you know them.'

'I'm afraid I don't really,' she bit her lip and looked uncomfortable. Peter could see that she felt much the same as he did about the prospect of explaining to a group of bereaved relatives that the burial could not go ahead as planned and that it might be several days before they could finally lay their husband, brother, father or whatever to rest. 'It's one of those difficult funerals where none of the family had ties to any particular church and they left it to the funeral director to find a minister.'

'The widow was clear that he wouldn't have wanted the Church of England involved,' Raymond added. 'So ...'

'So I'm a random non-conformist brought in to co-ordinate the proceedings and say a few words,' Mandy finished for him, with a wry smile. 'I'm in the Methodist circuit. I look after Kidlington, Bladon and Woodstock.'

Of course! Peter now realised that she must have preached on one of the occasions when he had accompanied his wife to the Methodist church that she attended in East Oxford.

As far as the family is concerned,' Mandy continued, 'I've met the widow and the younger son, but that's all. The rest of the family live at some distance and have travelled specially.'

'OK.' Peter braced himself to face the unwelcome task. 'Well, we'd better get on with it. They must be wondering what on earth is taking so long. Do you think you could ask the widow to come out here, so we can speak to her in private? I mean – it's all very well us coming up with a plan, but she may have different ideas. She might prefer to abandon the funeral altogether for the time being and do it all at a later date, for instance.'

In the end, the business of explaining to the widow that her late husband's burial would have to be deferred proved less difficult than either Peter or Mandy had anticipated. Mrs Pemberley, a spritely eighty-seven-year-old with a lively sense of humour and a keen liking for detective fiction, seemed excited rather than upset at being told about the trespasser in the grave. She readily agreed with the suggestion that they should complete the service in the cemetery chapel and then go back to her home for refreshments as per schedule, leaving the interment to be carried out on a separate occasion.

Her older son, Brian, was not so easily mollified. He had made the journey from Darlington for the purpose of seeing his father laid to rest, and he did not understand why this was not possible. His first suggestion was that the police should remove the offending corpse forthwith so that there need be no delay. Surely, he maintained, it would only take a few minutes to carry it away and prepare the grave for its rightful occupant. Peter patiently explained that there was rather more to it than that, at which Brian conceded that perhaps it would be more realistic if the funeral party were to partake of their refreshments and come back for the burial later that morning. He shook his head in disbelief when Peter told him that it could be several days before the cemetery was back to normal and the police cordon around the grave could be removed.

Fortunately, his mother was firm with him and it was not long before Peter found himself leading the way into the chapel to make the official announcement of the new funeral arrangements. The organist, an elderly man with white hair and blue-veined hands, looked up with an expression of relief on his face as they entered, a few bars into the slow movement from Mozart's clarinet concerto, which he was playing for the fourth time. He had also treated the waiting mourners to three renderings each of *Air on the G-string* and Handel's *Largo*, and he was beginning to become anxious that there would be complaints that he had not brought a more extensive repertoire of voluntaries to fill the lengthy waiting period before the service began.

Peter processed down the aisle followed by Mandy and Raymond, who took up positions on either side of him at the front of the chapel. He waited while Brian helped his mother into a seat on the front row and then raised his hand for silence. He delivered his message briefly and then walked back down the aisle without allowing any time for questions or protestations. As he hastened to make his exit, he overheard some of the muttered conversation among the funeral guests.

'I *told* Margery that she ought to have him cremated,' an elderly man in a dark trench coat remarked to the small woman standing next to him, whom Peter took to be his wife.

'It was hardly worth us coming,' a middle-aged woman in a pinstriped business suit complained on the row behind.

'Disgraceful!' came the verdict of a tall woman in a black hat, whose face was obscured by a black netting veil. 'But what can you expect when you put one of those lady vicars in charge?'

Peter, thankful to be able to escape back to the normality of an investigation into a suspicious death, came out into the weak early November sunshine to find that a police van had joined the vehicles clustering around the chapel. Scenes of Crime Officers were busily getting their equipment ready and setting off towards the grave to begin a forensic examination of the site.

Jordan Fox was waiting for Peter. He was accompanied by a man in a grey suit, who said that he was from the council and had oversight of all four cemeteries within the Oxford City Council area. Peter explained to him that the cemetery would have to be closed until further notice and then dispatched Fox to close the gates and guard the entrance to turn away anyone seeking to come in.

The grey-suited man pursed his lips and shook his head lugubriously, but did not argue. He followed Peter as he strode briskly over to where he could see Anna and Andy in conversation with two men dressed in overalls bearing the Local Authority logo. Anna made the introductions.

'This is Luke Thompson,' she said, indicating a scrawny lad in his teens or early twenties with greasy hair hanging untidily over his face. 'He found the body.'

'No I never,' Luke protested. 'I found the grave'd been opened and I went and got Eric, and *he* found the body.'

'I'm sorry,' Anna gestured towards the other man, who was older, with grey hair very thin on top. 'This is Eric Parkinson. He oversees the preparation of all the graves here.'

'We dug the grave on Friday,' Eric explained. 'We had to do that, because the funeral was supposed to be first thing this morning.'

'So the grave was left unattended over the weekend?' Peter asked.

'Unattended, yes,' Eric agreed. 'But it was covered and locked down. That's what young Luke here found – the padlocks had been broken off.'

He showed Peter the heavy black cover and the four padlocks, which fixed its corners to the steel panels shoring up the sides of the grave. Peter peered down into the depths and found himself looking into the cheery face of his old friend Mike Carson, the pathologist.

'I thought I heard your dulcet tones,' Mike greeted him. 'It's an interesting case this. I'd say that the death occurred elsewhere and the body was brought here some time afterwards. I should be able to give you a better idea of the timings after the post-mortem. I hope I'll also be able to tell you how she died, which isn't obvious just at present. One *very* interesting feature is *this*.' He held up a spray of small red roses for Peter's inspection. As he did so, several of the petals dropped down on to the boards surrounding the grave, looking to Peter eerily like drops of blood. One of the SOCOs[8] stepped forward and carefully enclosed the flowers in an evidence bag.

'It was lying on her chest,' Mike explained, 'with her hands across the top of it holding it in place. You'll be able to see how it was from the photos.'

'So, it's as if whoever put her here was trying to treat the body with some sort of respect,' Peter suggested. 'That looks like a floral tribute of some sort.'

'As you know, I don't go in for that sort of speculation,' Mike answered. 'I don't try to guess motives. I just record the facts and make scientific deductions. All I can say is that it must have been placed there after death and most likely, after she was put in the grave. There were a couple of petals lying outside of the plastic sheet that she's been wrapped in. And yes,' he added, seeing Peter about to ask a question, 'we did get photographs before I unwrapped her.'

'Right! Well, I'll leave you to get on.' Peter turned to look at Luke and Eric. 'Is there somewhere more comfortable where we can go and talk? I need you to take me through exactly what happened this morning.'

---

[8] Scenes of Crime Officers (also known as Crime Scene Investigators): specialist personnel skilled in preserving, recording and recovering evidence from the scene of a crime.

13.00 MONDAY 2ᴺᴰ NOVEMBER

'Right!' Peter called the room to attention. His team of officers from the Oxford division of Thames Valley CID looked up attentively. 'We're treating this as a murder enquiry. It's certainly a suspicious death and an attempt to prevent lawful disposal of a body. We've opened an Incident on HOLMES 2[9]. You should all have been given access to it – check after this briefing and make sure. Here's what we know so far. Anna – can we have the picture of the grave as it was when the SOCOs got there?'

A photograph appeared on the screen in front of them. It showed a pale face surrounded by some sort of light green material. The eyes were closed as if in sleep, but there was a deathly quality in the complexion that made it clear that this young woman would never wake up again.

---

[9] HOLMES 2 (Home Office Large Major Enquiry System) is an Information Technology system used by police forces across the UK to collate and manage data relating to criminal investigations.

Her body was completely encased in the same glossy, green material and partially covered with loose soil.

'The body was found early this morning by two grave-diggers,' Peter told them. 'Their statements have been uploaded on to the computer, but here are the main points. They prepared the grave on Friday and secured it to prevent anyone tampering with it or falling in accidentally. When they went to open it up this morning, to make it ready for the funeral, they found that someone had been there before them. The padlocks securing the grave cover had been forced – with a crowbar or something similar, we think – and the earth that had been excavated had been disturbed. They looked inside and saw a lot of loose earth in the bottom of the grave. At first, they thought it was just youngsters who'd drunk too much larking about and making some of the earth fall back into the grave, but when they got in to clear it out again, they found this.'

'What's that green stuff?' asked Monica Philipson from the back of the room. She had only recently been promoted to Detective Sergeant, after a longer time as a constable than she had expected when she joined the police service on a "fast-track" scheme for high-flying university graduates, and she was always keen to make her presence felt in front of senior officers.

'Visqueen,' Peter told her. 'Builders use it. It's a sort of thin plastic sheeting. It looks as if the body was wrapped in a sheet of it before being put into the grave and then covered with a thin layer of soil from the pile that the gravediggers had left for filling in after the official burial. Presumably whoever did it was hoping that nobody would notice the body under the soil and would just lower the coffin down on top of it.'

'But surely they must've known someone would check the grave after finding the locks smashed.' Monica pointed out. 'If they were hoping to hide the body, it wasn't a very good way of doing it.'

'Not a particularly easy place to put it either,' Peter agreed. 'They couldn't risk being seen carrying a corpse around during the day and the gates are locked at night. So they must somehow have got it over the fence. There's a chain-link fence all round the boundary, with a hedge as well most of the way and the original metal railings in places. There are playing fields bordering it on one side, which may be where they got in from. They'd have been less likely to be seen climbing over from there than from the Banbury Road. Can we have the map, Anna?'

Anna obligingly displayed a map of the cemetery and surrounding area.

'There are roads on three sides,' Peter said, pointing. 'The main entrance, where the funeral cars come in, is on Banbury Road. There's another entrance on Five Mile Drive. Banbury Road and Five Mile Drive are both residential, so it would be risky to be seen climbing over the fence there, even at night. Jordan Hill is a little business park – mainly publishing companies but some small IT outfits and other businesses. I imagine it's pretty deserted outside working hours. We've got people checking all round the perimeter to see if we can find where they got in. As soon as we finish here, Sergeant Davenport is going to lead on house-to-house enquiries to find out if anyone saw anything suspicious between Friday evening and Monday morning. I'll need some of you to help her with that. Meanwhile, the rest of us need to get to work on identifying the body. She wasn't carrying any documents, so the best bet is probably the distinctive tattoos that she's got on her forearms. Andrews, I'm putting you in charge of searching the Missing Persons database to see if you can find a match.'

Anna brought up a sequence of pictures showing the inner surfaces of the wrists and forearms of the young woman whose body had been found in the grave. Both arms were decorated with floral designs. The right arm had thin green stems winding up from the wrist almost to the elbow, with curling tendrils, delicate leaves and a few bluish purple flowers. The plant adorning the right arm was unmistakeably red clover. The distinctive trefoil leaves, trailing stems and purple-pink flowers were recognisable to anyone who had been for a walk in the countryside in summer or who had struggled to maintain a weed-free lawn.

'Are those the *only* tattoos?' asked Rupert Andrews, a tall detective sergeant with a mop of unruly black hair.

'Yes. Why?'

'I was only thinking, sir, that it's a strange place to have them. I mean, people usually either have tattoos where they'll be noticed – on the face or the outside of the arms, for example – or else hidden away so that only intimate friends know about them. On the inside of the arms, they'd have been visible, except when she was wearing long sleeves, but nobody could see the designs properly unless she held out her arms specially to show them off.'

'Andrews is right,' Anna agreed. 'It would be more natural to have them on the outside of the arms. Perhaps that tells us something about her psychology, but I'm not sure what exactly.'

'Well, the main thing is that they are very distinctive,' Peter said, not wishing to be diverted into speculation about the victim's state of mind. 'If she hasn't been reported missing they may still help us in finding out who she is. Philipson?'

'Yes sir,' Monica answered eagerly.

'I'd like you to do the rounds of local tattoo studios, asking them if they remember doing either of these. You may have to go back a few years. Mike reckoned she's at least twenty-five, probably older, so she could have had them done up to about ten years ago.'

'Right you are,' Monica said brightly, pleased to have been given a distinct role in the operation. 'I'll get on to it right away.'

'We'll know more after the PM,' Peter went on, 'but

that won't be until tomorrow, so in the meantime, here's a basic description to go with the photographs.'

Anna displayed a form on which were recorded basic data about the victim. The woman was five feet six inches tall and of slim build. She was white, with long straight hair which was black but showing a mousey brown at the roots. Her eyes were light brown. She was wearing a pink off-the-shoulder evening dress and red court shoes. Wrapped around her body, between her skin and the green plastic sheeting, was a long purple coat made of a woven woollen fabric. Her age was estimated as being between twenty-seven and thirty-two.

'That's about all we've got to go on for now,' Peter concluded. 'Andy – I want you to help Andrews. It'll be good experience for you to get to grips with the database. Everyone else – apart from Monica – you're to assist Anna with the house-to-house. I've got to get off to a press conference. The media are clamouring to know what's going on to warrant closing the cemetery.'

18.00 MONDAY 2ND NOVEMBER

'What's this case that old Peter's heading up?' Jonah demanded when Bernie brought Lucy to give him his dinner that evening. I just saw him on the news giving a press conference about a body turning up in an open grave. What's it all about?'

'You know Peter isn't allowed to gossip to me about his work,' Bernie answered, pleased to see that their friend appeared more cheerful than he had done for some time. 'I don't know any more than what's been put out in the official statements.'

'Come off it! You must at least know whether it's really as big as the media are making out it is. Are they treating it as murder? Why haven't they released any pictures of the body yet?'

Bernie smiled at the excitement in Jonah's voice. It was almost like the old Jonah who used to appear unannounced each year on Lucy's birthday, spend a few hours – or sometimes, when he was pressed for time, only a few minutes – playing with her, and then depart. While he was there, whatever game Lucy wanted to play always appeared to be the most important thing in the world to him and he entered into it with energy and enthusiasm. Now, it seemed, he was equally enthusiastic to join in Peter's new game of *pin the name on the corpse*. Bernie wished that she had more information to offer him, to feed his interest and stop him slipping back into the lethargy that had become his normal state in recent weeks.

'As you will have heard in the press conference,' she said, 'they are keeping an open mind and ruling nothing out.'

'That goes without saying. It's part of the standard press conference spiel, along with *I am not prepared to comment on such speculation*, whenever a journalist makes a suggestion about anything – especially if we think they may be right. But you didn't answer my question – why haven't they released a photograph, or at least a description, to get the public to identify the body? Does it mean that they have an idea who it is?'

'No, I don't think so. As far as I know, it's more that they aren't ready yet and they don't want to release a description that turns out to be misleading. You know how people's minds work – once you get an idea fixed in your head, it's hard to change it. So if, for example, they told everyone that it was a woman in her twenties and then, at the post mortem they concluded that she was actually over forty …'

'So they haven't done the PM yet? What's taking them so long?'

'A backlog of other jobs, I expect. Mike's promised to fit it in tomorrow. I think Peter's quite pleased to have the excuse for delaying launching a public appeal. He doesn't want to have to divert manpower away from finishing at the crime scene and getting the cemetery back into operation. Apparently, the family of the man who was supposed to be being buried in that grave have been remarkably understanding and co-operative, but I imagine there's going to be a lot of angst if more funerals are cancelled and if people are kept away from visiting their family graves for more than a few days. And, in any case, wouldn't it be better if they manage to identify the body from the Missing Persons register without a public appeal? If she were my daughter or sister or best friend, I'd far rather find out through a call from the police than by seeing her face splashed across my television screen.'

'I suppose you're right,' Jonah smiled his lop-sided smile. 'And careful old Peter will have thought about all that. I expect that's why they put him in charge, when you might have expected them to go for a DCI. The Chief Super will know that he'd think about all those things instead of just pressing on to solve the case. It could backfire though,' he added thoughtfully, 'if it turns out to be a serial killer and they strike again while Peter's still footling about trying not to upset anyone.'

'I'm quite sure Peter never footled about in his life!' Bernie said with exaggerated indignation. 'Just because he doesn't jump into everything feet first without considering the consequences …'

'Well, get *him* to bring Lucy tomorrow night, so he can tell me all about it. I'm still a serving police officer, even if I am stuck in here for the time being; so there's no reason that he can't discuss the case with me. I'll give him a few pointers to get him started!'

10.00 TUESDAY 3RD NOVEMBER

After calling in at the incident room to review progress, of which there seemed to be very little, Peter spent the morning watching the post mortem examination of the unidentified cadaver.

He decided to take young Andy Lepage along with him. It was time he got to know what actually went on to produce the sanitised report that would be entered on to the computer and sent to the coroner. It was now a little over three years since Peter had been chosen as the safe pair of hands into whose care Trainee Detective Constable Lepage had been placed. Although any formal training role was now over, Peter still felt responsible for giving him opportunities to develop his skills as a detective and encouraging him to progress in his career.

Pathologist Mike Carson greeted them warmly. He had worked with Peter ever since the days when Peter and Jonah both had Lucy's father, Richard Paige, for their boss. He knew the whole family well, including being aware of the reason that Peter felt a particular concern for DC Lepage's wellbeing. Seeing the two of them standing together in the doorway, he was immediately reminded of the photograph that stood on Peter's office desk. In it, Peter stood proudly next to his son Eddie, who was clad in a gown and mortarboard. Behind them rose the grand frontage of Whitworth Hall in Manchester, where Eddie had graduated a few years earlier. This picture had replaced a portrait of Peter's first wife, from a time before her violent death had made it too painful for him to be constantly looking into her smiling face. Like Peter's son, Andy Lepage had smooth, caramel-coloured skin, dark brown eyes and frizzy black hair – all in stark contrast to Peter's greying red hair and pale complexion. Neither Peter nor Mike would ever dream of asking Andy about his ancestry, but it seemed fair to assume that his racial heritage was mixed.

'We're all ready to go,' Mike told them, showing them into the cool room where the young woman's body lay covered by a thin sheet. 'Is this your first PM?'

'Yes,' Andy admitted, closing his mouth and taking deep breaths through his nose in a conscious effort at inducing calm and combating any sign of nausea.

'OK. Well try not to let anything we say bother you. Remember, we're doing this sort of thing every day of our lives, so we can't afford to take everything deadly serious.'

'And if you need to take a break at any point to get some fresh air,' Peter added kindly, 'just go ahead. There's nothing to be ashamed of about … I mean, there'd be something wrong with you if you didn't find all this … unpleasant.'

'Yes sir,' Andy nodded.

Peter and Andy took up their positions at the side of the room and watched as Mike and his assistant began their work. To Peter it was largely routine to begin with. Mike commented on the appearance of the body confirming that she was a white female aged between twenty-five and thirty-five years, thin, but without any obvious signs of malnutrition. There were signs of trauma to the trunk, legs and arms, but these looked to have occurred after death. They worked systematically, measuring, recording and photographing bruises, lacerations and potentially identifying marks. Peter had half-expected that there would be more tattoos to be discovered on the parts of the body that had been covered by her dress, but that was not the case. The young woman had restricted herself to those two floral decorations on her two forearms.

'Now this is interesting,' Mike said, as he peered down at the woman's left arm. 'See this?' He pointed to a slit in the skin just below the elbow. 'I'd say that this was a knife wound. There's no sign of healing, so probably inflicted shortly before death.'

'But not serious enough to have *contributed* to her death?' Peter queried.

'Oh no. It's quite superficial.'

'But it could suggest that she was attacked?' Andy suggested nervously. 'And maybe hurt herself trying to get away?'

Mike shrugged and carried on working, lifting the eyelids to peer closely at the brown eyes staring up lifelessly at him, and shining a light into each orifice of the body in search of clues to indicate how, when and where the young woman's life had ended.

'Here's a funny thing!' he said suddenly, holding up a pair of tweezers, with which he had been probing the woman's nostrils. 'It looks like a piece of plant material. I wonder ...,' he added thoughtfully, bending down and inspecting the inside of her mouth. A few moments later, he was showing Peter a larger tuft of greenery, which he had retrieved from her throat.

'See this?' he said. 'This is waterweed. I can't say for certain, but one possibility is that she drowned.'

'Drowned?' Peter and Andy chorused in surprise.

'Or at least spent some time in the river,' Mike corrected himself, conscious that he had abandoned his usual cautious approach and speculated ahead of the evidence. 'I'll get this checked out. There's probably someone in the university who'll be able to tell us exactly whereabouts it grows. Unfortunately, drowning is one of the most difficult causes of death to confirm with any certainty, so we'd better proceed with the process of eliminating everything else. I'll take some blood samples and get the lab to run toxicology tests and so on. Then, after that, we'd better open her up and take a look at the internal organs.'

'I'll get a detailed report typed up and sent across,' Mike told Peter, as they sat drinking coffee in his office a few hours later. 'But, I'll go through the main points now, if you like.'

'Please!' Peter urged. 'Especially anything you can say about likely time of death and this drowning theory of yours.'

'As for time of death,' Mike began, pausing to take a draft of coffee from a mug bearing the logo of a pharmaceutical company, 'I'm afraid I can't be at all precise. Rigor mortis had completely worn off by the time I examined the body yesterday morning, which means that death can't have occurred later than, say, Saturday lunchtime. Actually, I'd put it maybe a day or two earlier than that, based on the progression of putrefaction of the body tissues, but I could easily be wrong about that. It probably wasn't more than a week ago, but again I could be wrong. The trouble is that there are so many unknown factors. Assuming that I'm right about the body having spent some time in a river during the perimortem period, how long was it in the water? After it was taken out, was it transported straight to the cemetery or kept somewhere for a period? If so, what conditions was it kept in – temperature, humidity and so on? The forensic entomology report may give us an idea of how long it is since the body was retrieved from the water, but that isn't the same as telling us when she died.'

'But you're basically saying that we're looking at some time last week?' Peter queried.

'Yes,' Mike confirmed, 'and if I had to be more precise, I'd go for the latter half – Wednesday onwards, say.'

'Good. Well, that's a start. And you still think that she probably drowned?'

'I still haven't found any other likely cause of death,' Mike answered cautiously. 'But until the tests come back we won't know whether she could have taken drugs or had one of a number of medical conditions that could have contributed to her death.'

'But you definitely don't think she died as a result of a physical assault?' Andy asked. 'You think it was probably either drug-related or natural causes – an accident, maybe?'

'It's not for me to say. If we assume for the minute that she did drown, it's your job to find out whether she fell in the river by accident, jumped in of her own volition or if someone pushed her.'

'Oh! Yes, I suppose so,' Andy said, sounding a little deflated.

'Which is why we'd better be getting off back to the incident room,' Peter said quickly to cover Andy's embarrassment. 'Thanks for the coffee, Mike. Get that report over to me ASAP, won't you!'

They seemed to be getting nowhere fast. The house-to-house enquiries had yielded nothing. Nobody remembered having seen anything unusual going on in the vicinity of the cemetery during the course of the weekend. Monica's systematic investigation of tattoo studios in the Oxford area had drawn a blank. None of them recognised the pictures that she showed them of the tattoos on the arms of the body in the grave; and none recalled a young woman answering that description enquiring about having her arms embellished with such pictures.

Peter patiently drew up rotas of officers to widen the

area of the enquiries and to approach tattoo artists across a larger region. Then he set to work preparing for a public appeal for information that might help them in identifying the dead woman and discovering how her death had come about. Much as he disliked appearing in front of journalists, another televised press conference was clearly called for and this needed to be co-ordinated with appeals in the press and across social media. He sifted through the photographs that had been taken of the body, and selected one of each of the tattoos and one of the woman's face, chosen as being the most likely to give an indication of what she had looked like in life. Then he reached for the phone to arrange the press conference and to assemble a team of call handlers in readiness for the public response that could be expected to follow.

18.00 TUESDAY 3RD NOVEMBER

'Now then, Peter,' Jonah said when he saw that Bernie had brought her husband with them that evening. 'You're not to go sneaking off to chat to Jeanette. I want the low-down on this unidentified body of yours. I saw you on the TV news appealing for witnesses to come forward. What's the latest?'

Peter took one of the plastic seats from a pile at the side of the room and set it down in front of Jonah, who was sitting up in his high-backed chair looking far more alert and attentive than Peter remembered him from their previous visit. Lucy, seeing that the dinner tray was already there on the mobile table, squeezed past and took up her position next to Jonah, ready to feed him while they talked. Bernie took her accustomed seat in the corner of the room and got out her laptop, intending to catch up on her emails.

'There's not a lot to tell you,' Peter began. 'We really don't know much more than what we put out in the press-release.'

'What about cause of death?' Jonah asked, swallowing a

136

mouthful of ox-tail soup that Lucy had expertly inserted into his mouth while Peter was talking. 'I suppose Mike's being his usual cagey self?'

'Not really. Unusually for him, he's come up with a theory before waiting for all the tests to come back.'

'And?' Jonah prompted, sensing that Peter was holding back something sensational. 'Go on! Spill the beans!'

'Mike thinks that she may have drowned. He's pretty definite that the body spent some time in a river, and there's waterweed in her windpipe that most likely got there as a result of her inhaling while she was underwater in other words, she was still alive at the time. Mike's sent a sample of the weed off to the university Botany Department. He thinks they may be able to suggest which river it was and even perhaps whereabouts in it she must have been.'

'I may be able to help you with that,' Jonah said enigmatically. He opened his mouth to go on, but was prevented from speaking by Lucy's soup spoon.

'How? You didn't even know about it until just now.'

'I have my methods,' Jonah murmured, smiling complacently. 'But don't let me interrupt you. Go on! What else did Mike have to say? Did he estimate a time of death?'

'Sometime last week. He couldn't do better than that without having the forensic entomology report.'

'What's ent- … ento- … what you just said?' Lucy asked. She was keen to learn more about her chosen career and this was a term that she had not come across before.

'Entomology is the study of insects,' Jonah told her. 'Forensic entomology means using insects to discover things about a crime.'

'But how do insects help with working out when someone died?'

Both men hesitated, unsure how to explain. Bernie looked up from her computer screen and decided to take a hand in the conversation.

'Do you remember that dead sheep we found when we were walking on the Ridgeway that time?'

Lucy nodded.

'And it had all maggots wriggling around in it?'

Lucy nodded again.

'Well maggots are the larvae of blowflies that lay their eggs in dead bodies. The eggs take a certain time to develop and hatch out into maggots, and they can't get into a body before death so ...'

'So a forensic entomologist can tell by the age of any eggs or maggots that are in the body the minimum length of time that it must have been dead,' Jonah finished for her.

'I see,' Lucy nodded slowly, temporarily forgetting to ply Jonah with food while she thought about this newly acquired knowledge. 'But the flies might not find the body right away. So it doesn't tell you *when* the person died, only the *latest* time they could have died.'

'That's right,' Peter agreed. 'You're spot on there! And in this case, we have the added complication that she could have been under the water, where the flies couldn't get at her, for some time after she died. I can't honestly see it getting us much closer than what Mike's already told us based on looking at the body.'

'And he says that death occurred sometime last week?' Jonah asked eagerly. 'So last Thursday, for example, falls within his window?'

'Yes,' Peter answered, with a puzzled frown. 'But why pick on Thursday specifically?'

'Aha! Well that's all to do with *my* theory about where she drowned,' Jonah said mysteriously, his eyes lighting up as he relished the chance to baffle his colleague. 'My money's on her falling in the Isis somewhere between Port Meadow and the Gostow Road Bridge, sometime on Thursday.'

'Because that's the stretch of the Thames closest to Wolvercote?' Bernie asked, ostentatiously ignoring Jonah's use of the local name for the part of the River Thames that flowed through Oxford, something that she considered to be an affectation.

'No,' Jonah answered, still maintaining an air of secrecy. 'I have my own more cogent reasons for that.'

'And they are?' Peter asked, becoming irritated with Jonah's cryptic assertions. 'If you've got any basis for all this speculation you ought to tell me about it.'

'All in good time,' Jonah said in what seemed to Peter to be a very patronising way. 'Bernie! Bring that computer of yours over here and find those pictures that the Press Office released this afternoon of the tattoos on the corpse's arms.'

Bernie obediently opened a browser on her laptop and searched for the news report. Then she unplugged the power cable and carried the machine over to where Jonah and Peter were sitting. She set it down on the bed, where they could both see the screen. Lucy looked over Jonah's shoulder and gave a little gasp as she saw the two photographs, each showing part of an arm decorated with a tattoo.

'That's the same as on the woman who hit me!' she said in surprise, gesturing at the screen with the fork that she had been using to feed Jonah with spaghetti Bolognese.

'I was hoping you'd say that,' Jonah told her with an air of satisfaction. 'That's precisely what *I* thought when I saw it. It's just exactly how you described it to me.'

'Hang on! Let me get this straight,' Peter intervened. 'You're saying that this is the same woman as the one that Lucy saw on the riverbank on Thursday morning?'

'That's right,' Jonah agreed, smiling up at him complacently.

'I told you she was frightened and running away from those men!' Lucy exclaimed triumphantly. 'But Constable Ferrar wouldn't listen,' she added in an aggrieved tone.

'That's right,' Jonah said again. 'My guess is that they could be people-traffickers and they were holding her somewhere nearby and she escaped.'

'And they came after her with a knife,' Lucy added, putting down the fork in her excitement and picking up a knife from the tray in front of her and waving it around to illustrate her point. 'And she was frightened and ran away. And then I frightened her some more and she ran away again and ...,' she paused at the enormity of what came next, '... and fell in the river,' she concluded.

'There was a knife wound,' Peter added excitedly. 'You can just see a bit of it in that picture there. On the left arm, look! Just above the tattoo of the pink flowers. We tried not to show it on the photos in case it confused people, but it was there alright.'

'There you are then!' Jonah cried exultantly. 'It all fits! They came after her with a knife and slashed her arm, but not seriously, and she manages to get away. And then Lucy spots them and calls out. They see her watching them and get scared, because they don't want any witnesses to what they're up to, so they turn round and run off. But the woman doesn't know they've gone, and she goes and hides in the bushes, thinking that they're still after her. And then Lucy comes up behind her to try to help her and she thinks it's the men coming to get her and she lashes out with a bit of old wood that she's found lying around, and then runs off again.'

'And falls in the river,' Lucy added again, sounding rather guilty. 'I didn't mean to scare her.'

'Of course you didn't!' Peter said emphatically.

'We know you didn't, love,' Bernie added. 'You were only trying to help. It wasn't your fault, whatever happened after that.'

'There's no reason to assume that she fell in right away,' Jonah added, trying to reassure Lucy that no blame was attached to her. 'In all likelihood, the men waited until the coast was clear and then came hunting for her again. For all we know they may even have pushed her in deliberately.'

'This is all very fine,' Peter said after a short pause, 'but it doesn't help us to find out who she is. And if you're right about the people trafficking then it's unlikely that anyone's going to come forward to say they recognise her. The traffickers will have kept her hidden, and her nearest and dearest are probably all back in Eastern Europe or wherever it is she's been brought from. I'd better get the pictures sent out through Interpol and see about searching missing persons databases in all the likely countries. And we've probably been wasting our time looking for tattooists locally, because the chances are she'll have had them done before she came over here.'

'I'm not so sure about that,' Jonah said, with another enigmatic smile. 'I rather fancy I may be able to help you on that front too.'

'How on earth?' Peter exclaimed, not knowing whether to be pleased or annoyed that Jonah seemed to have been able to make more progress in the case from his hospital bed than Peter had done with a whole team of police officers to help him.

'Well, I had the advantage that I started before you. After Lucy described the tattoo that she'd seen, I got to thinking that probably each tattoo artist has their own range of designs. So I spent some time browsing around the web. Bernie! Put "Petra's Piercings and Pics" into Google, will you?'

Bernie reached over and typed in the words. A list of websites appeared on the screen. She selected the first, which was the homepage of a tattoo studio in Swindon.

'Now click on "Gallery",' Jonah instructed, 'and scroll through the pictures one at a time.'

Bernie did as she was told and soon they were all looking at a picture of red clover flowers and trefoil leaves.'

'This is an all-woman group of tattoo artists,' Jonah explained. 'They pride themselves on high-class tattoos for the more discerning customer. One of them specialises in designs based on British wildflowers. If you carry on going, you'll find one of vetch, which is almost identical to the one on the other arm of the corpse. That had already caught my eye because it seemed like what Lucy described to me; and then after the photographs were released, I had another look and found this one. It looks pretty conclusive to me.'

'You're right,' Peter agreed. 'I'll get someone over there first thing tomorrow. We were working outwards gradually in circles from Oxford, so we'd have got there in the end, but it might have been a while. I was surprised just how many tattoo studios there are out there these days.'

'And you need to do a proper search of the area where Lucy saw the woman,' Jonah added. 'It's a pity nobody followed up on the assault properly the day it happened. The crime scene should have been preserved and a proper search done for the woman then and there.'

'Yes, well there's nothing we can do about that now,' Peter said, with a touch of annoyance in his voice at the way that Jonah had begun to behave as if he were in charge. True, he was senior in rank to Peter, but he was also currently on sick leave and confined to the hospital ward. 'At least that gives us a starting point for searching the river. We'll have to take statements from Martin and Lucy, I suppose. Anna had better do that, so nobody can say I influenced what Lucy says. And I suppose I'll have to declare a potential conflict of interest,' he sighed, 'although it's quite tenuous really.'

'Surely they won't take you off the case just because you happen to know two of the witnesses?' Bernie asked. 'I don't see how that's going to affect your judgement.'

'That'll be up to the Chief Super to decide.'

'Adrian?' Bernie's long association with the police meant that she knew a good many of the senior officers. 'He won't want to replace you. He told me that it was a mystery to him that you hadn't made it to DCI yet – *been ripe for promotion for years* were his precise words.'

'Too late now! My next step is much more likely to be retirement. But meanwhile, are we about done here? I'd better be drawing up a plan of campaign for tomorrow. We can't start searching the river until it gets light, but the sooner we can get started the better. Someone had better get over to Swindon to talk to Jonah's tattoo artist and we'll need proper statements from Lucy and Martin – and from PC Ferrar and the ambulance crew, in case they saw anything when they came. That's going to be a bit awkward. Ferrar is bound to think she's being criticised for her handling of the incident.'

'And so she should,' Jonah said firmly. 'She botched the whole thing and she needs to take responsibility for it.'

'I'm sure she had the best of intentions,' Bernie began.

'That's not the point,' Jonah insisted. 'She should have kept an open mind to all possibilities – including that Lucy might have been telling the unvarnished truth – instead of allowing her obsession with domestic violence to cloud her judgement. She wouldn't last long in my team, I can tell you!'

'We can't go yet,' Lucy said, in the pause that followed. 'You haven't eaten your pudding.'

Bernie closed the lid of her laptop while Peter retired to a chair in the corner of the room with a notebook and pen. Lucy picked up a spoon and started cutting up a portion of jam roly-poly pudding into bite-sized pieces.

'How did you get on with Ken's students this morning?' Bernie asked, deliberately changing the topic of conversation. 'He seemed to think the meeting went well.'

'They seem nice enough,' Jonah said warily.

'Dean's certainly very nice,' Bernie agreed. 'Very quiet and thoughtful. I don't know Wayne; he's at another college, but Ken speaks highly of him.'

'They make an odd pair,' Jonah tried to keep the conversation going while his mind was busy thinking about the dead woman and the actions that he would have been taking now if he had been in charge of the case. 'Dean's so small and soft-spoken and Wayne's this big, loudmouthed Brummy[10].'

'According to Ken, he's a gentle giant,' Bernie told him. 'But apparently he plays prop forward[11] for his college, which makes that hard to believe!'

It was not long before the pudding was finished and they all got up to go.

'You'd better get on to Mike and ask him to take another look at that knife wound,' Jonah called out to Peter as they left. 'It's probably more significant than he realised, now that we know she was attacked shortly before she died. And get him to check again for any signs of drug-taking. And see if you can hurry up the botanists with that weed sample. It ought to be easier for them now you can tell them approximately which bit of river to look at. And-'

'Jonah,' Peter cut in, keeping his temper with some difficulty. 'You may out-rank me, but *I'm* the Senior Investigating Officer on this case – at least until they decide to take me off because of Lucy's involvement – and besides, I've already got all those things down on my to-do list.'

'Sorry,' Jonah apologised, treating Peter to one of his endearing lop-sided smiles. 'I wasn't meaning to criticise. It's just … it's just so frustrating being stuck in here all day when I ought to be out there solving crimes. I've never been away from the job for more than a fortnight since I joined the force. You will come again, won't you? And tell me how things pan out?'

Peter sighed and shook his head slowly. He was not at

---

[10] A native of Birmingham or the wider West Midlands region.

[11] In Rugby Union, the two prop forward positions are typically occupied by the largest and strongest players in the team.

all sure of the wisdom of allowing Jonah to get involved, but he could see how much more cheerful the prospect of being involved in a criminal investigation, albeit vicariously, had made him. It would be cruel to refuse the request.

'Alright. I'll keep you posted,' he said at last.

08.30 WEDNESDAY 4TH NOVEMBER

Peter decided that the three women who were partners in
Petra's Piercings and Pics would be likely to respond better to
an approach by female officers. So he despatched Monica
and Anna to Swindon to interview Bella, the artist who
specialised in wildflower designs.

'The senior partner is a Petra Alcock,' Peter told them.
'And there are two other partners, all women. I think they
consider themselves a cut above your average tattoo
studio. According to their website, Bella studied Fine Art
at Goldsmiths College before deciding to put her talents to
work decorating people. Try to get her to talk about why
our mystery woman might have chosen to have those
tattoos done and what her state of mind was, as well as any
information she may have about who she is.'

'I knew that course I took on *the role of body ornamentation
in the culture of indigenous peoples* would come in handy one
day!' Anna said with a smile. She had studied *Archaeology
and Anthropology* at the University of Cambridge before
joining the police. 'I remember a guest lecturer coming in
to explain to us some of the different methods of tattooing

and the symbolism of various designs. She'd had some tattoos done on herself, so that she knew what it was actually like. And then she went on to write a paper about tattoo culture in the UK. She said that the relationship between a tattooist and their clients is a very intimate one. She reckoned that people would say things to their tattooist that they wouldn't *even* talk about to their hairdresser!'

'Let's hope she was right,' Peter said, 'and that our Miss X told Bella her life story. Judging by the level of response to the media appeal, she hasn't made much impression on anyone else. We haven't had a single credible witness coming forward to say they know her.'

Anna and Monica left, and Peter turned to Andy.

'OK,' he said briskly. 'Now I want you to come with me to interview Martin Riess. I rang him last night and arranged for us to meet him in his room in Lichfield College. He'll be waiting for us and, if I know Martin, getting anxious wondering what it's all about, so we'd better get over there and put him out of his misery.'

The room occupied by Dr Martin Riess, Fellow in Geology, was at the top of a narrow winding staircase in a building that dated back to the foundation of Lichfield College at the tail end of the mediaeval period. When Peter and Andy arrived, they saw that the thick oak outer door was standing open, indicating that the don was inside and ready to receive visitors. Peter knocked on the inner door and then stepped back waiting for a response. It opened almost immediately to reveal Martin's diminutive figure and anxious face.

'Come in!' he called, throwing the door wide open and standing back to allow them over the threshold. 'Coffee anyone?' he added, gesturing towards a glass jug keeping warm on the hotplate of a filter coffee machine.'

'Thanks. Mine's white with no sugar,' Peter answered, judging that Martin would find answering their questions less stressful with a calming mug of coffee to keep his hands occupied.

Peter and Andy sat down on two rather sagging easy chairs. Andy took out his notebook and prepared to document the conversation. Martin poured coffee for them all and then sat down on another chair, facing them across an untidy coffee table strewn with copies of "Nature" and "Terra Nova" magazines.

'You said that you wanted to ask me about that woman that we saw by the river last week,' he said, looking anxiously at Peter. 'What's this all about? I thought that … well, that nobody was taking her existence seriously.'

'We have reason to believe that she might be the same young woman as the body that wound up in an unoccupied grave in Wolvercote Cemetery over the weekend,' Peter told him. 'You must have seen the news reports.'

'Yes. I saw you talking about it on the TV. What makes you think she's the same person as we saw on Thursday?'

'We'll come to that later. First, I need you to tell us everything that you can remember about her and about the men she was with. Can you describe them to me?'

'Not really. They were the far side of the field and they didn't hang about long.'

'Take your time. Close your eyes and try to picture what you saw.'

Martin followed Peter's instructions. In the silence, they all became aware of a clock ticking way the seconds as he struggled to remember what he had seen.

'The woman was wearing a pink dress,' he said at last. 'It was made of some sort of shiny material. The sun was low in the sky and it caught the light.'

'Good. That's a good start,' Peter said encouragingly. 'Let's concentrate on her for the moment. Can you remember anything else about her?'

'She had long hair – long, dark hair.'

'Good,' Peter said again. 'What about her build? Was

she tall, short, fat, thin?'

'Difficult to judge her height. I only saw her when she was running across the field and disappearing into the bushes. She definitely wasn't fat. As far as I can remember, she looked rather skinny.'

'Could this have been her?' Peter took out one of the photographs of the body from the graveyard.

'I suppose the hair's about right,' Martin said, gazing down at the face in the picture. 'But that's all I can say. I never saw her face. I never got anywhere near her.'

'OK. Now can we go back to the two men? Is there anything at all that you can tell me about them?'

'The thing is: I didn't notice them at all until Lucy pointed them out. And by the time I looked up and saw them, they must have heard her shouting and they turned round and scarpered.'

'So by the time you saw them, the woman had already got away and was running across the field?'

'Yes. Well, no. No. I do remember seeing one of them with his arm raised as if he was going to hit her. And then she got away and he lowered his arm and they looked across at us and then turned and ran away.'

'Good. Now the man who had his hand up – was he holding anything in it, did you see?'

'I know Lucy says she thought he had a knife, but I didn't honestly see anything. I just saw a man with his hand up above his head and a woman cowering down. I think maybe the other man grabbed the first one by the shoulder. Maybe he was remonstrating with him – telling him not to hurt her. And then she ran off towards the river and they ran the other way.'

'And is there anything else – anything at all – that you can remember about them?' Peter asked again. 'Their clothes, for example?'

'No,' Martin shook his head. 'They weren't wearing anything particularly striking – not like the woman's bright pink dress. Dark colours, I think. And …,' he tailed off as he strove to remember something that, until now, he had not been aware that he had noticed.

'Yes? Go on,' Peter urged gently.

'One of them – the other one, not the one that had hold of her and looked as if he wanted to hit her – was carrying something. Well, not exactly carrying – he had something over his arm – like the way you carry a coat if you take it off because it's getting too hot to wear it. But he had a coat on as well. I'm sure he did.'

'So you think he may have been carrying a coat?' Peter asked eagerly, remembering that the corpse had been found with a coat wrapped around her. 'What was it like? What colour?'

'Darkish,' Martin said cautiously. 'Blue maybe, or maybe black. I can't honestly say. I wasn't really looking. I was concentrating on steering the boat.'

'That's OK,' Peter said reassuringly. 'You're doing fine. Now, can you show us exactly where you were when all this happened?'

He got out a large-scale map and spread it out on the coffee table on top of the array of journals. Martin looked down and traced his finger along the line of the river from where they had joined it from the Oxford Canal, northwards to a point where it bent round to the left.

'We'd just come in sight of the house at Godstow lock.'

'If we took you there, would you be able to identify the bushes where the woman hid?' Peter asked.

'I'm not sure. Probably. There should be marks in the bank where I tied up the boat. If we can find those then I think I'd be able to work out which bushes it was from there.'

'Good. I think that's the next job then. Are you OK to come now? You're not supposed to be giving a lecture or anything this morning?'

'I've got a DPhil student coming at eleven, but I can put her off – if it's important.'

'It is rather. The sooner we find the place, the more

likely it is that any evidence there may have been of what happened will still be intact.'

While Martin made a short phone call to rearrange the supervision meeting, Peter called Sergeant Andrews, who was leading the team that was scouring the riverbank for signs of where the woman might have entered the water, and agreed that they would meet on the Godstow Road bridge.

'We'll leave Dr Riess with Sergeant Andrews and then head back,' Peter told Andy as they drew up by the entrance to the path that ran along the river from the bridge. 'I want you to get those notes into the computer. You need to create a record for each of the two men, even though we haven't got much on either of them yet, and we'd better have a new record for the woman, even though we *think* she's the same as the body in the grave. If they turn out to be two different people after all, it will be tricky untangling them unless we keep them separate at this stage.'

'Right you are, sir.'

'And then see if you can find out what happened to that lump of wood that the woman hit Lucy with. It's not very likely, considering the way Constable Ferrar was handling it, but you never know, there could still be some fingermarks that would help to identify her.'

12.00 WEDNESDAY 4TH NOVEMBER

Do you mind taking your lunch on the move?' Peter asked Anna, later that day. 'There's someone I'd like you to meet.'

'Not a problem. I've got my sandwiches in my bag and I'm not fussed where I eat them.'

'Good. Monica! We're going out, but we'll be back by three at the latest, so can you make sure you've got all that stuff from Swindon entered up? And when you've done that, get on to Missing Persons to see if it matches anything they've got on their database.'

'Yes, sir,' Monica took out her notebook and placed it on the desk next to her computer. She watched, rather regretfully, as Anna left the room in the company of their commanding officer. She wondered where they were going. It would be nice sometimes to be singled out like that instead of always being left with the boring jobs to do.

'You'll have heard of DCI Porter,' Peter said, as he backed the car into a parking space at the regional spinal injuries unit. 'He's based down in South Oxfordshire. He was shot in the neck a few months ago and he's still on the rehabilitation ward here.'

'I haven't only heard of him,' Anna replied. 'I've met him. Don't you remember? It was a couple of years back – that case where that journalist got himself killed on a narrowboat[12]. There was a second killing over in Didcot and DCI Porter was in charge of the investigation. He came over and spoke to us all about how the two cases might be linked.'

'So he did! I'd completely forgotten.' Peter got out of the car and Anna followed suit. 'Anyway, as I was saying, he's stuck in here at the moment, but he still managed to be the one who found out about *Petra's Piercings*, so it's only fair that you tell him all about what you and Monica discovered this morning.'

'She'll be green with envy. She fancies him!'

'Does she indeed?' Peter raised his eyebrows. 'I hope she's aware that he's a happily married man with two grown-up sons.'

They headed off across the car park towards the hospital building.

'Actually,' Peter began tentatively, unsure how to put into words what he wanted to say to prepare his colleague for what she was about to see, 'perhaps I ought to warn you.' He paused. 'You mustn't expect … Well, let's put it like this … After this injury of his, DCI Porter isn't quite the hunk that you girls were all swooning over two years ago.'

'I wouldn't ever have described him as a hunk, exactly – more of a slim wiry type.'

'Yes, well, slim maybe, but taken to the extreme these days; and as for wiry? Well, I suppose it's the difference between a tightly coiled spring and what happens when you put something too heavy on a spring balance and it

[12] See Murder of a Martian © 2016. ISBN 978-1-911083-10-8.

stretches and then won't go back again.'

'Oh.' Anna sounded doubtful. 'I think I see.'

'Look. The main thing is not to look shocked when you see him. Just behave as if nothing had happened. The only thing he'll be interested in is what you can tell him about our mystery woman, so just stick to that and you'll be fine.'

When they got to Jonah's room, Margaret was there feeding him with tapioca pudding. She looked up and smiled at Peter, who muttered an apology and turned to leave.

'No! Don't go,' she said hastily. 'Come in and sit down. We're nearly finished.'

'I don't want to intrude,' Peter said anxiously. 'I didn't know you were here. I should have thought …'

'Stop faffing about and come and sit down,' Jonah instructed. 'And introduce me to your …,' he paused and stared intently at Anna. 'Don't I know you? You're that Detective Sergeant who was working with Old Peter on the canal boat murder a year or two back, aren't you? I'm sorry; I don't remember your name.'

'Anna Davenport. And yes, that's right.' Anna tried to keep herself from staring at the sunken cheeks and veined hands that made the man who sat before her look so very different from the energetic officer that she remembered striding about the scene of the crime in Didcot and snapping out orders for photographs to be taken and bloodstains sampled.

'Pleased to meet you again, Anna. Now, I'm quite sure that Old Peter wouldn't have brought you here if you didn't have some news on this unidentified corpse of his, so take a pew and spill the beans.'

'Are you sure you wouldn't rather we came back later?' Peter asked, looking towards Jonah's wife. 'We can easily go and have our lunch first. I know how difficult it is for Margaret to find time to come over.'

'Don't you mind me,' Margaret insisted. 'I'm just grateful to you for giving him something to keep his mind occupied. He's been a right pain in the whatsit these past few weeks, until you came up with your mystery woman. Just wait while we finish this pudding and then I'll take the empties back outside and leave you three to talk shop.'

Peter unstacked two plastic chairs from a pile in the corner of the room and they both sat down. Taking care not to watch as Margaret spooned the remaining pudding into Jonah's mouth, Peter fumbled in his jacket pocket and brought out a plastic bag containing two rather squashed sandwiches. He opened it and began eating. Anna looked at him for a moment before reaching into her small shoulder bag and getting out her own lunch. They ate in silence while Margaret continued to feed Jonah.

As soon as the pudding was gone, Jonah dismissed his wife and looked towards Peter and Anna.

'Come on! I'm waiting,' he urged. 'I'm agog to hear your news.'

Peter opened the door to allow Margaret to go through it with the tray of empty dishes.

'Are you sure you don't mind?' he asked in a low voice as she passed.

'Mind! Are you joking? You're welcome to him!' Then she continued in a lower voice so that Jonah would not overhear. 'This is the first time in weeks that he's actually seemed to enjoy his food. If your gruesome corpse can give him his appetite back and motivate him to be bothered about things again then bring it on!'

Peter closed the door behind her and sat down again.

'Anna has been over to Swindon to interview the three women who run *Petra's Piercings*,' he told Jonah. 'I thought you'd like to hear what she found out, seeing as you were the one who put us on to them.'

'Monica – that's Sergeant Philipson – and I spoke to Petra Alcock herself and to the artist who specialises in wildflower designs. Her name is Bella Makin.' Anna said, trying to speak and act normally, but uncomfortably aware that she was addressing a space in the air just above and to the right of Jonah's head, to avoid looking at his cadaverous face. She had never seen a living person looking so gaunt and haggard.

'And did they remember doing those tattoos?' Jonah asked, becoming impatient as Anna paused to collect her thoughts.

'Yes. At least, Bella remembered.' Anna forced herself to look directly at Jonah and their eyes met. He smiled back at her in the strange lop-sided way that she remembered from two years earlier. His eyes – despite their sunken appearance the clearest blue that she had ever seen – twinkled back at her. Suddenly she felt more at ease. His body might have changed dramatically, but she could see that, underneath, the energetic police officer determined never to allow a case to defeat him was still there.

'She keeps a record of when she uses each design. There was only one person who had both the red clover and the common vetch done. We cross-referenced with the electronic diary that the company has for booking appointments and they were done about two and a half years ago. The customer was a woman in her twenties.'

'Did she have a name?' Jonah asked.

'She told them she was called Emma. They didn't know any more than that. So long as a customer is clearly over eighteen, they don't ask for any sort of ID; and she paid with cash, so no credit card details or anything.'

'Oh well. Emma will just have to do. Did she leave any other details? A telephone number, for example?'

'No. Bella thinks that she said she lived in Oxford, but she didn't know any more than that.'

'Hmmm. Not much to go on,' Jonah said thoughtfully.

'There was one thing that may help,' Anna added. 'Bella was very keen to tell me that every tattoo that she does is a one-off. She has a portfolio of basic designs for clients to choose from, but then she adapts them to suit their particular requirements. So every one is a unique work of art.'

She reached into her bag and took out four photographs, which she laid down on the table in front of Jonah.

'See here. That's the red clover design from her catalogue – and that's the tattoo on the left arm of our corpse. The stems curve differently and Emma's tattoo has an extra flower bud.'

'I see what you mean.' Jonah bent his head forward slightly and looked down intently at the pictures. 'The vetch is even more striking. There are more stems in the tattoo than in the original design. It's much more crowded, almost as if they didn't want there to be any gaps.'

'And that's because Emma wanted the tattoo to cover up scars on her arms,' Anna told him.

At this, Jonah looked up and their eyes met. He raised his eyebrows interrogatively.

'According to Bella, Emma had a history of self-harming, which involved cutting herself on her arms. Apparently, it dated back to her childhood. Bella thought that it was something to do with an abusive father, but she wasn't sure about that. Emma told her that she'd managed to kick the habit and had a new partner and wanted to make a fresh start. She'd been recommended to *Petra's Piercings* by someone who'd told her that they'd be able to cover up the scars so that nobody would know.'

'Now we're getting somewhere,' Jonah said eagerly. 'There should be medical records. Have you circulated GPs? What about casualty units? Or mental health services?'

'Hang on!' Peter protested. 'Give us a chance! We've only just found out about all this ourselves. I've been on to Mike to ask him to have another look at her arms to see if he can see the scars, now that he knows to look for them. He's also going to look out for any other signs of self-harm. After that, we'll start talking to the medical people – when we know more about what it is they may have been treating.'

'And she may have come to the attention of the police too,' Jonah went on. 'Either as a result of the emergency services being called out when she injured herself or earlier, if there's anything in the suggestion that she was abused. You'd better check out domestic abuse cases going back twenty or thirty years. Now what was it you said about the woman having a new partner?' He turned to Anna. 'Did the tattooist know any more about him – or her?' he added as an afterthought.

'Not really. She did seem confident that it *was* a man, but whether Emma had been specific about that or Bella just assumed, I don't know. She was very definite that Emma didn't mention any name. She just said that she was making a fresh start and she didn't want anyone to be able to see what she'd done to herself before.'

'That's a pity. If we could have nailed the partner, that might have really got us somewhere. Now, what about the person who recommended the tattoo studios in Swindon? Was that someone that Bella knew?'

'No. I got the impression that it may have been someone acting in some sort of professional capacity. I thought maybe a counsellor or a psychologist who had been involved in treating Emma's self-harming. They might easily have heard about *Petra's Piercings* through other clients and then passed the information on to Emma. Bella said that she does quite a bit of work disguising scars and birthmarks and things with tattoos.'

'No new leads there then,' Jonah said briskly. 'So now let's see what light this all throws on what was going on down by the river on Thursday morning. What do you reckon, Peter? Was one of the men that were chasing Emma her partner? Or could one of them have been the abusive father whom she thought she'd got away from years ago?'

'Or may they have been two completely different people that we don't know anything about?' Peter suggested. He was feeling a little put out that Jonah was behaving as if he were the officer in charge of the case, and this made him disinclined to encourage any of his theories.

'Indeed,' Jonah agreed. 'Especially as it's more than two years since Emma talked about her new relationship. For all we know it could have ended some time ago, and if it did ...,' his voice trailed off as a new hypothesis occurred to him. 'Do you remember Lucy saying that she thought one of the men was holding a knife?'

'Yes,' Peter answered. 'But Martin said he didn't see anything in the man's hand and even Lucy said it might have been a stick.'

'But supposing it *was* a knife. Could he have grabbed it from Emma to stop her cutting herself? You said there was a knife wound on her left arm. Could that have been self-inflicted? And then the two men come along and snatch up the knife, and she runs off.'

'But Lucy said the man was holding up the knife as if he was going to slash at the woman with it,' Peter argued. 'And Martin said it looked as if he was going to hit her.'

'That's how it *looked*, but that may have been because they didn't see what happened from the beginning,' Jonah insisted. 'Let's try it shall we? Sergeant! You be the woman crouching down, intent on cutting at her own arm. Have you got something you can use as the knife?'

'Will this do?' Anna asked, rummaging in her bag and bringing out a nail file.

'It's a bit too small. It needs to be big enough for someone to snatch out of your hands.'

'How about this pen?' Peter held out a blue ballpoint.

'Still a bit small, but it'll have to do. OK, Sergeant, you take the knife and cut your arm just below the elbow. Then you're just about to make another cut when Peter comes up behind you and snatches the knife, grabbing it from you and holding it up as high as he can to make sure you can't reach to grab it back.'

Peter stepped forward and took the knife from Anna as Jonah described. For a few seconds they remained frozen in position, with Anna crouching on the floor and Peter standing over her with his arm raised holding the pen above her head.

'I see what you mean,' he said, relaxing his arm and sitting down again. 'You're saying that the two men might have been trying to help Emma, not to harm her.'

'Precisely!' Jonah agreed. 'I may be wrong.' ('Perish the thought!' Peter muttered under his breath.) 'But that seems to me to be a perfectly feasible explanation of what Lucy and Martin saw.'

'But if that's what they were doing, why haven't they come forward?' Anna asked, scrambling to her feet and returning to her seat. 'Why didn't they report her as missing, after she ran off? And why didn't they respond to the appeals for information after she was found?'

'There could be all sorts of reasons,' Jonah answered. 'Maybe she often ran away. They may have thought she'd be safe, once they'd got the knife off her. Then, after the body was found, they may have got frightened that they'd be held responsible. Or they may even not have recognised her.'

'With those distinctive tattoos?' Peter asked, perversely pleased to have found a flaw in Jonah's reasoning.

'They may not have seen the appeals. Not everyone watches the news.'

'OK. So, let's suppose for a minute that you're right. If the men weren't criminals threatening her with the knife, who were they? And how are we going to find them?'

'One of them might be this new partner, she said she had,' Anna suggested.

'Anyway, we'd better be getting back,' Peter said, looking at his watch. 'I want to catch up with Andrews, in case they've found anything by the river. And I think we need to start looking for where the two men – and Emma for that matter – could have come from to get down to the riverbank. It's all open country round there. How did they get there so early in the morning? We'd better check all the farms in the area.'

'Or could they have been staying on a boat?' Anna suggested. 'That would explain how they got to the river so early.'

'You're right,' Peter agreed. 'It's a pity we didn't think of that before. I should have asked Martin whether he saw any other boats out on the river that morning. Right!' he turned to Jonah. 'We're off. Thanks for the tip-off about Petra's Piercings.'

'Just sort the computer out for me before you go, will you?' Jonah requested. 'Then I can see what else I can find out for you.'

Peter set up Jonah's laptop computer on the table in front of him, switched it on and plugged in the specially adapted keypad and rollerball mouse.

'Is that OK?'

'Yes thanks. But you'll have to put my hand on it for me.'

Peter hesitated. He felt strangely embarrassed at the prospect of touching his colleague's paralysed arm. This was the first time that he had been called upon to assist Jonah physically and he was not at all comfortable with doing so. For the first time, he was acutely aware of how demeaning Jonah's condition was. How could he bear to be so utterly dependent on other people, especially when he had always been one of the most independent people that Peter could think of?

However, there was nothing else for it. He reached out and took hold of Jonah's left arm, holding the hand in his own left hand while supporting the elbow with his right. The limb felt unexpectedly heavy as he carefully moved it and placed it so that the lower arm was resting on the table with Jonah's first two fingers over the mouse-keypad combination.

'Is that right?'

'Yes. Thanks.' Jonah immediately started moving his fingers, manipulating the controls to open a web browser and begin an internet search. Then he looked up and gave Peter a brief smile in recognition of the milestone that they had passed in their relationship. 'Thanks,' he repeated.

14.00 WEDNESDAY 4TH NOVEMBER

I'm sorry Peter,' Superintendent Alison Brown greeted him when he entered the incident room on his return from the spinal injuries centre. 'The Chief Super has decided that we can't afford to have you named as the Senior Investigating Officer on this enquiry now that your stepdaughter may be a key witness.'

'You're taking over then?'

'Not entirely. We still want you taking care of the side relating to the body in the grave, but I'll be in overall charge and take responsibility for investigating the incident at the river. That way you'll still be on the case, but kept at arm's length from anything involving your family.'

'OK.' Peter nodded acquiescence. 'Do you need me to take you through what we've got so far?'

'Andy and Monica have been filling me in; so I think I'm pretty well up to speed. Now, I gather Lucy is coming in to be interviewed later this afternoon?'

'Yes. Her mum's going to collect her from school and bring her straight here. I'd got Anna in mind to do the interview, with either Monica or Andy.'

163

'I'll do it myself,' Alison said. 'With Anna,' she added, seeing Peter opening his mouth as if to argue. 'I've read the report on your interview with Dr Riess this morning, so it should be a simple matter of checking that Lucy corroborates what he told you.'

'I'm not sure that Lucy will see it quite like that,' Peter warned. 'She's quite upset at the way Constable Ferrar appeared not to believe her before. If I were you, I'd try to get hold of that piece of wood that the woman hit her with and get it fingerprinted, to show that the police are taking her story seriously now. Nobody seems to know what happened to it.'

'Umm,' Alison pursed her lips and frowned. 'I've been on to her sergeant. It turns out that the piece of wood is still in the back of Louise Ferrar's car. Apparently, she was so convinced that the whole story was a fabrication to protect Dr Riess that she just threw it in there and forgot about it. I'm going to have to have words with that young officer about jumping to conclusions and failing to secure a crime scene. If she'd got a team down there right away, we might have found the woman before she went into the river.'

'And we might have caught the men who were chasing her too,' Anna added.

'Indeed,' Alison agreed. 'However, it's too late to start worrying about that now. The important thing is to find them as soon as we can, before they get the chance to attack any other young women.'

'If that's what they were doing,' Peter put in. 'I've got some ideas on that, which you might like to hear. They're not mine. DCI Porter came up with a theory that those men could have been trying to help her, not to harm her.'

'DCI Porter?' Alison looked questioningly at Peter.

'Jonah Porter. Maybe you don't know him. He and I worked together under Richard Paige, when we were both detective sergeants; but that may be before your time. He got promoted to a DI post down in South Oxfordshire and he's been there ever since.'

'The name sounds familiar, but ... oh! Isn't he the officer who was shot in the back a few months ago and crippled for life?'

'Yes. He's on the rehab ward in the spinal injuries centre. He's been following the case from there. He was the one who discovered the tattoo studios in Swindon. We've just been over to see him.'

'Why?' Alison asked sharply.

'To tell him about what we found out from the tattooists. It seemed only fair, seeing as he'd put us on to them. And he *is* still a serving police officer after all. He picked up on the woman's history of self-harm and suggested that the men might have been trying to stop her cutting herself. His version of events is that Lucy saw them just after one of them had snatched the knife away from her.'

'Sounds a bit far-fetched to me,' Alison said sceptically.

'I know. That's Jonah all over. He has these massive leaps of imagination. The thing is, surprisingly often they turn out to be right. Look, I'm not saying that's what happened, I just think maybe you ought to bear the possibility in mind when you're interviewing Lucy – in case anything she says either fits with that idea or contradicts it. Oh! And that's another thing. Be sure to finish with Lucy by five at the latest. She needs to get away by then to give Jonah his dinner.'

'I'm sorry.' Alison looked puzzled. 'You've lost me, I'm afraid.'

'Lucy fancies herself as being part of Jonah's nursing team. One of her duties is feeding him once a day, now that he can't do it for himself.' Watching Alison's face, Peter realised that she still did not understand. 'You've never met Lucy, have you? Prepare to be surprised. I suppose you'd probably describe her as precocious, but it's really just that she's always been surrounded by adults and her mother never excluded her from any of their conversation. So she tends to have a rather mature turn of phrase for a nine-year-old. The other thing you need to know about her is that, when she takes a thing on, she sticks with it. So, for example, she got interested in forensics through talking to Mike Carson, and by now she's become pretty knowledgeable on the subject. You can expect a few scathing words from her about Constable Ferrar's casual attitude towards preserving the evidence, when you talk to her. She is only nine, after all, and she still sees everything in very black-and-white terms, and Ferrar didn't do things the way Mike said they should be done.'

'I'd have to agree with her about that,' Alison observed drily.

'Where Jonah's concerned,' Peter continued, 'Lucy considers herself responsible for seeing that he gets at least one square meal a day and she's not going to let anything – including your interview – get in the way of that. She believes that she's helping him to get better; and from what the nursing staff say, she may well be right.'

'It's a big commitment though, travelling over there every day,' Alison said. 'Aren't you worried about it spoiling her childhood?'

'Yes. But we'd be more worried about putting our foot down and stopping her and then having him take a turn for the worse. Lucy would never forgive herself – or us – if she thought she'd let him down. And that reminds me: the other thing you need to be aware of is that she thinks it's her fault that she got hurt the other day, because Martin told her not to approach the woman, but she went ahead and did it anyway. So if you could see your way to putting the emphasis on finding out what happened to the woman after she ran off, rather than seeming to be bothered about what happened to Lucy, we'd be grateful.'

'I'll do my best.' Alison was beginning to think that this was going to be a particularly challenging interview to conduct. 'Now, I'd like you to get on to the press office and organise another appeal for information about the identity of the body in the cemetery. I think we ought to release the name "Emma" in the hope of jogging a few memories. Probably best not to mention the self-harming yet. Save that for later, if we need it; but get someone on to doctors and mental health services. And remember that she may well have accessed treatment *before* she had the tattoos done, so they need to be concentrating on just the name and the face.'

15.30 WEDNESDAY 4TH NOVEMBER

Lucy and Bernie arrived promptly at half past three. Alison led them into one of the interview rooms. They sat down, with Lucy and Bernie on one side of the table and the two police officers on the other. Andy Lepage, having been instructed to do so by Alison, put his head round the door and offered to get drinks for them all. Would they like tea or coffee? Or they had some orange squash that Lucy might like.

Bernie, Anna and Alison all opted for tea. Alison smiled kindly across the table at Lucy and suggested that they could get her a bottle of coke from the vending machine if she didn't like squash.

'I'd rather have tea, thank you,' Lucy said politely. 'Like everyone else.'

Peter, excluded from the interview, tried to concentrate on studying reports from the team who had examined the cemetery crime scene. The Crime Scene Manager had now declared the examination of the ground surrounding the grave to be complete. The cemetery was once again open for business, except for a belt of ground six feet wide on either side of the boundary fence, which was still being scrutinised for signs of where the body could have been brought in.

The area around the grave had been well trampled, before the police had arrived, by the two cemetery staff who had found the body. However, the Scenes of Crime Officers had managed to identify one footwear print that did not match any of the people who were known to have been there on Monday morning. It was from a size-ten work boot, slightly down at heel, but still with a well-defined tread pattern. It was currently being checked against the recently-created *National Footwear Reference Collection*, to establish the make and model. That might be useful for establishing that a suspect was present at the scene if only they could find some suspects to investigate!

'Excuse me sir!' Andy called across the room. 'The desk sergeant's on the phone saying there's a man downstairs who claims to have known the victim.'

'Tell them I'll be right down,' Peter said at once, grateful to have something more active to do, to take his mind off the grilling that Lucy was undergoing at the hands of Alison Brown. 'And you'd better come with me.'

Jamie Corcoran was an unassuming man with unruly dark brown hair that kept falling over his face and which he kept pushing back with his hand. He was dressed in jeans and a tee shirt, beneath a brown duffle coat with two of the toggles missing. He told them that he was a software developer with one of the small companies based on the Jordan Hill business park in Wolvercote. He was currently living in a flat in Kidlington with his girlfriend of some six months. He gave Emma's full name as Emma Sutcliffe and told them that she was two years younger than his own age of thirty-two.

'I met Emma in a nightclub,' he recounted. 'I can't remember which one it was now. She was one of the dancers. We started seeing each other and then, after a couple of months, she had some trouble with her landlord and had to give up her flat, so then she moved in with me.'

'And when exactly was this?' Peter asked.

'2007. She moved in, in the March. We were together for seven, no eight months – until the middle of November.'

Peter calculated in his head and concluded that Jamie must be the new partner that Emma had mentioned to Bella. The tattoo had been done in May 2007.

'And what happened to make you split up?'

Jamie took a deep breath and then let it out again in a sigh. Peter looked at him in silence, waiting for him to answer. Jamie took another breath and looked round at Peter and Andy, who sat with his pen poised ready to write down his answer.

'I broke it off,' he said at last.

'Why?'

Jamie looked round at them again with an anxious expression on his face.

'Don't take this the wrong way. I – I just couldn't stick it any longer.'

'Couldn't stick what?' Peter asked quietly.

'The way she was.'

'And how was that?'

'Don't get me wrong. She was a nice girl.'

'But?'

'But she was too – too …,' he sighed again. 'It wasn't her fault. She told me about how her dad treated her when she was a kid. It made her very insecure. And she had very low self-esteem. Sometimes she used to really hate herself. She even used to hurt herself deliberately.'

'Oh? How?'

'Well, mostly she used to cut her arms with a knife. At least that's what she told me, but she hadn't done that for a while when we met and she didn't do it while we were together. I remember her biting her lip so that it bled and pulling out handfuls of her own hair and actually banging her head against the wall of the bedroom. I mean, you talk about head-bangers, don't you? But I never knew people really did it!'

'I see. So you told her it was over, and presumably she moved out of your flat?'

'No. I let her keep the flat. It was rented and we'd had her name added to the tenancy agreement, so I just moved out and arranged for my name to be taken off. And I paid two months' rent before I left, in case she was short, with it being coming up to Christmas and everything.'

'That was very generous of you,' Andy commented.

'I was trying to do the right thing by her. I felt guilty about leaving her, but I just couldn't cope any longer. It was like walking on eggshells. She needed reassurance that I loved her all the time. And if I said something that she took as criticism, she'd be off into the bedroom hurting herself.'

'Did she get any professional help?' Peter asked. 'Counselling, perhaps?'

'I tried to persuade her to see a doctor, but it only upset her to think that I didn't believe that she'd got over it. I think that, because she wasn't cutting herself any more, she thought she was cured. I don't think she saw the other things as part of – of her illness. Anyway, it got so as I was afraid to mention it. But then there were a lot of things that I was afraid to mention.'

'Alright. You went off and left her living in your flat. Where is that, by the way?'

Jamie gave an address in East Oxford.

'And have you seen her at all since then?'

'No. I deliberately kept away from all the places we used to go to together. I wanted a clean break. I didn't want her trying to persuade me to go back.'

'Did she carry on working in the nightclub after she met you? Was she working there when you left?'

'Not when I left, no. She gave it up a couple of months after we moved in together. It's not like a proper job. The girls are all self-employed. They pay to be allowed to be there and they make their money from the punters paying for dances. I never realised that until I knew Emma. I tried to get her to stop when she told me, but she wouldn't. I think she sort of liked … no she *needed* to have the men paying to watch her. It was a sort of validation of her desirability, I suppose.' Jamie sighed. 'I think she could only believe in her own worth if she could see people being prepared to pay for her. Does that make sense?'

'But she did give it up eventually?' Peter asked.

'Yes. She got a job in a supermarket. It was better because the income was more reliable and it meant that we could have time together in the evenings. She *said* she was making a fresh start and putting all that behind her, but …'

'But?' Peter prompted.

'I do wonder now if she only did it because I nagged at her about it. If she thought she had to do it or I'd leave her. And if that marked the beginning of … her illness coming back. I can't help wondering if she'd have been happier if she'd … well that's what I meant when I said she *needed* to do it.'

'And the name of the club?' Andy asked, holding his pen poised to write it down.

'There were a few,' Jamie shrugged. 'And sometimes she'd fall foul of the management in one and have to move on. They had all sorts of rules that the girls had to stick to, and if you broke them, you were out. Or at least,' he amended, 'if you got caught breaking one of the ones that the management cared about. There were others – the *no touching* rule for instance – that they turned a blind eye to, because it brought in the punters. I don't go to those places any more, now I know what goes on.'

'Did Emma have any particular friends? Is there anyone who might be able to tell us where she's been since you split up?'

'No. I suppose some of the girls she worked with might know, but there wasn't anyone in particular. She never saw any of them outside of work.'

'And her family?'

Jamie shook his head. 'She wouldn't talk about them. All I know is her dad used to abuse her. Once she said that I stopped asking about them.'

'Physically? Sexually?' Peter asked.

'A bit of both, I think,' Jamie shrugged again. 'To be honest I wasn't that keen on hearing about it.'

'And she never spoke about her mother, or any siblings?'

'No. Just her dad. And, like I said, all she told me was that she never wanted to see him ever again.'

'So you can't think of anyone else who might know where she's been or what she's been doing for the last two years?'

'No. Sorry.' Jamie shook his head.

'Never mind. Now, is there anything else you can tell me about her? Do you know the name of her doctor? Or her dentist?'

'No.' Jamie shook his head again. 'I don't remember her seeing a doctor or a dentist while we were together.'

'Never mind,' Peter repeated. 'You've been a great help. Just knowing her full name will make things a lot easier. Now, I'm sorry to have to ask this, but, just for the record, can you tell me where you were between Friday afternoon and Monday morning?'

It took some time to piece together Jamie's movements during the weekend. He stated confidently that he had gone for a drink with mates from work on Friday, and then remembered that this had been the previous week. He was vague about the time that he and his girlfriend, Rebecca Gibbon, had returned from a visit to her mother's house in Chipping Norton. Eventually, however, Peter managed to draw up a rough schedule, which Jamie agreed was an accurate account. Significantly, according to him, he had been constantly in Rebecca's company from six-thirty on Friday, when she arrived home from work, until he left for work on Monday morning. On the face of it, unless she too were involved, he could not have killed Emma and deposited her body in the cemetery.

'Presumably your girlfriend will be able to confirm that you were with her?' Peter asked, trying to sound casual and not as if Jamie were the only suspect that they had so far identified.

'Yes. Of course. But, do you have to talk to Becky about this? I mean ...,' Jamie looked round at Peter and Andy.

'You haven't told her about Emma?' Peter asked.

'Yes, of course I have. I mean I've told her about us living together, but she doesn't know that she's the same as this dead woman you've found. I mean I didn't even know that myself until I heard the name on the radio this afternoon.'

'So you didn't recognise her from the tattoos?'

'No. Well ... yes. I suppose I did. But I didn't want to believe that it was her. The face looked different. And the hair. She had her hair dyed blond when we first met. She reckoned the punters preferred it and she got more dances. Then, when she made this big *fresh start*, she started dying it red – just to be different, I think. So I told myself that it couldn't be her and the tattoos were probably just standard designs that lots of girls had.'

'I see.' Peter sat looking at him in silence for a second or two. 'Well, that's very useful information. I think that's everything now – unless there's anything else that you think we ought to know?'

Jamie shook his head.

'Then you can go. DC Lepage will show you out. But a word of advice before you go. If I were you, I'd tell your girlfriend everything. Once Emma's full name is made public, it won't be long before some journalist starts probing into her background and there's a very good chance they may dig up something about your relationship with her. It will be better if Rebecca hears it from you

174

first.'

09.00 THURSDAY 5TH NOVEMBER

Detective Superintendent Alison Brown called the meeting to order.

'As you all know, we appear to have two related incidents. A week ago today, a young woman was seen running away from two men somewhere in the open ground between Binsey and the river.' She pointed at a large-scale map of the area on the wall behind her. 'And then, a few days later, what looks like the same woman turns up dead in a grave in Wolvercote Cemetery, a little less than two miles away.'

She moved her hand to indicate an area of green on the map.

'Dr Martin Riess was out in his narrowboat with nine-year-old Lucy Paige. They saw the woman hide in some bushes along the bank and Lucy went to help her. The woman assaulted Lucy with a piece of wood and then ran off again. We've got officers out doing a house-to-house in Binsey, in case the men came across the fields from there. Nothing from that so far. It's mainly farms and isolated houses, so people keep themselves to themselves and don't take much notice of what their neighbours are doing. They all claim to be fast asleep in bed or in the process of getting up at six or seven in the morning, which is the sort of time we're talking about, if we allow twenty minutes to half an hour for the men to get from there to the river. We got one complaint from a farmer saying that people have been cutting across her fields and leaving gates open, but she couldn't be specific about which day that was, so it's probably not connected. Andrews has been with the team searching the part of the bank where the woman was seen.' She turned and caught the officer's eye. 'Tell us what you found in the bushes.'

Rupert Andrews got to his feet and looked round the room, rapidly gathering his thoughts at this sudden summons.

'Dr Riess showed us some bushes that he thinks are the ones where the woman hid,' he began, tentatively at first and then with more confidence. 'The SOCOs have been over the area and we think we may have prints of the woman's shoes in the soft mud under the bushes. We need to cross-reference with the shoes the little girl was wearing to be sure about which are which. Forensics say they'll try to get us details of the make and model of the shoes by the end of the week.'

'We ought to compare the prints with the shoes that the woman in the grave was wearing when she was found,' Peter pointed out. 'And get forensics to look for any traces of mud from the riverbank on them.'

'Yes,' Alison agreed. 'Lepage! Make a note of that, will you? And keep a list of anything else we decide needs doing, so we can get on to it right away after we're done here. Now, carry on Andrews.'

'They also found some more pieces of wood,' Andrews continued. 'Similar to the one the woman used to hit the little girl. It looks like there used to be a field boundary there, which was pulled down but no-one bothered to get in amongst the bushes to rip it all up, so bits of it were just left to rot.'

'Did the footprints lead anywhere?' Monica asked from the back of the room. 'I mean, could you see which way the woman went when she ran off?'

'It looks as if she came out of the bushes on the upstream side – towards Godstow Lock,' Andrews answered. 'But we knew that anyway, from what Riess and the girl told us. Once you're out from under the bushes, the ground isn't as soft as it was in the shade there, so we couldn't tell where she went after that. And lots of people walk their dogs there and go jogging and stuff. We've got people out all along the river, up as far as the Western By-Pass, looking for evidence of where she may have gone in, but nothing so far.'

'So that's about where we're up to with the woman by the river,' Alison concluded. 'Now Peter, can you summarise what we know about the body in the cemetery?'

Peter stood up and came out to the front of the room. Andrews resumed his seat with a look of relief on his face.

'As you know, the main identifying characteristic of the body is the pair of tattoos on her arms. They were done by a tattoo artist in Swindon called Bella Makin. She was able to give us a name for our victim: Emma. Yesterday a man came forward saying that he and Emma used to be a couple, but they split up about two years ago. He gave her name as Emma Sutcliffe, last known at an address in Temple Cowley. Monica has been trying to track her down.' Peter looked towards Sergeant Philipson, who stood up and looked round the room, evidently pleased to be asked to address the group.

'I found three Emma Sutcliffes living in the Thames Valley region,' she told them, 'but none of them match the age of our victim. The flat that she was living in two years ago was sold last year. The current owner says that it was unoccupied when he bought it. It's rented to a Polish couple who say that they've never had any post delivered for anyone of the name of Emma or had anyone enquiring about her. I eventually found the previous owner and he said that there had been an Emma Sutcliffe living there, but she fell behind on the rent and he told her she had to go. That was in February of last year, so a year and nine months ago. I showed him the pictures of the body and he said it might have been her, but he wouldn't like to swear to it. He reckoned he'd never seen her arms, so he couldn't speak for the tattoos.'

'Thank you, Monica.' Peter indicated to her that she should sit down. 'Emma's ex-boyfriend, Jamie Corcoran, also told us that she used to work as a dancer in some of the nightclubs. Andy has been following up on that. Andy!' He nodded towards DC Lepage, who hastily put down his pen and got to his feet.

'I've been round to all the clubs in Oxford,' he reported. 'But none of them remembered having employed a dancer by the name of Emma Sutcliffe, and none of them recognised the tattoos. However, we think she probably stopped working in the clubs before she had the tattoos done, so that may not be significant.'

'Don't they have records of all their employees?' Monica asked. 'You'd have thought-'

'The dancers aren't exactly employees,' Peter put in quickly, anxious to quash any implied criticism of the thoroughness of Andy's work. 'They're self-employed and they actually pay the club for the right to be there. They do have a contract – or most of them do, anyway – but it's not a contract of employment and most of the payments are made in cash with rather few records kept.'

'Might she have had a stage name?' Andrews suggested. 'For working in the clubs, she might have thought *Emma Sutcliffe* didn't sound exotic enough. Or she might not have wanted her real name associated with that sort of work. I mean, I know it's supposed to be all above board and respectable, but well …'

'You mean, it isn't the sort of job that a father would want to find out that his daughter was doing?' Alison suggested.

'Something like that,' Andrews agreed.

'The boyfriend also told us that she changed her appearance after she met him,' Peter added. 'So I'd like us to get mock-ups done of how she might have looked with blond hair and the sort of makeup she'd have been wearing when she was working the clubs. I can't say I blame them for not recognising her from the photos of the body. I think we need to do a second public appeal for information, this time with a few different pictures of how she might have looked when she was alive, and making it clear that we're interested in hearing from anyone who knew her, going back several years.'

'Right,' Alison agreed. 'We'll do that. Should we release her full name do you think? It might jog a few memories.'

'I'm still a bit concerned about the effect it could have on her family, hearing about it like that,' Peter said dubiously. 'And there's also this idea that she could have had another name. If we're too definite about it we could deter anyone who knew her by a different name from coming forward.'

'Alright. I'll leave the final decision to you. Go ahead with getting the artist's impressions done and then decide on the wording for the appeal. I think that for the time being, it will be better to keep the two incidents separate as far as the public are concerned; so I'm planning to put out a completely independent appeal for help with finding the men on the bank – as witnesses to an assault – and the woman, as Lucy's attacker.'

'Do you think the boyfriend could have killed her?' Monica asked. 'Does he fit with the description of either of the men on the riverbank?'

'As far as the men on the bank are concerned,' Alison answered, 'we don't have a clear description. What do you think, Peter?'

'Well, for a start, we don't have any evidence that anyone killed her,' Peter said patiently. 'Cause of death is probably drowning – although Mike Carson will hedge that opinion around with all sorts of caveats about drowning being one of the most difficult causes to be definite about – in river water. So the question is: how did she come to be in the river? The waterweed that she had inside her is a kind that's common in lots of parts of the Thames and the Cherwell,[13] which means that she could have fallen in near Godstow lock last Thursday morning or somewhere else later that day or on Friday. It could have been an accident – maybe caused by her running away in panic – or suicide, or she could have been pushed in. We simply don't know.'

'But someone must have been there and pulled out the body and taken it to the cemetery,' Monica pointed out. 'And why would they do that if they hadn't pushed her in, in the first place?'

'On the face of it Jamie Corcoran has an alibi for all that,' Peter told her. 'He says that he was with his new girlfriend for the whole time from when the cemetery closed on Friday evening to when the body was found on Monday. And as for why someone would pull a body out of the river and transport it to a cemetery and deposit it in a grave …? Well! It doesn't make a lot of sense however you look at it. If you pushed her in, why not scarper and try to establish an alibi? If you didn't, why not report the accident? Or, if you don't want to get involved, why not just walk away?'

'Have you checked out his alibi?' Alison asked.

'Not yet. I'm hanging fire on that one for two reasons. One is that his current girlfriend may well confirm his story regardless, out of loyalty to him, so her value as a witness is limited. The other is that I think he may well be more co-operative if he doesn't think that he's under suspicion. We're going to need some more evidence before it's worth trying to break his alibi, but I can't help

[13] Pronounced "Charwell" this is a tributary to the Thames, flowing into it at Oxford.

wondering if he could have been the one who moved the body, even if he didn't have anything to do with Emma's death.'

'Any particular reason?' Alison enquired.

'The way the body was laid out in the grave: wrapped up in a coat, with the plastic sheet to stop the earth getting in, and with the arms placed across her chest with those roses clasped in them. It all looked as if whoever put her there was trying to show respect to her body. And the mere fact that they chose a proper grave to put her in bears that out. I think that, whoever it was who put her there, they were trying to give her a proper burial, but for some unknown reason they had to do it in secret. Jamie Corcoran is the first person we've found who actually knew Emma and felt something for her.'

'But there could have been others,' Monica chimed in. 'People who knew her more recently than he did. People who *didn't* come forward because they were afraid of being suspected of killing her.'

'Yes,' agreed Peter. 'And that's why I'm not rushing to any conclusions about Jamie Corcoran. However, there is one other thing. He works on Jordan Hill.' He stepped forward and pointed to the map on the wall. 'It's a tiny business park on the northern side of the cemetery. The access road runs along the cemetery boundary, *and*,' he paused dramatically, 'there is evidence that a vehicle was parked there at some time during the last week or two near to a place where the vegetation next to the fence has been disturbed and the chain-link was bent, as if someone had been climbing it. It's entirely possible that the body was manhandled over the fence and into the cemetery from there.'

18.00 FRIDAY 6ᵀᴴ NOVEMBER

'I thought old Peter might have come with you today,' Jonah said in a complaining voice as Bernie settled into her usual chair in the corner of the room, while Lucy began her task of feeding him with a thick Scotch Broth, which was today's soup. 'I haven't had a proper update on the case for days now.'

'He's working late again,' Bernie told him. 'They're doing the rounds of all the pubs and clubs, talking to the girls who work there, trying to find someone who remembers Emma Sutcliffe.'

'I saw the TV appeal yesterday. Haven't they got any leads through that?'

'You know that Peter couldn't tell me about them if they did; but I don't think so. Peter was worried about releasing her name, in case her family got to know about her death that way, but it looks as if either they don't watch television appeals from the police or they assume it isn't the same Emma Sutcliffe.'

'Or maybe that isn't her real name,' Jonah suggested. 'Have they thought of that?'

183

'You know they have,' Bernie said, detecting a hint of disparagement in Jonah's tone and leaping to the defence of her husband. She knew that Jonah viewed Peter's approach to his work as pedestrian and lacking the insight and intuition that he prided himself in bringing to the job. 'The press release specifically said that she might have used a different name in her work.'

'Yes, but that implied that her real name was Emma Sutcliffe and she may have had a pseudonym for her dancing. I was thinking more that she *changed* her name from something else.'

'Does it really matter?'

'Probably not. I was thinking about this self-harming business and the tattooist saying that Emma was wanting to cover up the scars in order to make a fresh start. I was just thinking that maybe that could have been when she changed her name.'

'*If* she changed her name. It's only conjecture that she did. Maybe none of her family have come forward because they haven't seen the appeal or they don't recognise the pictures. Those two artist's impressions looked to me like two completely different people, and neither of them look like the photo of the corpse. Or maybe she doesn't *have* any family. My closest living blood relatives are uncles and aunts, and I haven't seen any of them for the best part of thirty years – not since my dad's funeral. Which reminds me,' Bernie added, reaching down into a bag that she had brought with her and getting out a small cake tin. 'I brought this to celebrate our anniversary!'

She opened the tin and lifted out a tiny cake, covered with white frosting. It had a large *10* written across the top in blue icing. Jonah looked puzzled.

'It's exactly ten years ago today that we first met,' Bernie explained. 'And I thought we shouldn't let the occasion pass without marking it in some way. It's date and walnut underneath, which Margaret tells me is your favourite, so I'm expecting you to have a piece with us after you've finished your tea.'

'Oh I get it,' Jonah said, trying to sound annoyed but unable to suppress a grin. 'She's put you up to this. She's obsessed with getting me to eat more. But it seems a bit macabre celebrating the anniversary of your husband's funeral.'

'I told you, it's not that. It's celebrating the first time I clapped eyes on you. I can't help it if that happened to be at Richard's funeral. What made you decide to come? Peter said he could never make that out.'

'Curiosity I suppose, I got a shock when the news of Richard's death came out and especially when people started saying that he'd left a widow. I hadn't even known he'd had a wife. I wanted to find out what sort of woman would have been willing to take on a man who'd been married to the job for the best part of forty years.'

'I hope I lived up to your expectations!'

'I don't know about that. I'm not sure that I had any expectations, but even if I had some, the reality was something completely different.'

Lucy set aside the empty soup bowl and took the lid off a plate of steak-and-kidney pie. She cut it up into bite-sized pieces while Jonah continued to reminisce.

'I remember asking Peter to introduce us and then thinking afterwards that he seemed a bit put out at us engaging in conversation, and quite pleased when you had to rush off to speak to someone else. And then he let slip that you were pregnant and I could see he was regretting it right away, but I still made him promise to let me know when the baby was born.'

'And then you started coming to see me on my birthday every year,' Lucy chimed in. 'We've still got the plastic train set you gave me when I was two. It's up in the loft waiting for when Peter has grandchildren.'

'Doesn't he have any yet?' Jonah asked in surprise. 'His kids are both older than mine so I'd rather assumed that he would. Well, well, well! That's another thing that I've beaten old Peter to. Who'd have thought I'd have become a granddad before he did?'

'I don't think Hannah and Laurence are as financially secure as your Reuben.' Bernie felt irrationally obliged to defend her husband's family against what somehow felt like a slur. 'They've been busy saving up for a house these last few years. And Eddie and Crystal only got married last year, so it's early days with them. Besides, it's not a competition you know!'

'No, of course not. It just seems odd somehow. When I first met Peter, I was a raw PC still living with my parents, and he was married with a baby on the way and already a Detective Sergeant. I kind of expected him to be always a few steps ahead of me; but I passed my inspector's exams and got my DI post down in the South Oxfordshire division while he was still a DS, and by then Margaret and I had our own family, so I seemed to have caught him up.'

'Peter's more laid back. He doesn't have your raging ambition. And he enjoyed working with Richard.'

'Mmm,' Jonah nodded. 'Loyalty always was one of Old Peter's hallmarks – that and not taking any risks. I'm surprised at you going for him. I wouldn't have thought his cautious approach to life would have suited you. You're much more willing to jump into things feet first and worry about the consequences later.'

'Has it not occurred to you that we might perhaps be complementary in that respect?' Bernie suggested, with a smile. 'Your home life must be like a perpetual roller coaster ride, what with you and Margaret both rushing headlong into everything the way you seem to!'

Jonah laughed, looking briefly like the old cheerful Jonah that Bernie remembered from his annual visits to their house in Headington.

'Do you think that's what's made Nathan so paranoid?' he asked facetiously. 'We always say that he does all the worrying for the rest of the family as well as for himself.'

His words conjured up in Bernie's mind a picture of Nathan's anxious face as they sat in the canteen the previous Sunday, when he had suggested that it might be for the best if his father did not survive to spend the rest of his life severely disabled. For a moment or two, she was lost for words. Then she forced a nervous laugh.

'I'm not surprised, the way you go on sometimes. If you took proper care of yourself, he wouldn't need to worry, would he?'

10.15 SUNDAY 8TH NOVEMBER

'It's really good of you coming over like this,' Margaret greeted Peter in the car park outside the spinal injuries centre. He noticed that her hair was different today. It was dyed a deep plum colour that matched her lipstick and nail varnish, and it had been trimmed shorter and stuck up in jagged peaks on the top of her head. The pale foundation and dark eye shadow on her face masked any redness about her eyes, but he could see a few thin streaks of black just above her cheeks where her mascara had run. 'I'm sorry to call you at home, but I just couldn't think of anything else.'

'Don't worry about it,' Peter brushed her apologies aside. 'It's no bother. I'm just not sure what you're hoping I can do.'

'As I said on the phone, I just want you to talk to him about this murder case you've got on. Give him something to take his mind off this stupid medical retirement business.' Margaret sighed as they started across the car park towards the hospital building. 'I blame myself. I should have opened the letter instead of just bringing it here for him to read without knowing what was inside. But I don't like to look as if I'm prying into his private affairs.'

'You couldn't have known that he would take it like this,' Peter pointed out. '*I* wouldn't have expected it. He's always been such a fighter – especially when it comes to unnecessary rules and red tape.'

'But I knew how badly he'd been affected by the visit from HR,' Margaret argued. 'If I'd realised that this was the follow-up to that, I'd have been more careful.' She sighed again. 'But even so … He'd been so much better these last few days – ever since he had this case of yours to get his teeth into – that I would have thought he'd have been able to take it. I never thought …'

'Don't you think it's just   I don't know …,' Peter struggled to express himself. 'I mean, don't you think it's just a passing phase? It must have been a shock for him to get the letter, but when he thinks about it, he'll-'

'But I'm afraid that may be too late!' Margaret's voice had a frightened quality that Peter had never heard in it before. 'He hasn't eaten or drunk anything since yesterday lunch time, when Lucy fed him. If we don't get some fluids into him soon he'll be left with kidney damage on top of all his other problems. That's why they called me this morning and asked me to come over. I've tried reasoning with him, but he just isn't listening.'

'Well I'll do my best,' Peter tried to sound reassuring, while feeling distinctly unsure of himself. 'But, if he won't listen to *you*, I can't really imagine he'll take much notice of anything *I* say.'

'I'm not asking you to argue with him about what he's doing to himself. What he needs from you is convincing that he's still got something to offer. For so long he's been defined by his work. Now that it seems as if that's being taken away from him, he can't see any point in going on. I want you to ask him for help with your investigation. Tell him you're stuck and need his advice. I know it's a big ask but …,' she trailed off, looking Peter full in the face as she held open the door for them to go inside.

'I'll do my best,' Peter promised.

'Thank you,' Margaret said with feeling. 'You coming and sharing with him was making a big difference. I had really started to think he'd turned a corner – until this! Try and get him interested in it again. And if you possibly can, try and make him feel that he's helped.'

'I'll do my best,' Peter repeated. 'And if he *can* come up with some ideas on how to tackle this case, I'll be genuinely grateful. We seem to be going nowhere fast.'

'Good. I mean … well, you know what I mean.' Margaret stopped outside the entrance to Jonah's ward. 'I'll have to go. I'm on call, which means I'm not supposed to be more than half an hour from the hospital. Good luck. And thanks again.'

She placed her hand on his arm briefly before turning to go. Peter watched her walking briskly away down the corridor, her plum coloured coat just reaching the tops of her black leather boots. Then, after a moment's hesitation, he pressed the buzzer to request entry.

He was relieved that it was Jeanette Slater who opened the door and welcomed him in. He knew her better than any of the other nursing staff and he admired the caring attitude that she always showed towards both patients and visitors.

'I'm glad you've come,' she confided in a low voice. 'He's really down in the dumps today – ever since he read that letter. I suppose Margaret's told you that the first thing is to get him to start taking in fluids again. There's water by the bed, but probably best not to try to give him any unless he asks for it. I'll come in after a few minutes with tea for you both, in the hope that he'll join you out of good manners.'

'Can't you give him fluids through an intravenous drip?' Peter asked, also speaking in an undertone. 'Just until this crisis is passed?'

'Not without his consent,' Jeanette sighed. 'Unless

we're convinced that he doesn't have the mental capacity to decide for himself. His wife thinks that any suggestion that we think he's mentally ill might push him right over the edge. So we're hoping he'll come round and give up this ridiculous hunger strike.'

'Lucy's coming at lunch time,' Peter reminded her. 'He always co-operates with whatever she asks of him.'

'Up until now,' Jeannette agreed. 'But this seems different somehow. He's never admitted before that he was deliberately starving himself. I'm not sure that even Lucy ... and that's another reason for asking you to come. We don't want her to see him ... to see him the way he is at the moment.'

She opened the door of Jonah's room and led Peter inside.

'Here's a visitor for you,' she announced. 'It's earlier than we usually let people in, but he says it's important police business, so I didn't like to refuse.'

Jonah was propped up in bed. At first, Peter thought that he was dozing, but then he realised that his eyes were open and staring, unseeing, into the distance. He looked hardly any less lively than some of the corpses that Peter had come across in the course of his career.

'Hi Jonah!' he said, trying to speak normally and to avoid both a false cheerfulness and betraying the discomfort that he felt. 'I was hoping that you might be able to give me a bit of help with this mystery corpse case. It's coming up to a week now and we don't seem to be any further forward than when we started.'

Jonah did not reply. He remained staring at nothing.

'I brought along the case file,' Peter continued, pretending that he had not noticed his colleague's lack of response. 'Can I show you what we've got?'

Jonah continued to ignore him, so Peter sat down in the high-backed chair next to the bed and took out a laptop computer from his briefcase. He set it up on the bed in front of Jonah.

'This is a sketch of the crime scene,' he continued, bringing up an image on the screen. 'The cemetery only has one vehicular entrance – here, on the Banbury Road.'

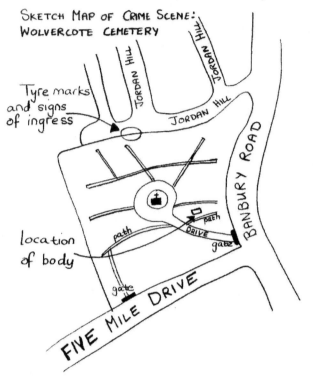

SKETCH MAP OF CRIME SCENE:
WOLVERCOTE CEMETERY

JORDAN HILL
JORDAN HILL
JORDAN HILL

Tyre marks and signs of ingress

BANBURY ROAD

path
DRIVE
path
gate

location of body

gate

FIVE MILE DRIVE

'It has gates that are locked at night. That's the only way of getting a vehicle inside the perimeter fence, which consists of chain-link and, most of the way, a hedge as well. There's a playing field down one side, with pedestrian access from Five Mile Drive. We thought that was the most likely way for whoever dumped the body to have got in, but there aren't any signs.'

Peter stopped speaking and looked at Jonah, who betrayed no sign that he had heard what he was saying. He decided to try another approach.

'Our big problem is trying to think of a reason for them to have gone to all the trouble of transporting a body from wherever she died to the cemetery and then manhandling it over the fence and dragging it across to the grave. I was hoping that you might have some ideas. You're usually good at working out motives. Come on! What do you think?'

'I don't know why you're asking *me*,' Jonah said at last, in a dry, husky voice that Peter had to strain to understand. 'I'm only fit to be put out to grass. It's official – look!'

Peter followed his eyes and saw a white envelope lying on the bedside locker.

'Go on!' Jonah urged, his voice still hoarse and unnatural. 'Open it and have a look.'

Peter hesitated, then reached over and picked up the envelope. He took out a letter and something that looked like an application form of some kind, with boxes for name, address and various other personal details. He started reading the letter, conscious that Jonah was watching him intently. As he expected, from what Margaret had told him, it was from the Human Resources department confirming that Jonah had been assessed as eligible for retirement on the grounds of ill health.

'You see?' Jonah croaked. 'They're saying …,' his voice cracked and he stopped, unable to go on.

He turned his head and tried to reach the long drinking straw that was sticking out of a plastic beaker standing on the bedside locker. Peter reached over and moved it closer so that he could drink. Jonah moistened his mouth just enough to continue speaking.

'They're saying that I'm not up to the job anymore.'

'No they're not,' Peter declared confidently, although he was secretly convinced that this was exactly what the HR department believed. 'They're just saying that *medically* you qualify for early retirement. That doesn't mean you have to take it, does it? I mean,' he added, sudden inspiration providing him with an argument that he had not thought of until then, 'they wouldn't have needed to send you this form to fill in if it was automatic, would they?'

Jonah looked sceptical but Peter thought that he detected a slight loosening of the tension in the muscles of his neck and a relaxation of the frown lines on his forehead.

'Anyway,' he went on resolutely, 'I didn't come here to discuss the finer points of the Police Pension Scheme. I came looking for ideas on tracking down who this mystery woman is and who put her in that grave in Wolvercote. Are you going to help me or not?'

'OK,' Jonah rasped. He took another draft of water before adding, 'fire ahead! Let's see what she looked like when you found her.'

Peter brought up on the screen a photograph of the grave, which one of the SOCOs had taken on arrival at the scene.

'This is the crime scene,' He said, rather unnecessarily. 'As you may be able to see, by the time we got there people had been trampling around all over the shop, but we did manage to identify one footwear mark that didn't match up to anyone who was known to have been there.'

'OK. We'll look at that later.' Jonah's voice sounded stronger now that his mouth was less dry. 'I'd like to see the body. That may give us some clues as to why she was put there.'

The door opened and Jeanette entered with a tray.

'I thought you might be in for a long session,' she said, smiling. 'So I've brought you a pot of tea and some biscuits.'

She put the tray down on the table-on-wheels and moved it to where Peter could reach it easily to pour tea for them both.

'Thanks,' Peter said, smiling back. 'I could do with a drink.'

'Well, I'll leave you two boys to it then.' Jeanette

headed for the door. 'Ring the bell if you need the pot topping up. I'm sure detecting must be thirsty work.'

Peter poured himself a cup of tea and then filled the plastic cup that Jeanette had left for Jonah. He fitted the lid carefully and stood up to place it on the bedside locker with the straw positioned within reach.

'I thought you were going to show me your famous corpse,' Jonah grumbled as Peter regained his seat. 'Stop faffing about and get on with it.'

Hiding the smile that came to his lips at this sign of the return of the impatient DCI who expected everything to be done by yesterday – or possibly sooner – Peter hastily selected the next photograph in the sequence, which was a view of the grave taken from above. Deep down below ground level, the woman's body was visible, wrapped in its green plastic winding sheet.

'This is how it was when Mike and the SOCOs arrived. The gravediggers partially unwrapped her to see what it was that was cluttering up their nice fresh grave. As soon as they realised it was a body, they dropped everything and dialled 999.'

'Any fingermarks or DNA on the plastic sheet?' Jonah asked, pausing briefly from taking long draughts of tea from the plastic cup.

'No. We assume that whoever parcelled her up was probably wearing gloves. Underneath the sheet, she was wrapped in a woollen coat. There were some hairs on that, which didn't come from the corpse, but none of them had the root, so no DNA. *However*,' Peter paused in order to add drama to what he was about to say, 'we do have one rather interesting piece of DNA evidence.'

'And that is?' Jonah asked eagerly.

'A tiny trace of blood.' Peter moved the computer mouse to select another photograph. 'See there! Whoever laid her out on top of the coat and plastic sheet put a spray of roses on her chest and then placed her hands across on top to hold it in place.'

Jonah gazed intently at the picture.

'Those aren't the sort of roses you get from a florist,' he observed. 'They tend to be large blooms, each on a long stem so you can put them in a vase. These came from someone's garden. They must be a late variety still to be flowering at the tail end of October.'

'Forensics found some blood on one of the thorns,' Peter went on. 'It didn't come from the body. So presumably, whoever put them there pricked themselves while they were doing it.'

'I take it you haven't found a match?'

'No.' Peter shook his head. 'We've got a DNA profile, but it doesn't match anything on the database. And, before you ask, we've taken samples and checked it against everyone who was at the crime scene, just in case any of them scratched themselves on the roses without realising.'

'That figures,' Jonah said thoughtfully. 'I'd be quite surprised if this turns out to be the work of known criminals. It has a very amateur feel to it, and you can't help thinking that they were trying to do their best for her. It was as if they wanted her to have a proper burial, but for some reason they had to keep it secret.'

'Yes. That was the sort of thing I was thinking too. But I can't think of a reason why. If they had a criminal record, then I'd say that it was to do with being afraid of involving the police, but …'

'My guess is that they *were* afraid of informing the proper authorities,' Jonah agreed. 'Could they have been afraid of being accused of killing her?'

'Seeing as Mike says the chances are she drowned, I don't really see why they should have been. All the evidence – apart from the body being moved – points to accidental death or, particularly taking into account her history of self-harm, suicide.'

'But supposing it wasn't,' Jonah suggested. 'Or, perhaps it *was* an accident but someone else was involved. You remember what I said about how the two men who were chasing her on Thursday morning might have been trying to help her?'

'Yes.'

'Well. How about this? She's threatening suicide … No! Not suicide. She's cutting herself with the knife that Lucy saw. They chase after her and get the knife away, but she runs off and they daren't follow right away because they know that Lucy and Martin have seen them and they're afraid that it looks as if they're trying to hurt her. But then, later, they catch up with her and there's a struggle and she falls into the river and drowns. They blame themselves and they think that they'll be accused of doing it deliberately, especially since they know that there are two witnesses who'll testify that they were chasing the woman with a knife earlier that day.'

Peter thought for a few moments.

'I think you must be on the right lines,' he said at last, 'but I'm not convinced about the struggle on the bank. Mike was very definite that there were no ante-mortem injuries apart from the one knife wound, which we're assuming was self-inflicted.'

'They needn't have laid hands on her. Maybe she just saw them and ran away and then tripped and fell in. Or it could even have been suicide, but they still thought they might get the blame. I mean, *we* know that the evidence suggests that she wasn't pushed in deliberately, but they mightn't realise that.'

'Yes. You're probably right. And, of course, there wouldn't necessarily be any evidence of her being pushed in, even if she was.'

'OK,' Jonah sucked up the last of the tea in his cup. Peter leaned over and refilled it. 'Let's assume that it's the two men that Lucy saw who found the body and decided to bury it in the cemetery. The next job is to try to find out who they are. Let's see that footprint that you were telling me about. But first, do you mind helping me to one of those biscuits? I'm starving!'

12.00 SUNDAY 8ᵀᴴ NOVEMBER

'So, to summarise,' Jonah said an hour or so later. 'You have footwear marks that suggest that at least two people – men, judging by the size of their feet – entered the cemetery from Jordan Hill by climbing over the fence there. You have another print, which matches one of those, in the loose earth by the grave where the body was found. There are marks that could have been made by a wheelbarrow on the ground between the fence and one of the paths that lead to the graves from the driveway. There are traces of mud on the path, which may, or may not, be signs that the boots, and perhaps the barrow, continued along it to where it meets the driveway, just outside the chapel. The drive goes from the chapel to the Banbury Road entrance, but the muddy marks only go as far as the path that leads to the grave where the body was found. Finally, you have a tyre mark suggestive of a vehicle having been parked on the verge on Jordan Hill, close by where the people probably climbed in. Does that cover it?'

'Yes. I think you've got the main points there,' Peter agreed. 'The tyre mark had traces of cement in it, which might fit in with the Visqueen wrapper around the corpse, because those are both things that are associated with builders or builders' merchants. And I've been told that the tyre is a size and type that could have been on a pickup truck.'

'Right! Now we're getting somewhere. Do we have any builders in our sights from any of the other enquiries?'

'No. I don't think so.'

'What about that ex-boyfriend you were telling me about? What does he do?'

'He works for an IT company. Interestingly, it's based on the Jordan Hill business park, which gave me pause for thought for a while. However, his current girlfriend has given him an alibi for the entire time from Friday evening to Monday morning, which means that unless she's shielding him, he can't have been one of the men who moved the body.'

'Hmm. I'm not sure that we can rule him out on that basis. It wouldn't be the first time that a woman has lied to protect her boyfriend. And the other possibility is that he didn't do it himself, but he got someone else to do it for him. He might well have wanted Emma out of the way – if she was causing trouble with his new girl, for example – and he might also want to give her a decent burial. I wonder if there's any way of finding out if he was one of the men that Lucy saw.'

'That reminds me!' Peter broke into Jonah's musing. 'There was something odd that they found when they were searching the riverbank. Did I tell you that there were footprints in amongst the bushes where the woman hid? They looked like a woman's shoe, so we assumed they came from Emma Sutcliffe – or whatever her real name is – but they didn't match the ones she was wearing when she was found.'

'When you say they didn't match, do you mean they were from someone else or were they the same size, but not the same shoes?' Jonah asked excitedly.

'The same size, but different shoes. Are you suggesting that she changed her shoes between when Lucy saw her and when she fell in the river?'

'Possibly. Or maybe whoever put her in the grave also replaced her shoes.'

'What an earth for?'

'Why did they do any of it? But think! They wrapped her in a coat, which you tell me was her size. So it looks to me as if they had access to her clothes. Maybe her shoes came off in the river and got lost, and they put some others on her to make it look more natural or because they didn't like the idea of her being buried without any or ...'

There was a knock at the door and Jeanette put her head round it.

'The lunches are here,' she told them, but Lucy rang to say they're stuck in traffic and might be some time. 'So I'll feed you, unless...,' she looked towards Peter.

'Peter'll do it,' Jonah said quickly. 'Then we can carry on talking shop.'

Jeanette collected the tea tray, smiling and winking at Peter as she noted the empty biscuit plate and took it away. A minute or two later, she returned with Jonah's lunch, which she put down on the table-on-wheels. She adjusted the backrest on Jonah's bed to bring him into a more upright position, tied a bib around his neck and checked that the table was at the correct height.

'There you are! Give me a buzz if you need anything.'

Peter lifted the cover off the plate and saw, with some relief, that it contained a type of stew made up of pieces of meat and vegetables small enough not to need cutting up. At least it should be fairly straightforward to feed this to Jonah using a spoon. Or should he use a fork to reproduce as closely as possible the way Jonah would have eaten it himself? He wished now that he had paid more attention to how Lucy went about the task, instead of carefully averting his eyes during Jonah's meals. He looked down at the cutlery provided: a knife, a fork and a spoon. If he used the spoon now there would be nothing left for the pudding. So he reached for the fork and speared a piece of meat with it.

Looking up anxiously, he saw Jonah watching him with what he thought – or hoped – was amusement on his face. Or was it embarrassment – like the embarrassment that he was feeling himself?

'Get a move on!' Jonah urged. 'Don't take all day about it. We'll both get what-for from Lucy if we don't manage to get this down me before she gets here.'

Peter raised the fork to Jonah's lips and somehow they succeeded in getting the meat inside his mouth. Jonah chewed it while Peter loaded the fork with a piece of carrot. Jonah opened his mouth and Peter lifted the fork, but he had to wait while Jonah spoke.

'Carry on telling me about Emma. What have you been doing to try to find out who she is?'

'We've hunted down all the Emma Sutcliffes within a two hundred mile radius,' Peter told him, inserting the carrot into his mouth and going back for some potato. 'None of them fit with what we know about our mystery woman. I'm beginning to think that what you said to Bernie about that not being her real name must be right.'

Jonah nodded agreement, swallowed and seemed about to speak again, but Peter was too quick for him and got the potato in first.

'None of the night clubs have any record of an Emma Sutcliffe working there, but then they don't seem to keep records beyond the current tax year and the staff change so frequently that not many of them date back that far. One or two of the dancers thought they remembered a girl called Emma who looked a bit like the pictures, but they didn't know anything about her. Most of *them* had started working the clubs after her time as well.'

Peter continued talking as he fed the rest of the stew to Jonah. As he struggled to get the timing of each forkful right, he became increasingly impressed at Lucy's efficiency in performing this task. She never seemed to spill gravy down Jonah's chin through attempting to introduce more food before he was ready for it or find herself haplessly chasing peas around the plate while Jonah waited impatiently for his next mouthful.

'We've come to the conclusion that she probably always calls herself *Emma*,' Peter concluded, putting down the fork and swapping the empty plate for a bowl of rice pudding. 'But that *Sutcliffe* is probably not her real name. Jamie Corcoran thought she was local, but none of the schools have records of an Emma Sutcliffe being enrolled at anything like the right time. And we've checked GP practices right across Oxfordshire and beyond, with no luck. The same goes for mental health services.'

'But she may not have gone to them,' Jonah pointed out. 'Lots of people with mental health problems don't want to admit it.'

'Corcoran seemed to think she had got help,' Peter began. 'No! It wasn't him. It was the tattooist from Swindon, who said that she'd talked about having therapy for her self-harming and wanting to cover up the scars now that she'd kicked the habit. Now, hadn't we better get started on this pudding?'

'Jonah! I'm sorry we're late!' The door burst open and Lucy ran in. She threw her arms round Jonah and hugged him round the shoulders. 'There was an accident. A motorcycle ran into a lorry and they stopped all the traffic.'

'Well, we're here now,' Bernie said heartily, not wanting Lucy to go into the details of an accident involving a motorcyclist. She knew that Jonah worried about Margaret's refusal to give up her motorbike and switch to less risky modes of transport.

'Yes,' Lucy agreed, looking across at Peter. 'Give me the spoon, Daddy. I'll do it now.'

Peter handed it across to Lucy, who settled down on the edge of the bed and began feeding Jonah with the rice pudding.

'As I was saying,' Jonah resumed, turning his head to avoid Lucy's spoon. 'Whatever help Emma got with her self-harming may not have been through the Health Service. There's something I've been wanting to show you for days, only you didn't come.'

'I've been busy,' Peter protested mildly. 'We've got a potential murder to investigate, you know!'

'Get my computer over here,' Jonah instructed.

Bernie fetched it while Peter made space on Jonah's mobile table for her to set it down. She powered it up and plugged in the mouse and keypad. Lucy paused in her feeding task to allow her mother to put Jonah's left hand into place so that he could manipulate it. A few minutes later, they were all looking at a photograph of a group of young people beneath the headline, 'Tackling Self-Harm Together.'

'It's a sort of self-help group for people who've been self-harming and want to stop,' Jonah explained. 'This article tells you all about it. Apparently, they've been very successful in helping people to quit without any medical intervention by doing things together to boost self-esteem. This picture is from getting on for three years ago. Now look carefully at the woman third from the left. Does she look familiar to you at all?'

'Mmmm. I see what you mean.' Peter leaned closer and peered at the screen. 'It does look very similar to our blond version of Emma Sutcliffe.'

'And look at the names across the bottom,' Jonah added. 'It's only got first names, but …'

'Rob, Stuart, Emma, Camilla, Millie, Jessica and Jo,' Peter read out. 'Yes. I really do think you may have found her there. I'd better get on to the organisation that runs the group and find out what this Emma's second name is and who all these others are.' He felt in his pocket for a pen. 'Has anyone got something I can write down on?'

'Here! Use this.' Bernie emptied the envelope containing Jonah's letter from the Human Resources department and handed it across to her husband.

'Rob or Stuart could be one of our size ten boot prints,' Jonah suggested. 'Or they could even both be involved. And John, the leader of the group, might be the older man out of the pair that Lucy saw.'

'Hmm. I think that's probably a leap too far,' Peter murmured as he hastily scribbled down the address of the website. 'But at least now we may be able to find out what Emma's real name is and maybe even speak to some people who knew her back then. I'd better get back and set the wheels in motion.'

He got up to go. Bernie looked across at him, frowning slightly.

'You're not supposed to be on duty today,' she pointed out.

'No. I know, but this could be a bit of a breakthrough. Don't worry. I'll be back in time for tea.'

16.30 SUNDAY 8TH NOVEMBER

'Bernie! Thank you for ringing. How is he?' Margaret's voice, with its unmistakable East Lancashire accent, sounded eager but tinged with caution. 'I rang the ward and they said he ate his lunch, which is a lot better than I expected after seeing him this morning.'

'By the time I got there he seemed to be on fine form,' Bernie assured her. 'Almost back to his old self. I reckon you were spot-on with your prescription. A good dose of *murder enquiry* appears to have done him the world of good. But that wasn't what I was ringing about. I have a confession to make.'

'Oh?'

'You know that letter you took to Jonah? The one from HR?'

'Yes?'

'Well … Peter needed something to write on, so I gave him the envelope to use. And, would you believe it? When we got outside Jonah's room afterwards I found I still had the letter in my hand!'

'Oh Bernie! What are you like?' Margaret exclaimed,

pretending to be annoyed.

'I know. It's awful isn't it? But that's not the worst. I'm so careless sometimes! On the way out, I managed to drop it in the confidential waste bin outside the nurses' office. I'm afraid that if Jonah wants to apply for early retirement he'll have to get on to HR to send him another one.'

'Oh dear! How tiresome,' Margaret held back her giggles with some difficulty. 'But there's nothing we can do about it now. I'm sure they'll be able to rustle up another form if ever he does decide to apply.'

'Yes. That's what I thought. Anyway, that's all really. I just thought you ought to know, in case Jonah starts wondering where it's got to.'

'Yes. Thanks. And thank Peter from me for going over there this morning. I felt bad about asking him, but I just didn't know what else to do.'

08.15 MONDAY 9TH NOVEMBER

'I've got the full names and addresses of the people in that photograph,' Monica greeted Peter as he entered the incident room the next morning. She had been on duty over the weekend and had been given the task of contacting the organisation that had published the picture. 'They were a bit cagey at first, but once they were convinced that our corpse really was one of their participants they were keen to help. I think they decided that was the best way of minimising any bad publicity. After all, it's not a great advert for them, having one of their supposed success stories winding up as a suspicious death, is it?'

'OK. Let's have a look at it.' Peter scanned down the list that Monica had put in front of him. 'This one looks interesting! *Crow's Acre* in Binsey Lane. And it's one of the men: Stuart Parsons. Which one was he?' He peered at the line-up of faces in the photograph on the computer screen. 'He's the one standing next to Emma. I wonder if that's significant. Maybe they were particular friends.'

'And we've got a new last name for her too,' Monica

said, eager to impart all the knowledge that she had acquired while the bulk of the team were taking time off. 'She registered with the group as *Emma Carr* and gave an address in Rose Hill.'

'Right,' Peter said decisively. 'I want someone to go out to that address and see if anyone there remembers her. It's presumably the flat she was living in before she moved in with Corcoran. The neighbours may have known her, and they may be able to tell us more about their relationship and about the sort of person that Emma was herself. What exactly was the problem with her landlord that made her move out, for instance? I also want to get interviews done with as many of these people as we can. They presumably all knew Emma Carr, as we'd better call her now, and may be able to tell us more about her.'

'The addresses are a couple of years old,' Monica warned him. 'Some of them will probably have moved on by now.'

'Yes, but they still give us a starting point. I'd like you to check them out and see how many of the faces from the photograph you can track down. Not Stuart Parsons, though. I want to look into that young man myself. I have a feeling that he may be one of the men on the riverbank or the owner of one of our size-ten boot prints from the cemetery or possibly both. I'm going to start by going through the Binsey house-to-house interviews.'

Peter was still sitting at his desk methodically studying the transcripts of interviews with residents of the scattered houses that made up the hamlet of Binsey when the phone rang. To his surprise, it was Jeannette speaking from the rehabilitation ward at the spinal injuries centre.

'I've got DCI Porter for you,' she said, speaking very formally but with a touch of amusement in her voice. 'He says he needs to speak to you urgently.'

'You'd better put him on then,' Peter answered, smiling to himself at the way that his colleague appeared to have drafted his nurse into acting as his secretary to enable him to behave as if he were back at work rather than imprisoned, unable to move, on a hospital ward.

'Peter!' Jonah's voice sounded excited. 'I've got something very interesting for you. I've been taking a stroll along Binsey Lane on Street View.'

'I'm sorry. I think I must have misheard. I thought you said you'd been for a stroll in Binsey.'

'Yes. That's right – a virtual stroll, using Google Street View. Haven't you seen it? It's a new extension to Google Maps. You pick a point on the map and it shows you what it looks like to someone standing there. As I was telling you, I've been up and down Binsey Lane looking at the houses and I found something very interesting.'

'Go on.'

'You remember those roses? The ones that were left with the body.'

'Yes?'

'There's a house in Binsey that has a climbing rose on its front wall that looks just the same to me.'

'Are you sure? What's the name of the house?'

'Hang on. There's a sign on the wall next to the door. I'll try to zoom in on it.'

Peter waited patiently, listening to Jonah's breathing as he manipulated the mouse in an effort to bring the name into focus.

'It looks as if it begins with a C,' he said at last, 'and it's two words.'

'Could it be *Crow's Acre*?'

'Yes! Yes, it certainly could. In fact, now you've suggested it, I can make out the other letters. Why?'

'One of the young men from that photograph you showed me lives there. I've got the interview that Anna Davenport did with his dad in front of me now. According to him, they were both tucked up in bed at the time that Lucy saw Emma down by the Thames, but I have a sneaking suspicion that the two of them could be the men who were chasing her. They're father and son, living alone together. The house backs on to fields, which they could have walked across to get to the river. And Stuart, the son, knew Emma from that self-harming group.'

'*And* they have a rose growing over their front door of the sort that someone put with her in her grave,' Jonah added triumphantly. 'Do you have enough yet to justify a search warrant, do you think?'

'Probably, but I don't want to rush in too fast. I've got a few more background checks I want to do first. We've got a new name and address for Emma, by the way, which Andrews is following up on. Apparently, she used to call herself Emma *Carr*. Don't forget, we still haven't officially identified the body.'

'OK. I'd better go now. We can't keep Jeanette here all day holding the phone for me. Let me know how you get on, won't you?'

11.10 MONDAY 9TH NOVEMBER

'Do you mind if I come in?'

Jonah looked up from his computer screen to see the bald head of Ian Stamford, one of the hospital chaplains, peering round the door. He nodded and beckoned with his head.

'Not at all,' he said, trying to sound welcoming, when in reality he felt somewhat resentful of the interruption. 'Take a pew.'

Ian came in and looked around. Then he lifted a plastic stacking chair off the small pile that stood against the wall in readiness for visitors and placed it a few feet away from where Jonah was sitting.

'How are you doing?' he asked casually. Margaret had left a message on the chaplaincy answering machine the previous day, asking him to call, but he did not want Jonah to know that they were anxious about him. 'We haven't seen you at Chapel for a few weeks, so I thought I'd call in and check you were OK.'

'I'm fine,' Jonah replied dismissively. 'I've been busy. That's all.'

211

'Doing anything interesting?' Ian asked, carefully hiding his surprise at this response.

'Identifying a corpse and tracking down the people who buried her.'

'Really?' Again, Ian tried to sound interested rather than incredulous.

'And I think I may have just made another breakthrough. Have a look at this.'

Ian got up and came round the back of Jonah's chair so that he could look at the screen in front of him. 'See there? This is the Facebook page belonging to the dead woman. She hasn't posted anything for about six weeks, but just before that … See there? She's talking about different ways of killing herself. And look at some of the comments. I don't know who these people are, but some of them look as if they're egging her on to do it.'

'That's very disturbing,' Ian said, bending closer to read the messages. 'I've never used Facebook and I don't know much about it. Is this sort of thing common?'

'I don't know the statistics, but some of my colleagues who specialise in cybercrime say they're coming across it more and more.'

'Are you telling me that she went on to kill herself?'

'Could be. Cause of death is still uncertain. However, the big question is what happened to her *after* she died, because, however she died, it wasn't in the place that she was found.'

'This is the woman who was found in Wolvercote Cemetery, right?'

'That's it. And now, I'd better let the officer in charge of the case know about what I've just found out. Can you go and fetch the ward telephone for me?'

14.15 MONDAY 9TH NOVEMBER

'This is the place,' Peter said as they pulled up outside a white-painted detached cottage on Binsey Lane. 'Crow's Acre. There are two people listed on the electoral roll as living here: Stuart Parsons and his father, Roger. It's also the registered address of Roger Parsons' building firm.'

'I can't see any sign of those roses you were telling me about,' Andy commented as they walked up the short flagstone path that led through a small garden to the front door.'

'Could this be it?' Anna asked, bending down to look at some upright stems cut off near to the ground. These look like the remains of a rose bush. Maybe they've been pruned back now that the flowers are over.'

'Or pruned back so that we won't see them,' Peter said drily. 'That's something else to add to the list of things that we need to be looking out for when we search the premises. Do you remember whether they looked the same when you came before?'

'No. But I didn't come up to the front door that time. Mr Parsons was just getting out of his car when I arrived and he took me round the back. There's a sort of builder's yard round there with a shed sort of thing with bags of concrete and sand and stuff piled up in it. He took me in through the back door and we sat in the kitchen.'

There was an old-fashioned brass bell hanging outside the front door, with a leather strap dangling from the clapper. Peter took hold of it and rang it vigorously. For a minute or so, nothing happened. He was about to try it again when a young man in work overalls appeared round the side of the house and called out to them.

'Hi there! Can I help you?'

'Are you Mr Stuart Parsons?' Peter asked, walking towards him and holding up his warrant card. The young man nodded and looked round anxiously at Anna and Andy, who were also displaying their police identification.

'I'm DI Peter Johns. I have a warrant to search these premises in connection with a suspicious death and an attempt to prevent the lawful and decent burial of a dead body.'

'I – I – I don't understand. What body?'

Stuart Parsons continued to look around as if in bewilderment. Then his eyes widened and his mouth dropped open at the sight of a police van drawing up outside and parking behind Peter's car. He stood staring as a team of officers got out and started to unload equipment from inside the van.

'The body of Emma Carr, who I believe used to be a friend of yours,' Peter told him. 'We have reason to think that you may have been involved in moving it from where she died to a grave in Wolvercote cemetery.'

'I knew Emma, but I haven't seen her for years,' Stuart said, speaking rapidly and rubbing his hands rhythmically up and down on his upper arms. Peter guessed that this might be some sort of ritual behaviour for coping with stressful situations. 'I never killed her. Why are you here? What are you accusing us of?'

'Is your father at home?' Anna asked, thinking that Mr

Parsons senior might be an easier person to deal with. 'I spoke to him last week about an incident down by the river, and there are a few things I'd like to clarify with him.'

'Yes. He's round the back. We were trying to fix the cement mixer. I'll show you.'

The young man turned and led the way back round the side of the house to a concreted area, on which were parked a shiny new four-wheel-drive car and a muddy pickup truck. There was a building down one side of this yard, which looked to Peter like an open-sided barn. Inside he could see a man bending down over an orange cement mixer. He straightened up at the sound of their footsteps and hurried over to greet them, wiping his hands on his overalls as he came.

'We're sorry to bother you again Mr Parsons,' Anna said, stepping forward. 'This is DI Johns and this is DC Lepage. We need to talk to you and your son again and we need to have a look round.'

'Why? What's this all about?' Roger Parson asked defensively. 'I told you we didn't see anything. And what do you mean *have a look around?*'

'We have a warrant to search these premises,' Peter informed him, holding out the paperwork. Parsons glanced at the document, taking in the name of the magistrates court and the description of the premises, which included the house, grounds, outbuildings and vehicles. Then he stood back with an air of resignation and motioned for Peter and his colleagues to go past. 'Be my guest. The back door's open. I don't know what you're expecting to find.'

09.30 TUESDAY 10TH NOVEMBER

'Now Mr Parsons,' Peter said, placing his hands together on the table that stood between him and his interviewee and looking him in the eye. 'Before we start, I'd like to check that you understand why you are here.'

'Because you think we killed Emma,' Roger Parsons replied promptly. 'But you've got it all wrong. We never laid a finger on her.'

'No,' Peter said quietly. 'You have been arrested on suspicion of attempting to conceal Emma Carr's death by hiding her body in a grave in Wolvercote Cemetery. We don't as yet know how she died. That's something that I'm hoping that you and your son may be able to help us with. However, before we go on, I need to remind you that you do not have to say anything; but it may harm your defence if you do not mention when questioned something which you later rely on in Court. Anything you do say may be given in evidence.'

'Yes, yes. We've been through all that.' Parsons sounded rather impatient. 'Can't we just get on with it?'

'I'm sorry, but we do need to have all this on the tape. Now, to get back to your role in the moving of the body of Emma Carr: where was she when you found her?'

'Like Stuart told you, we haven't seen her for years.'

'I see. So there's no chance that the blood that we

216

found on a spray of roses that had been left with the body will turn out to be from you or your son?'

Parsons did not answer.

'Our biologists are checking those roses against a sample taken from the bush growing outside your front door,' Peter went on. 'I'm no expert, but I'm rather expecting that they'll tell me that they are the same variety. When did you cut down that bush, Mr Parsons?'

'Last week. I always prune them back hard at this time of year.'

'And then you burn the cuttings?'

'Yes. It's a good way of getting rid of any pests. Roses are prone to diseases.'

'I see. We had a look at what was left of your bonfire. Rose cuttings wasn't all you were burning was it?'

'Of course not. It's a big garden. We get a lot of stuff that needs burning.'

'But it wasn't all garden waste was it? We found some very interesting things in there – the remains of a rucksack, for example, and a buckle that looked as if it came from a belt and something that might have been part of a jacket.'

'It was Guy Fawkes night last week, wasn't it? Stuart made a guy out of some old clothes stuffed with newspapers.'

'Alright, let's leave the bonfire for the time being. I'd like to talk about the roll of Visqueen that we found in your store shed.'

'It's what was left over from damp-proofing the floor of a conservatory we were building.'

'I see. So, can you explain this report that I have here, which says that the cut edge matches the edge of the sheet of Visqueen that was wrapped round Emma Carr's body before it was put in the grave?'

Parsons did not reply. He glanced towards his solicitor, who was sitting next to him. The lawyer raised his eyebrows but said nothing. Peter waited, watching Parsons' face intently. Parsons looked down, refusing to meet

Peter's eye. He appeared uncomfortable and confused.

'While we were at your house yesterday we took away two pairs of size ten work boots from the back porch. Can you tell me who they belong to?'

'They're mine and Stuart's. We both take size ten.'

'One of them has wear marks that match a print in the soil surrounding the grave where Emma Carr's body was found. We also found prints from size ten boots in the mud on either side of the boundary fence between the cemetery and Jordan Hill. Can you explain how they got there?'

Parsons did not answer. He remained staring blankly down at the table.

'Mr Parsons?' Andy Lepage prompted from his seat next to Peter. He was becoming impatient with their suspect's repeated refusal to answer. 'For the benefit of the tape, if you aren't willing to answer, please say so.'

'I don't know how those foot prints got there,' Parsons answered with a sigh, glaring across at Andy. 'Planted by you lot, I shouldn't wonder.'

'I think that my client would like to retract that last remark,' the solicitor intervened. 'Wouldn't you?' he added, looking Parsons square in the face.

'Yes. I'm sorry. I didn't mean to imply … I just don't understand what's going on.'

'Alright. How about this?' Peter said, referring to his notes again. 'We found tyre marks in the verge on Jordan Hill, just by where the footprints that I was telling you about were. Guess what? They match the tyres on your pickup truck. And when those tyres come back from the lab, I wouldn't mind betting there'll be traces on them of having been on that verge. The coincidences do seem to be piling up rather, don't they?'

Still Parsons did not attempt to explain the evidence that Peter had put before him. He remained staring silently down at the table. Peter sat watching him for a few moments, trying to think of a way of persuading him to open up. They had enough evidence to place at least one out of Roger and Stuart Parsons at the scene, and he was confident that the blood that they had found on the rose thorn would turn out to be from one of them. But if they persisted in refusing to answer, there might still be sufficient doubt as to which of them was responsible for moving the body that it would be impossible to convict either of them. Then an idea occurred to him.

'Mr Parsons,' he said, leaning across the table and speaking in a confidential tone. 'I know that you want to protect your son. But this isn't helping him. All this *refusing to talk* isn't doing him any good. We *know* that your pickup was parked on Jordan Hill sometime in the week before the body was found. We *know* that someone wearing one of those pairs of boots from your porch was there at roughly the same time. We will soon know which of you it was who put a spray of roses – from *your* rose bush – on Emma Carr's body before she was buried. If you really don't know anything about it then I can only conclude that it was all the work of your son, probably with one of his mates helping him.'

'No!' Parsons slammed his fist down on the table. Then he raised his head and looked Peter in the eye. 'You mustn't blame Stuart.'

'So what *did* happen?' Peter asked mildly, gratified to have gained Parsons' full attention at last. 'If your son wasn't involved, who was it that helped you get Emma's body over the fence and into the cemetery?'

'OK. I'll tell you what happened,' Parsons muttered. Then, louder, 'but first, you tell me where Stuart is and what you're doing to him!'

'He's being held in a police cell for the time being,' Peter told him. 'He says he wants your solicitor present when we question him, so we can't interview him until we've finished talking to you.'

'Can I see him? He'll be scared out of his wits.'

'I'm afraid that's not possible. The best thing you can

do for him is to answer all our questions honestly, so that we can get this all cleared up as quickly as possible.'

'But you don't understand. Stuart's ... He needs looking after. He's not mental – I don't mean that, but ... he might do something to harm himself, shut up in a cell.'

'Don't worry. The custody sergeant will be keeping an eye on him.'

'If you think he needs it, we could put him on suicide watch,' Andy added helpfully.

'Yes!' rather to Peter's surprise, Parsons jumped at this suggestion. 'You've got to understand, he gets worried about things and then he hurts himself. He can't help it. That's what I'm telling you. That's why you mustn't blame him for what happened to Emma.'

'OK. Andy – you go and have a word with the custody sergeant. Do you have any idea who's on duty?'

'Sergeant Gregson, sir.'

Peter waited for Andy to get to his feet and then added, speaking slowly into the microphone, 'DC Lepage has left the room.' Then he turned back to address Parsons.

'Pamela Gregson will see that your son doesn't come to any harm,' he assured him kindly. 'She has a boy with autism, so she understands how stressful some people can find it being in unfamiliar surroundings. Now, would you mind telling me the story from the very beginning? We know that your son met Emma Carr at a group for young people who were self-harming and wanted to stop. That would be three or four years ago, would it?'

'Yes. That'd be about right. But we need to go back further than that – right back to when Stuart was a kid. That's when it all started and that's why he can't be held responsible for ... And before we start, let's get one thing straight: he never did a thing to hurt her – not one thing! All he ever did was to try to help her. You've got to believe that!'

'OK,' Peter said quietly. 'I believe you. Now, in your own time, just tell me what happened.'

Before Parsons could begin, the door opened again and Andy returned carrying a tray on which there were four paper cups, two plastic spoons and some sachets of sugar.

'DC Lepage has entered the room,' Peter said into the microphone.

'I've brought tea for everyone,' Andy said. 'I hope that's alright?'

There was a short pause while the cups were distributed. Parsons took a few sips of tea and then looked towards Peter again. Peter smiled back encouragingly.

'Stuart's Mum had really bad post-natal depression after he was born,' Parsons began. 'It got so bad she was sectioned[14] for a while. After that, she was never really right again. She'd be OK for a few months – or even a couple of years – and then she'd stop taking her meds and she'd be right back to square one. Then, when Stuart was seven, she took an overdose. He found her. I hadn't realised how bad she'd got. I left her at home with him and she …,' he trailed off and stared down into his tea.

'That's fine,' Peter assured him. 'We don't need to hear all the details. Stuart's mother committed suicide and he found her body. Is that what you're saying?'

'Yes.'

'That must have been very traumatic for you both.'

'Yes. I don't think Stuart ever really got over it. But he tried to hide his feelings and I thought … I did my best. I tried to keep a lookout for signs … And everything seemed to be OK until after he went up to High School. I think some of the other boys must've been picking on him, though he would never say. Anyway, he started hiding away in his room and cutting himself with a Stanley knife. It was a while before I found out about it, because he was careful not to let it show. When I *did* find out I took him along to our GP and he got him referred to mental health.

[14] Detained in hospital under the provisions of the Mental Health Act 1983, as stated in section 2 or 3 of the Act.

It was like his mum all over again. He'd be OK for a while and then something would happen to spark it all off again. It got so I was afraid to let him out of my sight, so when he left school I told him he had to join the business, so that I could keep an eye on him. Then about three and a half years ago, he heard about these people who claimed to be able to help youngsters who were self-harming without using any medication. It was called, "Drama not Drugs". They reckoned they could cure people by getting them to do play-acting together. It sounded a bit far-fetched to me, but he was keen on the idea and I was just glad that he'd decided that he wanted to stop cutting himself.'

'I've seen their website,' Peter told him. 'They claim to have had a lot of success. Did it help Stuart?'

'Yes. I don't know whether it was anything to do with the acting stuff or if it was just meeting other youngsters who were feeling the same as he was. Anyway, that's where he met this girl, Emma Carr. He brought her home a few times. I wasn't that keen on him going out with her, to be honest. What with his mum and everything, I thought we could do without any more of that sort of problem in the family. But I didn't say anything, because I didn't want to upset him. That's how it's always been, ever since his mum died. I'm always watching myself to make sure I don't do anything that'll set him off. It's important that you know that.'

He paused to take a long draught from his cup. Peter waited patiently for him to continue.

'Anyway, I needn't have worried because it turned out this Emma had another boyfriend. After they'd finished the course at DND, she stopped seeing Stuart. I was afraid this would set him off again, but he seemed OK about it. So maybe I was wrong to think there'd ever been anything between them. I don't know. Anyway, that was that, until the week before last. Stuart had gone out clubbing with an old mate of his from High School. The club closes at three, so I was expecting him back by half past.'

'That's half past three in the morning, I take it?' Peter asked.

'That's right. We'd finished a job that day and we weren't due to start the next one until the Friday, so he was going to sleep in late.'

'Right. Sorry – I interrupted you – go on.'

'When he wasn't back by four, I rang him on his mobile and he told me he was at the train station and could I come and collect him? Of course, I said *yes* right away and off I went in the four-by-four. And when I got there I found that he'd got Emma with him.'

'Which day was this?' Andy asked, flicking through the notes that he had made of the hypothetical sequence of events that had led up to Emma's body being deposited in the grave.

'Wednesday.'

'Wednesday morning, you mean?'

'No. It'd be Thursday morning. Stuart went out on Wednesday night and then we had a day off on Thursday and the new job starting on Friday.'

'I see. Thank you.'

'Stuart said Emma didn't have anywhere to go and he wanted to bring her back home with us. He had this obstinate look on his face that he gets sometimes, so I didn't argue. Like I said before, I always have to be careful not to upset him in case … Anyway, we took her home and put her in the spare room and we finally got to bed just before five.'

18.30 TUESDAY 10TH NOVEMBER

'So they admitted everything?' Jonah asked eagerly. 'And did they explain *why* they did it?'

'It rather depends what you mean by *everything*,' Peter answered, smiling at his friend's enthusiasm. 'We're still none the wiser to exactly how she died. They both insist that they weren't there when she drowned, and I believe them. I think the inquest will come out with an open verdict. I don't see how we'll ever know whether it was suicide or an accident.'

'But if they didn't kill her, why didn't they just phone 999 when they found the body?' Lucy asked as she fed Jonah with the last spoonful of his portion of chocolate blancmange.

'It's all down to Stuart Parsons being convinced that nobody would believe them, and his father not daring to refuse to do whatever he wanted for fear of setting off his self-harming again.' Peter sighed. 'I feel sorry for Roger Parsons. He quite obviously didn't want to do any of it, but he was so focussed on keeping Stuart on an even keel mentally that he felt he had to go along with it. I think he was actually quite relieved that we'd worked it out, in a funny sort of way.'

'I still don't see,' Lucy complained, moving the table away from Jonah's chair and leaning forward to remove his bib. 'If they didn't want to report it, they could have just run away, couldn't they?'

'Yes,' Peter agreed, 'but the things is: Stuart knew Emma. He didn't like the idea of leaving her in the river. He wanted her to have proper burial.'

'I can't see why it matters what happens to you after you're dead,' Lucy argued 'You can't feel anything anymore.'

'No, but it matters to the people who are still alive,' Bernie told her.

Lucy looked puzzled, but did not argue further.

'You still haven't told us how they all came to be down by the river at seven in the morning a week ago last Thursday,' Jonah complained. 'You've been telling it all to us backwards. I want the whole story from the beginning, starting with when and how the Parsons met Emma.'

'Well, you know how Stuart Parsons met her in the first place,' Peter said. 'They both attended a course run by that *Drama not Drugs* organisation. According to Roger Parsons, they were close for a while after that, but Stuart claims that they were never more than friends and that he didn't see anything of her at all after she met Jamie Corcoran. Either way, he hadn't seen her for over two years when he ran into her in a nightclub. That was a week ago last Wednesday – the day before the incident on the riverbank.'

'If she'd gone back to working in the clubs, how come none of them recognised her when you talked to them?' Jonah asked sharply.

'No. She wasn't one of the dancers. She was just hanging around, hoping to …,' Peter stopped and glanced across at Lucy, who looked back with an interested expression. 'Stuart was concerned about the way she was behaving. He got the impression she was …,' he stopped again. It was very difficult thinking of a way to explain what had been going on, which was suitable for the ears of a nine-year-old and would not provoke a string of embarrassing questions. 'Well, to cut to the chase, it turned out that she was homeless and she'd taken to hanging around pubs and clubs on the lookout for men who might take her home with them for the night.'

'And Stuart took advantage of that, presumably?'

'No. According to him – and that's borne out by what his father told me – he just watched and waited until Emma decided to call it a day. She'd had plenty of men buying her drinks, but none of them offered her anything more than that. Stuart followed her to the cloakroom where she retrieved a coat – the same one that we found her body wrapped in – and a rucksack. Then he followed her through the streets to see where she went. He said that he'd got a feeling that there was something wrong, and wanted to be sure that she was safe.'

PART III GENERAL CONFESSION

03.15 THURSDAY 29TH OCTOBER

Stuart stood on the steps of the club and looked to right and left, waiting for his eyes to adjust to the street lighting after the brightness inside the foyer. For a moment, he thought that he had lost her. Then he caught sight of the incongruous figure teetering along on high heels with a bulging pack on her back. There was something wrong there. Why had she felt the need to bring the rucksack with her to the club? What did it have in it that she could not safely leave at home?

He followed her at a distance as she walked through the streets. She seemed unsteady on her feet, perhaps the consequence of those drinks that he had seen men buying for her. She stumbled and put out her hand to steady herself against the stone wall that surrounded the grounds of Worcester College. Stuart quickened his pace and caught up with her.

'Are you OK? Would you like me to give you a hand?'

'No. I'm alright.' Emma stuffed her hands into the pockets of her coat and walked away. Stuart followed half a pace behind.

229

'I could ring for a taxi,' he suggested. Getting no reply, he went on, 'or at least let me walk you home.'

'No. I told you – I'm alright. Just leave me, OK?'

'OK.'

Stuart stopped walking and watched as she turned the corner into Hythe Bridge Street. Then he started following her again, keeping well back so that she would not see him. She walked on down the street, across the bridge that spanned Castle Mill Stream, on past the modern buildings of the Said Business School, over the pedestrian crossing and into the cycle park outside the railway station. Was she going somewhere by train? Was that why she had her luggage with her?

There was nobody else around at that early hour, so Stuart watched from a distance until she was inside the station building, afraid that he would be conspicuous if he followed more closely. Then he hurried up the steps and in at the glass doors. He looked around. The departure board showed that there would be trains leaving for London Paddington at 04.00 and 05.01 and to Hereford and Banbury a few minutes after that. London seemed the most likely destination and if she was booked on the four o'clock train, perhaps that was why she had chosen to while away the preceding hours in a nightclub. Stuart still felt uneasy. Something still did not quite add up.

He looked around the concourse. There was a row of seats along one wall. And there was Emma! She was lying across them with her rucksack under her head to act as a pillow. Stuart hurried across and knelt down next to her.

'Emma!'

She opened her eyes and stared at him.

'Don't you have anywhere to go?' he asked anxiously.

'I could ask you the same thing,' she retorted with a scowl. 'Go away and stop following me!'

'I'm only trying to help. I don't like to think of you sleeping rough like this.'

'I told you – I'm OK. Just go away and leave me alone.'

Stuart hesitated. He did not like arguments, but he did not like the thought of leaving her there alone either. Then he was saved from the need to make a decision by the sound of his phone ringing in his pocket. It was his father, wanting to know why he had not arrived home yet.

'Sorry Dad. Something cropped up. Do you think you could come and pick me up? I'm at the train station.'

He turned back to Emma.

'That was my dad. He's going to come in the car to take me home. I want you to come with us.'

'I told you – I don't need you to do anything.'

'But I want to. Dad won't mind you coming to stay for a bit. We've got plenty of room. Just until you get somewhere of your own fixed up. Come on! It won't be that bad staying with us! It'll be better than here anyway.'

Emma sat up. She appeared to be thinking.

'OK,' she said at last. 'Just for tonight.'

Stuart was about to protest that the night was almost over and that she was welcome to stay for as long as she needed, but he thought better of it. They sat together for several minutes without speaking. Then he plucked up courage to ask the question that he had been wanting to put to her ever since he had seen her pathetic attempts to pick up one of the customers in the club.

'What happened? I mean, you seemed so happy. I thought you were all set to settle down – maybe get married and have kids. What went wrong?'

'I don't know.' Emma sighed. 'Jamie moved out. And then I lost my job and I couldn't pay the rent. And then … I just don't know!'

'You can stay with us as long as you like,' Stuart promised eagerly. 'I don't mean … I mean, no strings attached, just somewhere to stay until you're back on your feet again.'

'What about your dad?'

'He won't mind. Please Emma! Say you'll stay until you find somewhere proper to live. I can't bear to think of you like this.'

His phone rang again.

'I'm in the drop-off area outside the station. Where are you?'

'Sorry Dad. We'll be right out.'

'*We*?' Roger queried, but Stuart had already ended the call and put his phone away. He picked up Emma's rucksack and led the way outside to his father's waiting car. She tried ineffectually to snatch the bag back from him, but he was already out of reach walking briskly towards the doors. Emma turned up the collar of her coat around her face, pushed her hands into her pockets and followed.

05.50 THURSDAY 29TH OCTOBER

Roger Parsons lay awake in bed, trying to think of a plan for dealing with his unwelcome guest. It was all very well for Stuart to say that he didn't like to think of her sleeping on the streets. Roger was equally certain that *he* didn't like to think of her sleeping in his spare room! There must be somewhere they could take her – a homeless hostel perhaps? But would Stuart agree to that? He might see depositing her in some squalid place amongst the winos and drug-addicts as a betrayal. A women's refuge then? But maybe you had to have been beaten up by a man to qualify? In any case, he didn't know how to find such a place.

Did she have any family? They were the ones who ought to be looking after her. But hadn't Stuart said something once about her not getting on with her dad? Or was that one of the other girls from the *Drama not Drugs* group? He was not sure. Would suggesting that she went back to her family upset her? He could not take the risk. If he upset Emma, that would upset Stuart and Stuart might start his self-harming again. Or they might even go off

233

together! That was unthinkable. Whatever happened, he must keep Stuart here at home, where he could keep an eye on him and make sure that he was safe.

Did that mean that he had to resign himself to having Emma staying with them? For how long?

He became aware of movement in the house. A floorboard on the landing creaked. Straining his ears to listen, he made out the pad, pad, pad of feet on the carpet outside his room. Stuart or Emma must be visiting the bathroom. More footsteps. Wasn't that someone going downstairs? Then he heard Stuart's voice, calling softly but urgently.

'Emma? Where are you going?'

Roger sat up in bed and listened harder. That was definitely someone going downstairs. And that was Stuart's voice calling again, this time from down in the hall. What was going on now?

He got out of bed and went out on to the landing and then down the stairs. The hall was empty, but he could hear voices from behind the closed kitchen door. He went over and listened, not liking to go in. Stuart might resent his interference in their private affairs.

'No Emma,' he heard Stuart saying. 'Don't! Give me that!'

Emma replied, but Roger could not make out the words.

'You don't have to do this,' Stuart's voice came again. 'You're safe here. And you can stay just as long as you like.'

'Your dad doesn't want me – and why should he? It's better this way.'

'No don't! Come back!'

There was a bang, which Roger recognised as the sound of the door from the kitchen into the back porch being flung open and hitting the worktop. They really must get round to fitting the doorstop that he had been meaning to install ever since the new units were put in.

He went into the kitchen and was just in time to see Emma's bright pink dress disappearing out of the back door. He ran across the room to join Stuart, who was standing in the porch in pyjamas and bare feet, staring out after her as she headed off down the garden. She must be aiming for the gate into the muddy track that ran behind the garden and into the fields. She had been here before. Stuart must have shown her the way across the farmland to the river, from where the towpath led back to the city.

'Let her go,' Roger said, putting his hand on Stuart's shoulder. 'It's her choice. You did your best.'

'But she's got a knife! I've got to go after her.' Stuart attempted to pull away.

'Not like that. You haven't even got any shoes on. And like I said, you've done your best. If she doesn't want help, that's up to her. Come back to bed.'

'She's left her bag,' Stuart pointed at the rucksack, which Emma had put down on the floor while she rummaged in the kitchen drawers looking for a sharp knife. 'She hasn't got any of her things with her.'

'Then the chances are she'll come back for it,' Roger reasoned. 'Just leave the back door unlocked, and when she remembers it she'll come back. Now you come back upstairs to bed.'

'And she hasn't even got her coat,' Stuart continued, refusing to be mollified. 'I put it in the hall cupboard and she mustn't have been able to find it. We can't let her just wander the streets in that thin dress of hers. She'll freeze to death this weather.'

'OK. OK,' Roger sighed, realising that further argument was pointless. 'I'll come with you and we'll try to find her. But we're both going to go back upstairs and get dressed first. And we'll need lights so we can find her. We won't be any help to Emma stumbling around in the dark half naked.'

Stuart nodded. 'Thanks Dad.'

They went back up to their bedrooms. Roger hurried to

get dressed, fearful that Stuart might be unable to wait if he were to delay them. Then he went downstairs and got out thick coats for each of them from the cupboard under the stairs. He also found Emma's coat. By now, Stuart was standing in the hall waiting for him, so he handed it to him. We'll take this with us for her to put on when we find her.

They padded through the kitchen in stockinged feet and put on their work boots in the porch. Then Roger led the way out into the yard to collect two of the battery-powered lights that they used when outside jobs over-ran and had to be finished after dark. The powerful beams showed up the path that led down the garden to the gate into the back lane. They went through it and stood with their backs to the fence, shining the lights to right and left.

'There she is!' Stuart said eagerly, pointing to the right.

Roger looked that way and saw a flash of pink as Emma disappeared through the hedge. As he had guessed, she was taking the footpath across the fields to the river. They hurried after her. Once they had passed through the kissing gate into the open field, they could see that the sky to the east was glowing faintly red and orange. It would not be long before the sun rose above the line of trees that hid the river from view. Stuart flashed his torch across the field and they caught a glimpse of Emma's dress catching the light.

'Emma!' he called out, striding forward across the grass. 'Come back! You've forgotten your bag.'

She stumbled. Then she righted herself and continued across the field without looking back.

'Here! You take this,' Stuart said, thrusting Emma's coat into his father's hand and starting to run after her. 'Wait for me! We only want to help! Emma!'

She glanced back, then turned again and started to run. Stuart quickened his own pace. He had nearly caught up with her when he missed his footing and fell, dropping the torch.

Roger hurried to help him up. Together they located the torch. It had gone out and nothing they could do would make it come on again. Stuart put it in his pocket and set off again after Emma. She was on the far side of the field by now, beyond the reach of the beam from the remaining torch, but just visible now that the daylight was increasing.

Roger followed, struggling to keep up with his son's energetic strides. As it became lighter, he found himself relying less and less on the gleam from the torch. He switched it off and stowed it in the pocket of his coat.

They came to another kissing gate – very muddy underfoot and partially obstructed by the overgrown hedge – and then they were through and into one of the fields that bordered the River. Stuart gave a cry as he spotted Emma crouching down under the hedge, a hundred yards or so away. He ran to join her. Roger tried to follow, but his coat had become entangled in a bramble that was hanging across the gate.

He was still struggling to free himself when Stuart reached Emma. There they were! He could hear their voices, but he could not make out the words. He gave a final pull and the bramble sprang back as his coat ripped. Ignoring the damage, he hastened to join his son, whose voice sounded more agitated now, although it was still indistinct.

Then there was a sudden movement. Stuart bent down over Emma. What was he doing to her? Then a moment later, he was standing upright again with his hand raised above his head. What was it that he was holding in it? It looked a familiar shape, but he could not quite place it. Then a slight movement of Stuart's hand made it glint in the light from the rising sun. Of course! It must be the knife that Emma had taken from their kitchen drawer.

Roger's thoughts were interrupted by a sound from across the field. He looked towards it and saw a narrowboat on the river. There was someone on the roof shouting and pointing towards them. He looked back at Stuart and saw that he had seen the boat too. He had lowered his arm now and he was standing, staring towards the river, his eyes wide and frightened.

Emma, seeing that both men were distracted, got to her feet and ran off across the field towards the river. For a moment, Stuart looked as if he were about to follow, but Roger reached out and took hold of him firmly by the shoulder and turned him in the direction of home.

'Let her go. There isn't any more we can do for her. You've got the knife away from her; that's the main thing.'

15.15 THURSDAY 29ᵗʰ OCTOBER

Roger returned from taking measurements for a quotation on a house-extension in Eynsham, and found his son sitting in the kitchen eating a piece of toast. He had been reluctant to leave him at home alone, but they could not afford to pass up potentially lucrative jobs or to antagonise clients by breaking appointments. It looked as if he had only recently got up. Roger was back in time to prevent him from doing anything silly.

He was thankful that Stuart had offered only token resistance to his insistence that he should take one of the sleeping tablets prescribed by their family doctor before they both flopped into bed at around eight that morning. He could feel the bottle now, safe in the pocket of his jeans, where Stuart could not get hold of it and succumb to the temptation of using the tablets, as his mother had done, to quieten his anxiety and take him into permanent oblivion.

Was he wrong still to insist on taking charge of his son's medication? Was it time to recognise that he was an adult and should be trusted to take care of himself? Had his over-protectiveness contributed to Stuart's continuing insecurity and isolation? Was it time to let go? If he had been more welcoming to Emma during the time when they were going out together, perhaps by now they would be living together in their own flat. They might even have a family of their own. But that would have meant letting him out of his sight, taking the risk that he would not be able to cope.

Stuart's greeting, when he looked up as his father entered the kitchen, did not bode well.

'Good. You're back. I was going to leave you a note. I'm going out to look for her.'

'For Emma, you mean?' Roger asked, as if Stuart could have been referring to someone else.

'Yes. We shouldn't have left her like that. She must have been out all night.'

'Or maybe those people in the boat picked her up,' Roger suggested. 'You aren't necessarily the only Good Samaritan in the world, you know.'

'Why should they? They don't know her.'

'They may have done,' Roger argued, clutching at straws in the hope of dissuading Stuart from making any further attempts to befriend Emma. 'That could be why they called out. They recognised her and they were trying to get her attention.'

'But she ran away. She was scared of them.' Stuart stuffed the remainder of the toast into his mouth and got to his feet. Roger positioned himself between his son and the door to the back porch.

'Look Stu, face facts. She doesn't want our help. If she did, she'd have come back here. She knows where we are. You've done your bit, getting the knife off her. She can't hurt herself now, can she? You've got to let her go. It's her life.'

'But it's my fault!' Stuart's voice rose in pitch as he tried to put into words the guilt feelings that were threatening to overwhelm him. He started to move his hands up and down his arms in the repetitive way that Roger recognised as a sure sign that he was feeling stressed. 'I brought her here and now she's lost her coat and her spare clothes and she's out there in the cold with nowhere to go!'

'No!' Roger took hold of Stuart by both shoulders and looked him in the eye. 'It's – not – your – fault,' he said slowly and emphatically. 'You were only trying to help. It's not your fault that she ran off.'

'I've still got to try to find her,' Stuart said dogmatically. 'If something happens to her and I didn't even try …'

'OK,' Roger said, dropping his hands to his sides and giving a sigh of resignation. 'OK. We'll go out and have a look for her. Not that we'll find her. I bet she's back in town by now, snug indoors in a bar somewhere.'

'Thanks Dad.' Stuart's features visibly relaxed and his hands stopped their rhythmic movements. 'I'll get my coat. We'd better go right away. It'll be dark soon.'

They set out, leaving the back door unlocked in case Emma returned before they did. In the daylight, it was easier to see the path and they made rapid progress across the fields to the place where she had disappeared into the bushes.

'The chances are she went towards town,' Roger said. Stuart nodded. They turned to the right and headed off along the towpath in a southerly direction.

Roger's idea was that they would take a brisk walk along the river to the point where it went under the main road leading out of Oxford to the west, a distance of not much more than a mile. However, Stuart insisted on stopping to examine every hedgerow and clump of bushes, in case Emma had taken shelter there. They had not got far when dusk began to fall.

'It's no good,' Roger said. 'We'll have to go back now. There's no chance of finding her in the dark.'

'But we can't leave her out for another night,' Stuart protested.

'If we don't start back soon, *we'll* be the ones who are

241

lost outside at night. Come on, Stu. We don't even know that she's still out here. Like I said, the chances are she's safe and warm somewhere, while we're freezing our bollocks off out here looking for her.'

'Maybe she went the other way,' Stuart said as if he had not heard. 'She could've been heading for Godstow Road. Let's go back and try there.'

'Alright,' Roger conceded, thinking that this might provide a way of terminating the search. 'We'll just go up as far as Godstow Road, and if we don't find her by then, we'll go home, agreed?'

'OK,' Stuart nodded.

They retraced their steps along the towpath to the bushes where they had last seen Emma. Just beyond them, Stuart suddenly gave an excited cry.

'Look there! That's her scarf. There! On that branch, down near the water.'

Roger followed his pointing finger and saw a piece of flimsy pink material hanging from one of the trees that overhung the riverbank. It was moving gently in the breeze. It matched the pink dress that Emma had been wearing. They both hurried over to it. The tree was a hawthorn and the scarf was caught on numerous of the small pointed thorns and twined around several of the twisting branches. Roger put his hand up and started to disentangle it, trying not to tear the delicate fabric.

Stuart meanwhile plunged in under the trees, his eyes down; searching for signs that Emma had been there. When Roger finally got the scarf free and looked round for his son, he was nowhere to be seen.

'Stuart?' he called out, stuffing the scarf into his coat pocket. 'Stu! Where are you?'

'Here Dad!' the sound came from amongst the trees a little further upstream. 'Come quick!'

The hint of panic in Stuart's voice prompted Roger to set off at once, forcing back the twigs of the hawthorn tree and pushing his way through, ignoring the scratches that the thorns were making on his face and hands.

'What is it?'

'I've found her!'

Roger's heart gave a lurch. If Emma really was there, hidden amongst the dense mass of branches and tree roots at the very edge of the riverbank, it could not be good news. At best she would be cold and wet and in need of medical treatment. At worst …

He found Stuart standing up to his ankles in water in a shallow cove, overhung by the branches of an alder tree. He was bent over, staring at something in the water beneath where the twigs, with their distinctive small cones, touched the surface. The sun had already set by now and it was dark under the tree, but Roger caught sight of a flash of pink and his heart sank as he realised that they had indeed found Emma.

'Help me to get her out,' Stuart said, going a little further into the stream and grasping hold of Emma's body under her arm pits.

'I think it'd be better to leave her where she is. There's nothing we can do for her.'

Stuart took no notice of his father's words. Instead, he started pulling the body free of the dangling tree branches and into the shallower water of the cove. He panted with the exertion and almost fell. Seeing that he was not to be deterred from carrying out his resolve, Roger stepped down into the shallows and stretched out to grasp Emma's arms as soon as they came within reach. Together they managed to lug her on to the bank.

'I'd better call the police,' Roger said, taking off his sodden gloves and fumbling in his pocket for his phone.

'No!' Stuart leapt at him and, for a moment, they were in danger of both toppling over into the icy water. 'We can't let them … they'll think I killed her.'

'Don't talk nonsense! Why would they think that?'

'They'll see my record. They'll say, "He's mental. He must've pushed her in." You know they would. Everyone thinks if you've been diagnosed with mental problems you can't be trusted.'

'No they don't,' Roger protested. 'You're just-'

'Yes they do! Even *you* do! You're always trying to watch what I'm doing. Even on a night out with a mate, I get you ringing me saying "why aren't you back yet?" you don't trust me any more than everyone else does.'

'If I'm keeping such a close watch on you, then I can vouch for it that you didn't hurt Emma, can't I?'

'Oh yeah? Like they'll believe you? *You* can't be my alibi. Besides, you did go out and leave me, didn't you. They'd latch on to that and say I must've gone out and done her in this afternoon.'

'And then brought me here to see what you'd done?'

'Don't they say something about the murderer always returning to the scene of the crime?'

'Alright then,' Roger sighed, putting his phone away. 'If that's the way you want it, let's get back and leave her for someone else to find.'

'We can't just leave her here.'

'Well, what else *can* we do?' Roger was beginning to lose patience. '*You* insisted on getting her out. You don't want the police called. So she'll just have to stay here until someone else comes along.'

'But what about rats – or foxes? Or, I've seen magpies pecking at dead rabbits on the road.'

'You should've thought of that before you got her out.'

'We'll have to take her home. She'll be safe in the old wash house.'

'And then what will the police say if they find her?'

'They won't – not unless you tell them.'

'But we can't just keep a dead body in our wash house. It's no good. Either we leave her here and go home or I phone for the police.'

Stuart stood thinking for a few moments, still dissatisfied. Eventually he nodded and climbed out of the water.

'OK. I suppose you're right. It just doesn't seem right somehow, leaving her like this.'

19.45 THURSDAY 29TH OCTOBER

As he came downstairs from the bathroom, Roger noticed, through the window on the half-landing, that the light was on in the yard. That was odd! He was sure that they had not left it like that. He distinctly remembered fumbling around in the dark to find the keyhole of the back door after they returned from the river – and then remembering that they had left it unlocked in case Emma were to return.

He hurried downstairs and went out to see what was going on. Stuart was there, dressed in overalls and work boots. He was loading a roll of Visqueen into one of the heavy-duty navvy barrows that they used for carting building materials around a site.

'What are you up to?' Roger asked.

'I'm going back to get her.'

'What do you mean?'

'We can't just leave here there. I'm going to bring her back here, where she'll be safe.'

'Look Stu, we've been through all this. We can't keep her here. She's got to be buried properly – with a funeral and stuff.'

'I know. That's what I want to do.'

'If that's what you want, let me ring the police and they'll deal with all that.'

'But then they'll arrest me and have me put away for killing her.'

'No they won't. Look! I can do it anonymously. Then they won't know it's anything to do with you, will they?'

'They'll be able to trace the call.'

'Not if I do it from a call box.'

'Where would you find one of them working, these days? Anyway, somebody might see you.'

Roger sighed. He could see from Stuart's stubborn expression that he was not going to listen to reason. He decided to try another line of argument.

'What about if someone sees *you* with a dead body in your barrow? That'll be far worse than just calling the police.'

'There won't be anyone down by the river now it's dark. I'm going to bring her in the back way. There won't be anyone to see.'

'How're you going to get the barrow through the gates?' Roger asked, remembering the narrow kissing gates, designed to allow pedestrians through without livestock accompanying them.

'I'll go down to the farm gate. That's big enough. And there's a gap in the hedge into the next field wide enough to drive a coach and horses through.'

Stuart pushed past his father and headed off down the path, wheeling the barrow. Roger followed, putting his hand on his son's shoulder in an attempt to stop him. Stuart shook it off and quickened his pace. He reached the bottom of the garden and put the barrow down to undo the fastening on the gate that led out into the back lane. Looking down, Roger saw Emma's coat and one of the torches lying alongside the roll of Visqueen.

Stuart took up the barrow again and headed out down the muddy track. Roger followed, still full of misgivings but not knowing what else to do. It was very dark in the lane, where the lights from the house were unable to penetrate the fence that ran along the back of the garden. Roger picked up the torch and shone it ahead of them. Soon they reached the tubular steel farm gate that led into the field. Stuart stopped again, waiting while Roger pulled back the spring-loaded handle and pushed the gate wide open to admit the barrow.

They made their way across the field, peering ahead in search of the way through the hedge at the far side. When they arrived there, they discovered that the gap had been closed with sheep netting and barbed wire.

'We can't get through here,' Roger said, hoping that this setback would provide Stuart with an excuse to give up his mad scheme.

'We could lift the barrow over and then go through the small gate,' Stuart suggested.

'Not on the way back – at least not if you've got … I mean if the barrow's full.'

'No. I suppose not. Well, there must be a way through somewhere.' Stuart picked up the handles of the barrow again and started walking along parallel to the hedge. His father followed him, making mild protestations in an attempt to persuade him to come home, but without much hope that they would have any impact. Once Stuart got an idea into his head, it was always extremely difficult to change his mind.

After a hundred yards or so, they came upon an old wooden five-bar gate, tied together with thin wire and held closed by a loop of bailer twine. Stuart undid the fastening and lifted the gate up out of the muddy hole where it was resting. Panting with exertion, he pulled it open and set it down on the grass. Then he took up the barrow again and set off towards the river with Roger scurrying along in his wake.

It took some time to find the body. Roger was beginning to think that someone else must have found

Emma and taken her away, when Stuart gave a shout and pointed with the torch towards a clump of trees growing at the edge of the bank. Sure enough, the light glinted on something pink and shiny. She was still there: hidden among the brambles beneath the alders and willows.

Roger stood keeping watch, gazing round nervously, jumping at every sound, while Stuart methodically prepared Emma's body for the journey back. He had evidently been planning this in his mind in some detail. He unrolled the Visqueen and spread it out in a sheet on the ground. He laid the coat, with its lining uppermost, on top. Then he crouched down by Emma's body and slipped his arms under her chest and knees, so that he could lift her up. Roger noticed how stiff the body appeared to be. It was as if Stuart were carrying a plastic mannequin from a shop window display.

Staggering, but managing somehow to stay upright, Stuart carried Emma over to her prepared resting place and laid her down on the coat, which he wrapped around her, fastening two of the buttons to keep it in place. Then he folded the plastic sheeting over her and rolled her over repeatedly so that she was encased in several layers of Visqueen. Finally, he took out a knife from his pocket and cut the sheet off the roll.

'Give me a hand to get her in the barrow, will you?'

Roger positioned the torch on top of a convenient tree stump, to provide light for the difficult task of lifting the corpse into the barrow without knocking the barrow over in the process. At their third attempt, they succeeded in balancing their unwieldy parcel lengthwise, with the feet sticking out between the handles and the head overhanging at the front. Roger bent down, picked up the discarded roll of Visqueen and stuffed it in beside the body. Then he picked up the torch and shone it round, carefully checking for any other signs that they might have left behind, by which their presence might be traced. There were footprints in the mud and indentations caused by the navvy barrow, but nothing else that he could see. He waited until Stuart had pushed the barrow out from under the trees and then brushed dead leaves (from the piles that lay against the tree trunks, blown into drifts by the wind) over the marks to disguise them.

They made their way home as fast as they could, taking turns to push the heavy barrow across the grass. When they reached the back lane, Roger switched off the torch in case anyone might be looking out of an upper window in one of the other houses dotted at wide intervals along the road and might notice the light. They felt their way in the dark along the familiar track until they reached the open gate and the safety of their back garden. Roger closed the gate behind them and drew the bolt across. Then he turned and saw that Stuart had already reached the wash house and was attempting to lift his burden off the barrow. He ran to help him and together they carried the body into the outhouse and laid it down on a long wooden bench next to the deep old ceramic sink that still stood in the corner.

07.30 SATURDAY 31ST OCTOBER

Stuart was nowhere to be seen when Roger got up on Saturday morning. The dirty cereal bowl and mug in the sink showed that he had finished his breakfast, and the absence of his work boots in the porch indicated that he had gone outside. Roger went to seek him out. They had to decide what to do about the corpse in the wash house.

Friday had been taken up with digging the footings for the new job. By the time they got home, tired out with a hard day's work, it was already dark and he had no energy for considering how to dispose of Emma's body in a way that would satisfy his son and not attract attention from the authorities. He had been glad that Stuart appeared to have forgotten about her, and he had been only too pleased to push it to the back of his mind, telling himself that they would think of something. Now, they could put it off no longer. They had to agree on a plan of action.

He found his son in the outhouse, bending over Emma's body, which he had unwrapped, leaving the plastic sheet hanging down over the side of the bench. Coming closer, Roger saw that there was now a spray of

251

red roses lying on her breast. As he watched, Stuart took hold of her arms, one at a time and gently bent them so that they lay across her chest, holding the flowers in place. That was strange! When they had brought her in on Thursday night, her limbs had been stiff and unbending.

'Better wrap her up again,' he said, trying to speak normally, as if there were nothing unusual about keeping a dead woman in their outhouse. 'She'll be safer that way. Then come back in the house. I've got an idea.'

'Just a minute! I want to put her shoes on.'

For the first time, Roger noticed that Emma's feet were bare. Her shoes must have fallen off somewhere. He hoped fervently that they had been lost in the river and not on her journey home with them in the wheelbarrow. If one of them were to turn up in the lane behind their garden, it would be a clear pointer to their involvement in the removal of her body and could perhaps be interpreted as suggesting that they were responsible for her death.

Roger watched as Stuart rummaged inside Emma's rucksack, which was lying on the floor underneath the bench. He brought out a pair of red shoes and eased them on to her feet. Then he carefully fastened the coat around her body again before wrapping it in the green plastic sheet, folding it down neatly and sticking it together with tape. He stood in silence, looking at his handiwork for a moment or two before following his father back indoors.

'D'you remember Mrs Pemberley?' Roger said, sitting down at the kitchen table.

'The old dear with the patio we just re-laid?'

'That's right. Remember we had to get the job done quick, because she was anxious about having a load of people coming round?'

'Yeah. Her hubby's funeral or something, wasn't it?'

'That's right. It's first thing Monday. She told me all about it. Nine o'clock Monday at Wolvercote Cemetery.'

'What about it?'

'Well, that means there's bound to be a grave dug all

ready for him, isn't there? I mean, they won't be working Sunday will they? You said you wanted to give Emma a proper burial. How about putting her in there?'

'Then where's Mrs Pemberley's old man going to go?'

'On top. We'll put Emma in and cover her up with soil so no-one can tell she's there and then, on Monday, they'll just lower the coffin down on top and that'll be that.'

Stuart sat for several minutes turning over this suggestion in his mind. Roger watched him anxiously, hoping that he would not come up with any objections. He had an uncomfortable feeling that his son had been hoping to keep Emma permanently in their home. At last, Stuart's face cleared and he smiled back at his father.

'That's a great idea. When shall we do it?'

02.15 SUNDAY 1ˢᵀ NOVEMBER

'It's locked!' Stuart called out. 'What do you we do now?'

'Get back in and we'll drive round to the other side. We'll have to get over the fence. But not here – there's too much traffic and someone might see us from the houses.'

Stuart got back into the pickup truck and sat down next to his father, who immediately drove away from the cemetery entrance, up the Banbury Road and left into Jordan Hill. A row of shrubs on the left-hand side of the road obscured the boundary fence of the cemetery. To the right, the carparks in front of the offices were deserted. They drove slowly, peering out, looking for a place where they could get through the dense bushes and over the fence.

At last, the bushes on the left thinned out, giving way to a wide grassy area, beyond which they could see a line of railings and a tall chain-link fence. They pulled up on the verge and got out to survey the area. Roger was pleased to see that there was a convenient place to set up the ladder behind a large conifer, whose dense foliage would shield them from any prying eyes, in the unlikely event of anyone passing by.

They unloaded the truck, depositing their equipment, together with the grisly green plastic parcel, behind the tree. Roger set up the ladder against one of the supporting posts of the chain-link fence.

'I'll go first,' he said. 'Then you pass the barrow over, and after that …,' he trailed off, unwilling to put into words what would have to follow next.

'OK,' Stuart nodded, turning to lift the unwieldy parcel out of the barrow and lay it gently down on the ground.

It was a struggle to get the body over the fence. Emma had been slim – Roger would have described her as painfully thin – in life, and yet her body seemed surprisingly heavy. They began to think that Roger would have to return over the fence to help with the lifting; but eventually Stuart managed to climb the ladder with the corpse slung over his shoulder. Roger stood on the barrow and reached up to slow her descent as she toppled over the fence. At last, they were both standing inside the cemetery, staring down at what could easily have been a parcel of building materials for their next job, but which they both knew contained the mortal remains of a human being.

They got it into the barrow and Stuart picked up the handles, while Roger shone the torch round in a slow arc, searching for the path.

'How're we going to find the grave?' Stuart asked anxiously. 'There are hundreds of them!'

'The new ones are all over the other side,' Roger told him. 'This one won't be far from where we buried your Auntie Fran. Right! Let's go.'

It took both of them to get the heavy barrow across the soft ground to the path. Then the going became easier. Roger walked ahead, looking round all the time, trying to remember where it was that his sister-in-law had been laid to rest three months earlier. They came to the chapel. Yes, of course! They had to go past here and down the drive a little way.

'This way!' he whispered to Stuart. 'Not much farther now.'

They turned off on to another of the paths that led from the drive to the neat rows of graves. Now, when Roger shone his torch round it showed up mounds of orangey brown earth, some with heaps of flowers piled up on them.

'That must be it!' Roger said, shining the torch ahead of them and picking out in its beam a pile of earth, which he judged was waiting to backfill a grave after an interment.

They hurried on and soon found themselves looking down on an area of artificial grass, in the middle of which was what looked like a shallow rectangular box with a sloping black plastic lid. It was about eight feet long and 4 feet wide. Clearly it was covering the new grave.

'Right! We'd better get this off,' Roger said, as if he were talking about the preliminaries to a routine job in the course of their daily work.

Stuart put down the barrow and stepped forward to help his father to lift the cover. It was heavier than they had expected. Try as they might, they could not shift it. Panting, they stood back and Roger scanned it all round with the torch.

'Oh my god!' he groaned. 'It's padlocked. Look!'

They both stood in silence, staring down at the grave cover. There were two padlocks on each of the two longer sides of the rectangular lid.

'What're we going to do?' Stuart asked anxiously. 'Will we have to take her home again?'

'No, of course not,' Roger answered hurriedly. Having got the corpse this far, he was determined that whatever else they did, it would not include taking her back to lie awaiting discovery by the police in their outhouse. 'We'll just have to force the locks.'

'But then they'll know someone's been in,' Stuart argued. 'You said nobody would be able to tell. You said-'

'I know what I said,' Roger interrupted. 'I never

thought it'd be locked. But it's too late now. We'll just have to cover her up with soil and hope no-one finds her.'

He took hold of one of the heavy shovels, which they had brought for deepening the grave and burying the body, and started hacking at one of the padlocks with it. The jarring of metal against metal sounded loud in the stillness of the early morning and his heart began beating faster at the thought that someone might hear it and come to investigate. At last, the lock gave way and fell on to the artificial turf. Roger turned his attention to the next one. Stuart, who had been watching in silence, took up the other shovel and started working on one of the locks on the other side of the grave cover.

By the time they had all four locks broken and the grave cover lifted off, they were exhausted. Roger stood leaning on his shovel, looking down into the open grave.

'It looks plenty deep enough already,' he said, breathing heavily after his exertion. 'Let's just put her in and cover her up and then get out of here.'

That was easier said than done. Some of the tape had come unstuck during the journey from the truck to the graveside and the slippery plastic started to come apart. As they lifted the gruesome parcel off the barrow and placed it down on the artificial turf, two rose petals emerged from inside the wrapping. Roger hastily pushed them back between the folds and pulled the plastic sheet closer around the body.

'You take one end and I'll take the other,' he instructed. 'Hold the Visqueen tight together so she can't fall out and then we'll just have to let her drop.'

The green-covered parcel slithered over the side of the grave and landed with a thud on the earth at the bottom. Stuart and Roger peered into the gloom, flashing the torch to pick out the crumpled sheet of plastic. Satisfied that the body was completely obscured from view within the sheet, they set to work shovelling loose earth from the neat pile that lay next to the grave. Soon Roger was satisfied that nobody looking into the grave would be able to see that anything other than fresh earth had been deposited there. He called a halt to their efforts and declared that it was time that they headed back home. Stuart hesitated and gave one last longing glance down before nodding, stowing his shovel in the barrow and picking up the handles ready to go.

07.30 TUESDAY 3RD NOVEMBER

'What're you doing Dad?' Stuart asked. 'I thought you liked that rose. You always said it reminded you of Mum.'

'I do, son. Don't you worry. It'll grow again. I just don't think it's a good idea having it growing here where everyone can see it just now.' Roger had spent the night turning over in his mind whether there was anything that might link them to the "mystery corpse" that had been reported on local radio the previous evening. He had got up early to dispose of any evidence that there might still be around their house and garden, which the police might find and use against them.

'Why?'

'You heard on the radio last night: they've found Emma's body. That means they've found those roses you put with her. And if they see we've got the bush they came from …'

'Do you think they'll come here?' Stuart asked, opening his eyes wide in fear. 'Will the police come and arrest us?'

'No. There's no reason they should.' Roger wished that he had managed to finish the job before his son got up, so

259

that he could have avoided this explanation, which was certain to heighten his anxiety. 'But, just to be on the safe side, I thought we'd have a bonfire this evening and burn all Emma's things.'

'Everything? All her clothes and everything?'

'Yes. Just in case the police come poking about. There's no reason they should, but … better to be on the safe side.'

'OK … You *are* sure? You don't think …?'

'It said on the radio the police are mystified. They don't even know who she is, never mind how she got there. Don't worry. They won't come here. It's just … if they do, better we don't have anything that could link us to her, OK?'

19.30 TUESDAY 10TH NOVEMBER

'Well I think they were both very silly,' was Lucy's verdict when Peter finished his account of Roger Parsons' confession. 'Why didn't they just ring the police?'

'Stuart Parsons was afraid that they would think he'd killed Emma,' Peter tried to explain. 'And his father was afraid that he'd start hurting himself again if he didn't go along with whatever he wanted.'

Lucy still looked dissatisfied, so Bernie chipped in.

'I think it was a bit like the way *you* said that you wished Martin hadn't called the police when you got hurt. They were afraid of a misunderstanding. Maybe Stuart had had problems with the police before.'

'Your mum's right,' Jonah agreed. 'We don't always get it right and Stuart could have run into someone like your Constable Ferrar, who jumped to conclusions and wouldn't back down.'

'That doesn't mean that you shouldn't trust the police,' Peter added hastily. 'Mostly we're doing our best, and even Louise Ferrar admits now that she made a mistake.'

'Not that she had much choice, based on what you said

about the dressing down Superintendent Brown gave her,' Bernie added with a grin. 'Seriously though, Lucy, Martin did the right thing and the Parsons *were* rather silly, but only because they were frightened of what might happen.'

'Stuart was detained for a while under the Mental Health Act when he was only nineteen,' Peter continued, still trying to explain the younger Parsons' actions. 'That must have been pretty frightening for him. It probably explains why he found it hard to trust anyone in authority after that. And he may have remembered the same thing happening to his mum when he was a kid.'

'What does *detained under the Mental Health Act* mean?' Lucy wanted to know.

'When someone has a mental illness, sometimes they can't think properly and they do dangerous things – either to themselves or to other people,' Bernie explained. 'The Mental Health Act allows doctors to decide that someone needs to be kept in hospital, even if they don't want to go there, to stop them hurting themselves or anyone else. It's all to keep everyone safe, but I don't expect it feels like that to the person it's happening to. The Parsons lad probably felt a bit the way you did, when you were worrying that Social Services might take you into Care.'

'What you need to remember, Lucy, is that this is something that only happens as a very last resort.' Margaret, who had slipped into the room while Peter was telling his story, was anxious to assure Lucy that she had nothing to fear from authority figures. 'Usually people with mental illnesses agree to let the doctors treat them and they get better without being put in hospital.'

'Do *you* ever have to do that to people?' Lucy asked, becoming interested in this new aspect of a doctor's job.

'No. You have to be specially trained for that. I deal with patching up people's bodies. There are special doctors called psychiatrists who know about treating people whose minds are ill. Once or twice, I've had to refer a patient on to them. That was when they came into Casualty with self-inflicted injuries and I was worried they might do it again.'

'And what happens after that?' Lucy frowned as she tried to imagine what it might be like to be treated in a mental hospital. 'I mean, what do they do to make someone better when their mind's ill?'

'As I said, that's not my area of expertise,' Margaret answered. 'And it depends on the sort of mental illness – there are lots of different ones. There are drugs that help to make people less anxious or depressed. And there are what they call "talking therapies" where people are taught how to avoid thinking about things that make them upset or agitated or to think about them in a different way. Usually it takes a long time and quite often it never really goes away. This lad you're talking about, for instance: it sounds as if he was traumatised when his mum killed herself and seeing another dead body brought it all back to him and made him ill again.'

'I hadn't thought of it like that,' Peter said thoughtfully. 'Maybe that's what the flowers and the coat and wanting to bury her in a proper grave were all about. Maybe in a funny way he was doing it for his mother. I don't suppose he was allowed to have much to do with her funeral, with him being only seven at the time.'

'You never know,' Margaret agreed. 'The human mind sometimes works in a very strange sort of way. I'm glad I work with mending people's bodies. They don't take so long to heal up and it's easier to know when you've fixed them. Take Lucy's cheek, for example, now the stitches have gone, you'd hardly notice it.'

'Yes,' Bernie agreed, thinking of Martin and wondering how long it would be before he felt confident about his friendship with Lucy again. 'Physical scars aren't the ones that last the longest. That's what makes me so angry with Constable Ferrar. I know she thought she was doing the right thing, but she really did make a right mess of everything, and it's going to take ages for everyone to get back to normal and forget her stupid insinuations.'

'Getting back to the case in hand,' Jonah said, noticing the time on the clock that hung on the wall opposite his chair and determined to hear all the news before his friends had to leave, 'I suppose the inquest will be able to go ahead now?'

'Yes. We've finally had the body officially identified,' Peter confirmed. 'The leader of the *Drama not Drugs* group did that for us and we've also tracked down her father. He couldn't help with finding her mother. Apparently, she left home when Emma was only a baby and he hasn't seen anything of her since. I'll be sending my report to the coroner tomorrow.'

'And what outcome do you expect?' Jonah asked, with a glint in his eye that Peter recognised as signifying that he knew something and was building up to telling them about it.

'Probably an open verdict – or maybe suicide. The pathology report will say that she drowned and I don't see that there's any evidence to say whether she did it deliberately or if it was an accident, but her history of mental illness may just tip the balance.'

'I'd go for *misadventure* myself.'

'Oh yes? What makes you rule out suicide?' Peter asked, all the more convinced that Jonah had something up his sleeve that he was itching to reveal. 'You were the one who found all that stuff on Facebook about her wanting to kill herself.'

'I know,' Jonah smiled complacently. 'But then, afterwards, I read all the posts properly. Have a look at this.'

The sound of an electric motor whirred unexpectedly and the others watched in amazement as a computer screen, which they had not noticed high up against the wall over Jonah's chair, moved outwards on a jointed metal arm and descended to a position about eighteen inches in front of him.

Looking down, Peter noticed that Jonah's left hand was

264

manipulating a small joystick, which seemed to be an addition to the mouse-and-keypad combination that he used for operating his computer. He must have been using the computer before they arrived and nobody had moved his hand off the controls.

'Neat, isn't it?' Jonah grinned round at their open mouths. 'Those two students rigged it up for me. Now, so long as I've got hold of the controller, I can use the computer whenever I want, without having to call someone to set it up for me. But what I wanted to show you was this.'

Peter came round the back of Jonah's chair and watched over his shoulder as he navigated to a Facebook page and scrolled down to find a particular conversation

'This is one of the places where Emma discusses different ways of committing suicide,' Jonah told them. 'One of her so-called friends says that he's thinking of jumping off the Clifton suspension bridge.'

'Sounds like an attention-seeker to me,' Peter muttered. 'One of those idiots who want to make a dramatic gesture and get everyone looking at them. He probably never had any intention of actually jumping.'

'The interesting thing is Emma's reaction,' Jonah went on ignoring the interruption. 'Quite a lot of the others are egging him on and telling him to go for it, but Emma says she doesn't like the idea of drowning. Then there's a lot of discussion about whether, jumping from that height, you'd be dead before you hit the water or the impact would kill you and so on. Then further down, Emma comes back to the theme of drowning and says it's the one way she wouldn't like to go, because she can't bear the idea of being under the water and not being able to stop herself breathing it in. I almost wonder if she'd actually tried it in the past, it's so graphic.'

'So you think it was an accident?' Bernie asked. 'She was just running away along the towpath and she slipped and fell in?'

'Yes. That's how I read the evidence,' Jonah agreed. 'Based on what she says here, if she had decided to kill herself she'd have gone for an overdose of some sort.'

'OK, clever clogs. I'll put that in the report to the coroner,' Peter said, joking in an effort to keep the resentment out of his voice. 'I'll tell him, "DCI Porter, who is both omniscient and infallible, is confident that the victim fell into the water and drowned as a result of taking insufficient care when walking on the path along the riverbank." That will save him a lot of time weighing up the evidence and drawing his own conclusions!'

Jonah smiled back complacently. Bernie, pleased that Jonah seemed to be back to his usual ebullient self, but conscious of the annoyance that Peter was feeling at his smugness, decided to intervene.

'Time we were off!' she declared. 'It's Lucy's bed time. But we'll both be back tomorrow evening and we'll be expecting a proper demonstration of your new gizmo.'

THANK YOU

Thank you for taking the time to read GRAVE OFFENCE. If you enjoyed it, please consider telling your friends or posting a short review. Word of mouth is an author's best friend and much appreciated. Thank you,

Judy.

MORE ABOUT BERNIE AND HER FRIENDS

Bernie features in nine more books.

- **Awayday:** a traditional detective story set among the dons of an Oxford college.
- **Changing Scenes of Life:** Jonah Porter's life story, told through the medium of his favourite hymns.
- **Despise not your Mother:** the story of Bernie's quest to learn about her dead husband's past.
- **Two Little Dickie Birds:** a murder mystery for DI Peter Johns and his Sergeant, Paul Godwin.
- **Murder of a Martian**: a double murder for Peter and Jonah to solve.
- **Death on the Algarve:** a mystery for Bernie and her friends to tackle while on holiday in Portugal.
- **My Life of Crime:** the collected memoirs of DI Peter Johns.
- **Mystery over the Mersey:** a murder mystery set in Liverpool.
- **Sorrowful Mystery:** Jonah investigates a child abduction and Peter embarks on a new journey of faith.

Read more about Bernie Fazakerley and her friends and family at https://sites.google.com/site/llanwrdafamily/

Visit the Bernie Fazakerley Publications Facebook page here:
https://www.facebook.com/Bernie.Fazakerley.Publications

Follow Bernie on Twitter: https://twitter.com/BernieFaz.

ABOUT THE AUTHOR

Like her main character, Bernie Fazakerley, Judy Ford is an Oxford graduate and a mathematician. Unlike Bernie, Judy grew up in a middle-class family in the South London stockbroker belt. After moving to the North West and working in Liverpool, Judy fell in love with the Scouse people and created Bernie to reflect their unique qualities.

As a Methodist Local Preacher, Judy often tells her congregation, "I see my role as asking the questions and leaving you to think out your own answers." She carries this philosophy forward into her writing and she hopes that readers will find themselves challenged to think as well as being entertained.

DISCLAIMER

Most of the locations and institutions that feature in this book are real. Their inhabitants and employees, however, are purely fictional. In particular,

- The house in Binsey Lane where the Parsons family lives does not exist (and neither do they);
- The charity *Drama not Drugs* is pure invention and is not based on any actual organisation;
- The description of the night clubs where Emma worked is not based on any real club in Oxford or anywhere else;
- The behaviour of the police officers in this book should not be construed as in anyway representative of Thames Valley Police or any other police service;
- Lichfield College and St Luke's College are both imaginary and are not based on any specific college of the University of Oxford.

27431336R10158

Printed in Great Britain
by Amazon